"Sorry to disappoint."

She playfully slugged his shoulder. "You never could, Noah. Stop it. You are always the best surprise."

He turned to her then, so close she could breathe in his delicious scent. The moonlight made his dark eyes shimmer, and her heart tugged with familiar warmth. Noah. She didn't think she'd ever love anyone quite the same way she loved her best friend.

"Do you think you'll leave town if the bookstore closes?" he asked.

"I don't know, but I might need to leave. At least for a while."

"Why? I just got back."

"Noah, you're not the only one that thinks it might be nice to start over somewhere else." She swallowed hard. "Do you realize I still occasionally get referred to as Will's girlfriend?"

"You mean by someone other than my mother?" Noah shook his head. "If you want her to move on from your tragic love story, you need to give her something else to talk about. Give everyone something to talk about. Learn from my experience. Life is too short to please other people."

Dear Reader,

I have to admit, writing this book scared me a little bit. Let me explain. At the time I began to write this book, I'd just lost my father after a long illness. Later that same year, my husband lost his older brother quite unexpectedly and shockingly. I suppose it isn't any surprise that in 2022 I tackled the subject of grief. Writing, however, felt like a huge and agonizing undertaking because it hit a little too close to home.

But as with everything, there is the other side of the coin. Even with a great loss, there remain friends, family and faith to get you through. There is a comfort and joy found in books. I know I'm not the only one who has closed a book and walked away filled with a sense of hope and inspiration. That's what I set out to have a reader feel in this best-friends-to-lovers romance. So, we have the *Once Upon a Charming Bookshop* in Charming at Christmastime, our quirky senior-citizen poetry group, a literary-character costume contest, lights, decorations and heartfelt gifts.

And finally, we have two best friends who have experienced a great loss together. Twyla, our heroine, and Noah, our hero, discover that friendship endures through grief and guilt, and at times it even catches fire.

I always love to hear from you. You can reach me at heatherly@heatherlybell.com.

Heatherly Bell

Once Upon a Charming Bookshop

HEATHERLY BELL

ISBN-13: 978-1-335-59441-9

Once Upon a Charming Bookshop

For questions and comments about the quality of this book, please contact us at CustomerService@Harlequin.com.

Harlequin Enterprises ULC
22 Adelaide St. West, 41st Floor
Toronto, Ontario M5H 4E3, Canada
www.Harlequin.com

Printed in U.S.A.

Bestselling author **Heatherly Bell** was born in Tuscaloosa, Alabama, but lost her accent by the time she was two. After leaving Alabama, Heatherly lived with her family in Puerto Rico and Maryland before being transplanted kicking and screaming to the California Bay Area. She now loves it here, she swears. Except the traffic.

Books by Heatherly Bell

Harlequin Special Edition

The Fortunes of Texas: Hitting the Jackpot

Winning Her Fortune

Montana Mavericks: The Real Cowboys of Bronco Heights

Grand-Prize Cowboy

Wildfire Ridge

More than One Night
Reluctant Hometown Hero
The Right Moment

Charming, Texas

Winning Mr. Charming
The Charming Checklist
A Charming Christmas Arrangement
A Charming Single Dad
A Charming Doorstep Baby

Visit the Author Profile page
at Harlequin.com for more titles.

For those who believe that books can bring you joy

Chapter One

Twyla Thompson was thrilled to see a line out the door on the night of *New York Times* bestselling author Stacy Cruz's book signing. This was exactly what Once Upon a Book needed—an infusion of excitement and goodwill and the proverbial opening up of the wallet during the holidays for a book instead of the latest flat-screen TV. Even if Stacy's recently released thriller wasn't exactly Christmas material, the timing was right both for her, the publisher and certainly Twyla's family-owned bookstore.

The reading had been short due to subject matter—murder—and Stacy took questions from the crowd. As usual, they ranged from, "How can I get published?" To "I have an idea for a book. Would you write it for me?" To "My mother had a *fascinating* life. It should be a book, then a movie starring Meryl Streep." Stacy was a good sport about it all since the Charming, Texas, residents were her friends and neighbors, too.

Twyla, for her part, would never dream of writing a book. She barely had time to read everything she wanted to. Which was basically…everything. The heart of a bookseller beat in her and she recommended books like they were her best friends. Want an inspirational book? Read this. Would you like a tour de force celebrating the power of the human spirit? Here's the book for you. A little escapism with some romance and comedy thrown in? Right here. Want to be scared within an inch of your life? Read Stacy Cruz's latest suspense thriller.

The very best part of Twyla's day was getting lost in the worlds an author created. Her favorite books had always been of the fantasy romance genre, particularly of the dragon-slaying variety. She adored a fae hero who slayed dragons before breakfast. But honestly? She read anything she could get her hands on. Owning her four-generation family bookstore had made that possible. She'd grown up inside these four walls filled with bookshelves and little alcoves and nooks. She read all the *Nancy Drew* mysteries, Beverly Cleary and, when her grandmother wasn't looking, Kathleen Woodiwiss.

Twyla stood next to Roy Finch at the register as he rang up another sale of Stacy's latest book, *Vengeance*, that featured a serial killer working among the political power brokers in DC. Twyla had read it, of course. She could not deny Stacy's talent at terrifying the reader and making them guess until the last page. You'd never expect this from the married, sweet and beautiful mother of a little girl. She was as normal a person as Twyla had ever met.

"Nice crowd tonight," Mr. Finch said. "Too bad Stacy doesn't write more than one book a year."

Too bad indeed. Because while hosting yoga classes and book clubs, and selling educational toys had sustained them, it would no longer be enough. For the past two years, the little bookstore, the only one in town, had been in a terrible slump. Her grandmother still kept the books, and she'd issued the warning earlier this year. Pulling them out of the red might require more than one great holiday season. Foot traffic had slowed as more people bought their books online.

"I've got a signed copy of Stacy's latest book for you." Lois, Mr. Finch's fiancée, set a stack of no less than ten books on the counter by the register. "And I grabbed a bunch of giving tree cards."

The cards were taken from a large stack of books in the shape of a Christmas tree Twyla set up every season. Instead of ornaments, tags indicated the names and addresses of children who either wanted, or needed, a book for Christmas.

"We can always count on you, sweetheart." Mr. Finch rang her up.

It was endearing the way residents supported the Thompson family bookstore. They might have been in this location for four decades, but they'd never needed as much help as in the past two years.

Mr. Finch, a widowed and retired senior citizen, volunteered his time at the shop so Twyla could occasionally go home. For a while now they hadn't been able to afford any paid help. Her parents were officially retired and had moved to Hill Country. Their contributions amounted to comments on the sad state of affairs when a bookstore had to host yoga classes. But the instructor gave Twyla a flat rate to rent the space, and she didn't see *them* coming up with any solutions. They didn't want to close up shop. Of *course* not. They simply wanted Twyla to solve this problem for the entire Thompson family by selling books and nothing else.

"I don't know what I'd do without either one of you," Twyla said fondly, patting Mr. Finch's back. "Or any of the other members of the Almost Dead Poets Society."

Many of the local senior citizens had formed a poetry group where they recited poems they'd written. It had all started rather innocently enough—a creative effort, and something to do with all their free time. Unfortunately, they also liked to refer to themselves as "literary" matchmakers. Literary not to *ever* be confused with "literally." They'd failed with Twyla so far, not that they'd ever give up trying. Last month they'd invited both her and Tony Taylor to a reading and not so discreetly attempted to fix them up.

You're both so beautiful, it's a little hard to look at you for long, Ella Mae, the founder of their little group, had said. *Kind of like the sun!*

The double Ts! Lois had exclaimed. *Or would that be the quadruple* Ts?

Quadruple, I think, Mr. Finch had said.

You won't even have to change the initials on your monogrammed towels! Patsy Villanueva had clapped her hands. *I mean if it works out, that is.*

But no pressure! Susannah held up a palm.

Twyla didn't own anything monogrammed, let alone towels, but she'd still exchanged frozen smiles with Tony. They'd arranged a coffee date just for fun. Unfortunately, as she'd known for years, Tony batted for the other team. He even had a live-in boyfriend that the old folks assumed was his roommate. It was an easy assumption to make since Tony was such a "man's man"—a grease monkey who lifted engines for a living. And he hadn't exactly come out of the closet, thinking his personal life was nobody's business. He was right, of course. But…

"You really *should* declare your love of show tunes, Tony," she'd teased.

"I'm not a cliché."

"Well, you *could* get married."

"I'm not ready to settle down." He scowled.

Still, they'd had a nice time, catching up on life post-high school. He'd asked after Noah Cahill, and of course she had all the recent updates on her best friend. In the end they'd decided she and Tony would definitely be double-dating at some point.

When Twyla could find a date.

This part wasn't going to be easy because Twyla had a bad habit. She preferred to spend her time alone and reading a book. Long ago, she'd accepted that she wouldn't be able to find true love inside the walls of her small rental. But accepting invitations to parties and bar hops wasn't her style. She wanted to be invited, really, but she just didn't want to go. An introvert's problem.

This was why she'd adopted a cat. But, she worried, if she didn't get a date soon, she was going to risk being known as the cat lady.

"That's the last copy!" Stacy stood from the table, beaming, holding a hand to her chest. "My publisher will be thrilled. I honestly can't *believe* it."

"I can." Twyla began to clear up the signing table. "You're very talented and it's about time people noticed. I just wish you'd write more books."

"So do I, but tell that to my daughter." Stacy sighed. "She's a holy terror, just like her father. Runs around all day, throwing things. I'm lucky if I get in a few hundred words a day."

"That's okay." Twyla chuckled. "We can't exactly base our business plan on how many books you write a year."

Stacy blinked and a familiar concern shaded her eyes. "Are you…are you guys doing okay? Should I maybe ask my publisher whether they can send some of their other authors here for a signing?"

As a bookseller, she knew everyone in the business was suffering, and publishers weren't financing many book tours. Stacy did those on her own dime, hence the local gig. Twyla didn't like lying to people but she liked their pity even less. She constantly walked a tightrope between the two.

"As long as we have another great holiday season, like all the others, we should be fine!" She hoped the forced quality of her über-positive attitude wasn't laying it on too thick.

But Stacy seemed to accept the good news, bless her heart.

"What a relief! We can't have a *town* without a bookstore."

"No, we can't," Mr. Finch agreed with a slight shake of his head. "It would be a travesty."

One by one the straggling customers left, carrying their purchases with them. Not long after, Stacy's husband, the devastatingly handsome Adam, dropped by to pick her up and drive her home. Everyone said their goodbyes.

Mr. Finch and Lois brought up the rear, wanting to help Twyla close up.

"You two go home!" She waved her hands dismissively. "I'm right behind you."

"I'll be by tomorrow for my morning shift promptly at nine." Mr. Finch took Lois's hand in his own.

"Are you sure you don't want to take a break? Take tomorrow off." Twyla went behind them, shutting off the lights. "You worked tonight."

"I'll get plenty of rest when I'm dead," Roy said, holding the door open for Lois.

"Roy!" Lois went ahead. "Please don't talk about the worst day of my life a second before it happens."

"No, darlin'." He sweetly brought her hand up to his lips. "I'll be around for a while. You manage to keep me young."

These two never failed to fill her heart with the warm fuzzies. Both had been widowed for a long time, and were on their second great love.

Which meant some people got two of those, and so far, Twyla didn't even have one.

Twyla arrived at her grandmother's home a few minutes later, having stopped first at the bakery for a salted caramel Bundt cake. She and Ganny usually met for dinner every Saturday night and she always brought dessert. Was it sad that a soon-to-be thirty-year-old single woman didn't have anything better to do on a Saturday night? Not at all. She had her gray cat, Bonkers, waiting at home. He was mean as the devil himself, but he'd been homeless when she adopted him from the shelter, so she was all he had.

Twyla also had at least half a dozen advanced reader

copy books on her nightstand waiting for her. There were also all the upcoming Charming holiday events she'd agreed to participate in because that's what one did as a business owner. Ava had told her about a rare angel investor offering a zero-interest loan to a local Charming business. On top of everything else, Twyla had to prepare an essay this month to be considered. It wasn't as if she didn't have anything else to do. Too much, in fact.

"Hello, Peaches."

Ganny bussed Twyla's cheek. Occasionally she still referred to Twyla by her old childhood nickname. Once, she'd eaten so many juicy fresh peaches from the tree in Ganny's yard that she threw up. It wasn't the best nickname in the world.

"How was the book signing?"

"A line out the door." Twyla followed Ganny into the ornate dining area connected to the kitchen and set the cake on the mahogany table.

Ganny had been widowed twice and her last husband, Grandpa Walt, a popular real estate broker, had left her with very little but this house. It was too big for Ganny, but she refused to leave it because of the dining room. It was big enough to accommodate large groups of people, which she felt encouraged Twyla's parents to visit several times a year.

"It was a good start to the month."

"Good, good. Well, that's enough book business talk for tonight." Ganny waved a hand dismissively. "I've got a surprise for you tonight. An early Christmas present."

"You didn't have to get me anything."

But a thrill whipped through Twyla because her

grandmother was renowned for her thoughtful gifts all year long. It could almost be anything. Maybe a trip to New York City, where Ganny had promised to finally introduce her to some of the biggest booksellers in the country. People she'd met over a lifetime of acquiring and selling books. Twyla had wanted to go back to New York for years. She could still feel the energy of the city zipping through her blood, taste the cheesecake from Junior's, and the slice of pepperoni pizza from Times Square.

"Why wouldn't I give my only granddaughter the best present in the world?" Ganny smiled with satisfaction. "He should be along any minute now."

All the breath left Twyla's body. Just the thought of another blind date struck her with a sadness she had no business feeling during the holidays. Everyone in town was conspiring to fix up "poor, sad Twyla who can't get a man."

She could get a man, but she wasn't concentrating her efforts on this.

Please let it not be Tony again. And yet there were so few single men her age left in town. Hadn't her grandmother always told Twyla she'd do fine on her own? If she couldn't find the right man, she didn't need *any* man? Twyla had embraced this truth. She wanted the perfect man or no one at all.

"Life with the right man is wonderful. But a life with the wrong man might as well be lived alone. So many things in life can replace a spouse. Work, travel and books, to start with," Ganny had said.

Twyla, then, *could* lead a happy and fruitful life without ever being married.

"Oh, Ganny." Twyla slumped on the chair. "You didn't fix me up with someone, did you?"

"Of course not, honey!" She patted Twyla's hand. "But speaking of which, you're not going to meet anyone special if you don't get out more."

"I'm just like you. Books are my family."

It seemed to have skipped a generation, because though her father, Ganny's son, had loyally run the family bookstore, it wasn't exactly his happy place.

"Yes, but keep in mind I made myself go out and meet people. It wasn't like it is today. Certainly not. I used to have three dates on the same day. No funny business, of course, but your mother already told me things are different."

Twyla couldn't imagine going out three times in one day. She'd be lucky to go out once every three years. Okay, she was exaggerating. But still. Men weren't exactly lining up to date her. One of them had said she'd look prettier if she'd stop wearing her black-rimmed glasses. Twyla refused to go the contact lens route because if glasses stopped a guy from being interested in her, it wasn't the guy she wanted anyway.

"Fine, I promise I'll go out! But please don't fix me up." Her friend Zoey had bugged her to go out with her and her boyfriend, Drew, and Twyla hadn't yet.

"No blind date. This is someone you actually want to see."

"I can't even imagine."

There was only one "he" she'd like to see, and he was all the way in Austin, at home with his girlfriend. Probably planning their wedding.

"That's it. I'm having dessert first." Twyla opened the cake box.

The doorbell rang and Ganny rose. "You stay here and close your eyes! Don't open them until I tell you to."

Oh, brother. It was like being twelve again. She clasped her hand over her eyes, but not before taking a finger swipe of salted caramel frosting, feeling… well, twelve again.

"Okay, fine. My eyes are closed."

Twyla heard the front door open and shut, Ganny's delighted laughter, but no other sounds from this "he" man. Nothing but the sounds of boots thudding as they followed Ganny's lighter steps.

"Can I open my eyes now? I would really like to have a piece of cake. Whoever you are, I hope you like cake."

"I love cake," the deep voice said.

Twyla didn't even have to open her eyes to recognize the teasing, flirty sound of her favorite person in the world. She didn't have to hazard a guess because she knew this man almost as well as she knew herself.

And Ganny was right. It *was* the best present.

Ever.

"Noah!"

Twyla stood and hurled herself into the open arms of Noah Cahill, her best friend.

Chapter Two

There were few things in his life Noah enjoyed as much as filling his arms with his best friend. He held Twyla close, all five feet nothing of her. Her dark hair longer now than it had been a year ago when he'd left Charming. Today she was wearing her book-pattern dress, which meant the store must have had a signing. The outfit was a type of uniform she wore for those events. She had a similar skirt in bright colors with patterns of dragons, swords and slayers.

God, she was a sight. The old familiar pinch squeezed his chest. He almost hadn't come home this Christmas, thinking it would be easier. There was already so much he hadn't told her when he normally told her everything.

Almost everything.

Then he'd narrowly missed death, or at the least a devastating injury, and everything changed in the course of days. He would not waste another minute of his life doing a job he no longer wanted to do.

"I thought you weren't coming home this Christmas!" Twyla said, coming to her tiptoes to hug him tight. Her arms wrapped around his neck.

Automatically and before he could stop himself, he turned his head to take in a deep breath of her hair. She always smelled like coconuts. He set her down reluctantly, but he was used to this feeling with Twyla. It was always this way—the push and pull always resulting in the distance he'd created due to guilt.

And loyalty.

"Things have changed."

"Noah isn't just *visiting*," Twyla's grandmother said, sounding pleased. "He's come home to stay."

Bless Mrs. Schilling's kind heart. She'd always been pulling for Noah, against any and all reason, even if he could have told her a thousand times it was useless. He was destined to pine after Twyla forever. What he wanted to have with her would never work and the door had been slammed shut years ago. Now the opening might as well be buried under rubble. Like the roof that nearly fell on him.

"You're here to stay?" Twyla brightened. "But what about your job in Austin?"

"I quit." He held his arms off to his sides with a shrug. "It's not for me. Not anymore."

"It's *exactly* you. You've been an adrenaline junkie since you were a boy. How is it not for you?"

Yeah, best not to tell her about the roof that fell inches from him during a building fire. His entire squad had been lucky to escape with no fatalities. Three had wound up with minor injuries.

Noah could have sworn something, or *someone*, had shoved him out of the way. In that moment, with the heat barreling toward him and unfurling like a living thing, he'd felt his brother, Will, there in the room with him. Will, shouting for him to get out of the way.

His long-dead older brother was telling Noah, in no uncertain terms, to stop trying to be a hero. To, for the love of God, stop rescuing people and start living his own life. Noah had first worked as an EMT, and then later a firefighter in nearby Houston for the past few years. He'd saved some people and lost some, but "imaginary Will" had called it. No matter what Noah did, he'd never get another chance to save Will.

And he was the only save that would have ever mattered. Now it was high time to honor his life instead. Noah may have always felt second best to his much smarter and accomplished brother, but that feeling wasn't one encouraged by Will. His older brother had always had Noah's back. Even on their last day together.

"It was good, for a while, but it's time to move on."

"But—"

"Let's have some of that delicious cake." Mrs. Schilling urged them to take a seat at the table. "We have plenty of time to discuss all this."

"I never say no to cake." Noah took a seat, avoiding Twyla's gaze.

If he looked too directly at her, she'd see everything in his eyes, so at times like this he had a system in place.

Don't make eye contact.

Three serving plates were passed around and Twyla sliced off generous pieces.

"No matter what, we're glad you're home," Mrs. Schilling said. "Aren't we, dear?"

"Yes, of course. It's just such a surprise. So…unexpected." Twyla took a bite of cake.

Using an old trick, he purposely looked at her ear, to make it look like he was meeting her eyes.

"It's a career choice. I have a really great opportunity here."

"Where are you staying?"

It was a fair question since he'd given up his rental when he'd grown tired of the memories that haunted him here and moved to Austin to start over.

"I rented one of those cottages by the beach. Just temporary until I find a place. The place where I'll be living is far less important than what I'll be doing." Noah winked.

This was his biggest news: the culmination of a long-held dream. He'd squashed it for so long after Will's death that he'd nearly forgotten it. But in that fiery building, he'd *remembered.*

"What *are* you going to be doing?"

"Taking over a business here in town." He'd start with the easy stuff first.

"Wonderful!" Mrs. Schilling clapped her hands. "Obviously, I have always loved the entrepreneurial spirit. Why, it's the reason the Thompson family started Once Upon a Book."

"What kind of business? Fire investigation? Teaching safety? You would make a *great* teacher." Twyla smiled and took another bite of cake.

He hoped the news wasn't going to kill her like it might his own mother. But he couldn't live the rest of his life in fear. Or worse yet, accommodating the fears of others.

"No. I'm taking over the boat charter. Mr. Curry is retiring, and he's been looking for a buyer for a year or more."

When his news was met with such silence that he heard Mrs. Schilling's grandfather clock ticking, he continued.

"He actually wants someone local to take it over, so he'll work terms out with me. I have enough hours on the water, so I'll be taking the USCG test for my captain's license. I've obviously already had first aid training and then some. Until I get my license, I'll have Finn's help and he already has his license. Mr. Curry said he'd be around awhile longer, too, if we need help." He filled his mouth with a big piece of cake.

Twyla sucked in a breath, and Mrs. Schilling's shaky hand went to her throat. Other than that, Noah thought everything here would be okay. Nothing to see here. Sure thing. They'd all get used to the idea. Eventually.

Just give them a couple of decades.

"Are you serious?" Twyla pushed her plate of unfinished cake away.

Only he would fully understand the significance of the move. For Twyla not to finish a slice of cake meant that in her opinion, the world just might be ending.

"Yes, I'm serious. Ask yourself whether if anyone else said the same thing, you'd have this kind of a reaction."

"That's not even funny. You're *not* anyone else." She took a breath and whispered her next words. "You're Will's brother. You...you almost died out there, too."

"Now, Twyla…let the man finish." This from Twyla's grandmother, thankfully, the voice of reason.

She didn't let him finish.

"If this is my surprise, I don't like it." Twyla stood.

With that she walked right out of her grandmother's kitchen.

"Twyla!" her grandmother chided. "Oh, dear. Noah, I'm sorry. She's had a rough year. The bookstore isn't doing well, and—"

"Let me talk to her."

"Noah? Are you sure about this? If Twyla reacts this way, you can only imagine how your poor mother—"

"I know. *And* I'm sure."

He found Twyla outside on the wraparound porch's swing, bare feet dangling as she stared into the twinkling sky. Without a word, he plopped himself next to her and nudged her knee.

"Hey."

"Hey." She leaned into him, and he tamped down the rush of raw emotion that single move brought. "I'm sorry. I may have…overreacted."

She couldn't stay angry at him for long. Neither one of them could. Not since they'd been kids.

"You think? It's not that I don't understand the concern but everyone seems to forget I grew up boating. Will and I both did. I'm going to be careful and follow all relevant safety practices. Probably go overboard with them." He chuckled and elbowed her. "See what I did there?"

"Funny man."

"I just…can't pretend anymore."

Starting over had served its purpose. He'd lived in a city in which no one knew him as Will's younger brother. A new place where he'd excelled and never been second best. He'd tried to settle down into a stable relationship with Michelle. But he hadn't been happy even before the roof collapse.

"What are you pretending?"

"That I'm okay living someone else's life. I don't want to live in Austin. I want to live here. You do realize the ocean is not the only danger in life?"

"Sure, I'd prefer you do something normal like… I don't know, real estate? You'd make a killing. *Everybody* loves you."

Wind up the only surviving brother after a boating tragedy and you're bound to get a lot of sympathy. He was tired of that, too. Another reason he'd left town.

He grunted. "Real estate is not going to happen. Too much paperwork."

"Why now? Did something happen?"

While he could tell her, letting her realize that it wasn't only water that could kill a man, this didn't seem like the right time. Later, he'd tell her about the roof collapse. Later, he'd tell her about Michelle.

And everything else. Someday. Just…not now.

"I think Will would want this. And I want this. This was our dream when we were kids. We'd wake up every day and go fishing. Every day would be like a vacation."

"I know he would want you to be happy."

"*This* is going to make me happy. I'm tired of living for other people. You only get one life. This one is mine."

They both sat in silence for a beat. Will had been only eighteen when they'd lost him in the accident that nearly took Noah's life, too. Their family had never been the same. When Noah's parents divorced, his father left the state and now rarely spoke to Noah. His mother still lived in Charming and had never truly gotten over the loss of her oldest son. She'd laid her dreams at Will's feet, who had done everything she'd ever asked of him. He'd been the good son, the strong academic. Noah had been the classic bad boy, unable to live up to the impossible standard that Will set.

"Remember when you, me and Will would lie under the stars at night?" Twyla pushed her legs out to start swinging. "And Will renamed the Little Dipper 'Noah Dipper' after you, and the Big Dipper was 'Will Dipper'?"

"Yeah, even if 'Bill Dipper' would have sounded better."

Noah smiled at the memory. Will believed in the power behind words and used to play around with letters all the time. Mixing them up, creating new words. Like Twyla, he was a bit of a book nerd. The valedictorian in his graduating class of Charming High. He and Twyla had been so much alike it was no wonder that though Noah met Twyla first, it was Will who wound up dating her. His courtship with her might have been short and sweet, but at least he'd had one.

"He used to like renaming stuff. Combining two words together, shifting letters. Word play."

"Mine was easy. Twilight was hereafter renamed Twyla for short." She chuckled. "Totally made sense."

It had been a long while since they talked about Will. Remembered. He was that silent spot between them, keeping them apart but making Noah wish for nothing more than those good times.

"He had the biggest crush on you."

Of course, Noah had been the first to have the crush, except *crush* might not have been the right word. He'd been astounded. He recalled literally gaping when he first laid eyes on Twyla helping her mother at the bookstore, dressed in a pink dress and matching shoes. Pushing her horn-rimmed glasses up her nose and giving him a shy smile. She looked like an angel to an eleven-year-old boy.

"We should do that again sometime," Twyla said. "Lie under the stars together."

He almost jerked his neck back in surprise. She'd never suggested anything like this before. It amounted to doing something together that they'd only ever done with Will.

It was like…reinventing it.

"Why?"

"Why?" She spoke just above a whisper. "Because they're still there. Still twinkling. Is it okay with you if I want to look at them again and see them in a different way?"

He reached to lighten the moment. "Rename them, you mean?"

"Anything. Of course, maybe Michelle wouldn't like it. You and I spending so much time together."

Ah, that's why she'd brought it up. She didn't know about his breakup with the woman he'd dated while in Austin. He'd brought her to Charming once, where she'd met Twyla and the family. She thought Michelle was still there between them, a safe buffer from getting too close to him. There was no point in telling her the truth. Let her relax in her false belief. Their guilt had kept them apart this long. What was another decade?

Noah would throw himself into work. His dream.

He'd live his life the way he wanted to and reach for happiness wherever he could find it. Around every blind corner. Behind every rogue wave. Fake it till he made it. He was excited about the future for the first time since he could recall.

Life was too short and if Will hadn't taught him that, then certainly the roof collapse had.

"No, probably not. She wouldn't like it," he lied. "But I don't care."

Twyla took off her glasses and wiped the lenses on the edge of her shirt.

She didn't say anything to that—probably because they didn't usually talk about any of his girlfriends. It was better that way.

He changed the subject. "Is it true you're having problems with the bookstore?"

Twyla sighed. "Why do you think I want to lie under the stars like when I was ten? Yes, we're having trouble. What else is new?"

"I thought everything was better after the last holiday season. You always say December counts for ninety percent of your business."

"Welcome to the book world. A lot can change in a year. The ground is constantly shifting under my feet."

"Well, you can't close the bookstore."

"Everyone says that."

"We grew up in that museum. Reading dragon slayer books in those cozy corner nooks filled with pillows. I'll help. Just put me to work."

She smiled. "You're going to be busy if you insist on this madness."

"I'll figure out a way."

"Hey, does this mean you'll be at the tree lighting ceremony tomorrow?"

"Wouldn't miss it."

"Wait until you see the little book shaped ornaments we have for the tree."

She sounded excited and like her old self for the first time tonight.

"Let me guess. Dragon slayer books?"

"Among some others, of course. We can't ignore *The Night Before Christmas* and the other classics."

Sometimes, Noah could still see himself and Will sitting among the shelves of dusty books. They'd read quietly every afternoon after school because Twyla's parents didn't mind being an unofficial after-school center. It wasn't until much later, when he and Twyla had been in the depths of their shared grief, that they'd found "the book." The one that had defined the years after Will. They'd take turns reading chapters. One week the book stayed with Noah and he'd read three chapters, and one week it was with Twyla. He'd write and post stickers in the margins of the book, which had technically belonged to Twyla.

Noah would comment: *That idiot deserved to be killed by the dragon.*

And Twyla would answer: *Sometimes the dragon chooses the right victim.*

They'd mark significant parts, but almost never the same ones. Noah was far more impressed with dragon slayer tools while Twyla loved the mushy stuff about love and sacrifice. The book came to belong to them both, since they'd literally made it their own. Noah had never done this with any other book before or since and he'd venture she never had either. For reasons he didn't quite understand, they'd made this particular book, *A Dragon's Heart*, their own. They shared the words until the day Noah stole the book from Twyla. There was just no other way to put it.

He'd "borrowed" the book without returning it.

That, at least, was something he'd never tell her.

Chapter Three

The next day, having risen before dawn to drive to the docks, Noah watched the sunrise while he waited for Mr. Curry to arrive. The view was calming and soothing in the way a Gulf Coast native could appreciate. Gold mixed with shades of blue and painted the sky with morning. Noah found little more beautiful than a Gulf Coast sunrise other than a sunset accompanied by fireflies. Over the years, he'd been seeing less of them lighting up the coastal nights.

"You're early." Mr. Curry emerged from his brightly detailed pickup truck.

The truck itself was practically a Charming landmark. Granted, it had seen better days and could definitely use a paint job. But the etching of two dolphins meeting halfway, blending into sharp blue and purple hues still grabbed attention. The letters spelled *Nacho*

Boat Adventures and the phone number. Boat tours, fishing charters, diving excursions, water skiing, rentals. Group rates available.

A walking advertisement. Not that Noah would need to take out an ad because the business, decades old, was practically the apex of Charming tourism.

And if Noah was early, it was because he couldn't wait to get started.

He handed Mr. Curry a coffee cup. "Will you throw in the truck, too?"

"Let's talk inside." Mr. Curry put his key in the door of the unimpressive A-line shack on the pier.

Weather-beaten and somewhat battered, the outside could also use a makeover. So could Mr. Curry, for that matter, who had grown his white beard down to his chest and looked older than his sixty-five years.

"Are you doing okay?" Noah asked, watching him hobble inside.

"Ah, it's the arthritis. Makes me a grump most days. Don't take it personal." He took a swig of coffee, then held it up. "Thanks for this."

"No problem." Drinking from his own cup, Noah took in the shop he hadn't been inside of for years.

A handwritten schedule of boat tours hung on a whiteboard behind the register. Surf boards were propped against the rear walls, hung near boating equipment like ropes and clips. The smells of wood and salt were comforting. Noah inhaled and took it all in. It was his burden to have never had a healthy fear of the ocean. And even after all he'd been through, he still didn't shy away from the memories of long summer days boating. Their father had taught both of his boys everything he knew, and they'd manned the captain's wheel from the time they were thirteen and fourteen. Two boys, a year apart. Irish twins, his mother called them.

"You should know. I'm moving." Mr. Curry interrupted Noah's thoughts.

"I know. That's why you're selling."

"Me and the Mrs. We're headed west to Arizona."

"Landlocked?" Noah raised his brow. This he had not expected.

"Hell, yeah. They got lakes. Need the dry and hot weather for my stupid arthritis." He went behind the counter and seemed to be fiddling around back there. "That's all to say that while I want someone like you to take over, I also need someone who's going to stick around. Do I make myself clear? I can stay on awhile and take some of those boat tours we've already scheduled for the real die-hards, but there's no turning back. No second thoughts. Of course, you could sell, but you see how long it's taken me. This isn't the greatest moneymaker in the world."

"I figured." Noah had some ideas of his own to increase business but best not interrupt the man's flow of thoughts.

"You won't get rich owning this business, but you will also never be poor."

"I'm in this for the long haul. I picture myself a grandfather, like you, finally retiring someplace dry because I have arthritis." Noah reached for some other older person's ailment and came up with nothing. "Or something."

"That's what I want to see. You, growing old in this town. Safe. Giving tours. Teaching. Because, well, you know..."

Noah let the silence hang between them for only a moment. He knew where this would be going. Knew it far too well.

"I know," Noah completed the sentence. "And the accident still doesn't define who I am. Never did."

"My wife is going to kill me twice when she finds out who I sold to. I told her I had an offer from a local. That I'd offered financing to help the young man out. She thinks the idea is great. But she doesn't know it's *you*."

Noah sighed. He'd felt the protectiveness of this town come over him like a choke hold. It no longer felt like protection. It felt controlling. Unreasonable.

"It's time for all of us to move on."

"*If* you're sure." Mr. Curry crossed his arms. "Then this…is a done deal."

"I'm absolutely one hundred percent sure. I'm never going back to firefighting again. One roof nearly falling on me is enough."

Mr. Curry gaped. "Hot damn, son. You might be the luckiest man I've ever met. All right. Welcome aboard."

He chuckled, then went on to give Noah the speed version of the business he'd managed for two decades. It was all written down, of course…somewhere. Though good help was hard to find, Noah would have two staff members staying on through the transition. They were both part-time workers—teens who loved boating and were willing to be paid a microscopic salary for the pleasure of working for the new boss.

Concern hit Noah like a hot spike, but he forced himself to shake it off. Teenagers near water did not *automatically* mean danger.

"What do they do around here?"

"As little or as much as you want. Diana answers the phone and takes the bookings. Sells the little equipment we have for sale and the surf boards." He waved his hand in the air. "Tee, that's the ridiculous nickname he goes by, is working on a boating license. You can fire them both as far as I'm concerned but they're good kids and for a while they'll know more than you will about how we run things."

He had a point.

"Be at the bank tomorrow morning and we'll sign the papers. Owner financing the first year. It's all in the contract." He then reached under the register and came up with a small box. "May as well take these with you since you're here."

Noah accepted the box. "What's all this?"

"Christmas."

Indeed, dozens of tree ornaments in the shape of boats announced "A Merry Christmas from Nacho Boat." They were for the tree lighting ceremony tonight. This meant a couple of things. After tonight, almost everyone in town would know Noah was the new owner of Nacho Boat Adventures.

He was on borrowed time before his mother heard about the contract he'd sign tomorrow morning.

But he told himself one more day wouldn't hurt anything.

Just before the tree lighting ceremony, Twyla closed up shop and drove her sedan the short drive to the boardwalk. She carried her basket full of ornaments for the lighting of the Christmas tree. This had always been the first Charming event at the start of the month, which kicked off the season's festivities. This never failed to make her heart buzz with anticipation, even if the excitement was dulled tonight due to Noah's unexpected news. She didn't like the idea of him taking over Nacho Boat any more than his mother would. But, more than anyone else, she understood what it was like to live under the heavy weight of opinion.

Charming was a small town and its residents were similar to an extended family you loved to hate. Even if more than a decade had passed, she was still thought of as "Will's girl." Even though she and Will barely dated for a year before he broke up with her because he'd be going away to college. Of course, that never happened. He'd never made it to college. She was Will's *last* girlfriend and some people, Noah's mother included, saw her forever frozen in the tragic role. The reason, she understood, was that Will himself would remain forever eighteen.

Twyla, on the other hand, would be twenty-seven this year. Like Noah, who'd been trying to escape his role as town hero responsible for the biggest water rescue in Charming history, she'd been trying to move on from the role of grieving ex-girlfriend. She'd signed up for some of the dating apps and forced herself on the occasional date. She'd even expressed her interest in Adam Cruz when he'd arrived in town over a year ago. He'd been single for about two minutes, however, and then there went that opportunity.

Over the years, she'd dated men here and there that Noah interestingly always found fault with. Yet he'd never even tried to fix her up. Not even with his best friend, Finn. Noah would sing the guy's praises all the live long day but whenever he was single, Noah stopped talking about Finn. She and Noah had never been on dates together, keeping that part of each other's life separate. She never complained about guys to him, and he never complained about women. But as far as she could tell, Noah never had any issues with the female population, other than the fact that he'd never seemed ready to settle down. Michelle, someone he'd met in Austin, was simply the latest and Twyla wondered how long they'd last long distance.

Walking toward the boardwalk along the seawall, Twyla took in the holiday scene. As usual, the decor on the boardwalk was already in full swing. Many of the vendors would stay open through their mild winter, their shops decorated to the hilt with snowflakes, trees and more lights. Sounds from the roller coaster on the amusement park end of the boardwalk were as loud as on any summer night, only with residents and not many tourists. Families were out having fun, creating memories. She strolled along accompanied by the sound of seagulls cawing and foraging for food in the sand. Aromatic and delicious scents of fresh coffee, hot cocoa and popcorn competed. She would need some hot cocoa sooner rather than later.

Despite the lower tourism rate that tended to hit every business, winter in Charming was her favorite time of the year, when temperatures hovered in the low sixties and, on a good day, reached the high fifties. She loved sweater and boot weather. Finally, she could haul out her cowboy boots and wear them without anyone teasing her.

She waved as she passed the Lazy Maisy kettle corn store, selling their classic peppermint-flavored, red-and-green popcorn as they did every December, each worker dressed like an elf for the entire month. Strands of white lights hung from every storefront. A plastic model of Santa and his sleigh guided by a reindeer were suspended across one side of the boardwalk, cheery signs everywhere announcing a "charming" Christmas. Yes, thank you. Twyla would have a charming Christmas indeed.

Noah was back. Christmas would be even better now.

She had to keep telling herself that. Nacho Boat had a great safety record. Noah was bright and intelligent. He'd take all necessary precautions because he'd never want his mother to hurt again. For so long, they'd all walked on eggshells around Katherine Cahill. Twyla included. The woman had suffered enough, but Noah did have a point. His career as a firefighter wasn't exactly a desk job. At least here, they'd all be able to keep an eye on him. Keep him safe. Yes, she'd do that. For Will and for Katherine. But mostly, for herself.

"Hey, Twyla."

She turned to find herself face-to-face with Valerie Kinsella, a third-grade teacher and wife of one of the three former Navy SEALs who ran the Salty Dog Bar & Grill.

"Check these out. I think the ornaments are amazing this year. I found a specialty shop in Dallas with a great price." She handed the box to Valerie, who would mix it up with the others.

"You've outdone yourself as usual." Valerie smiled.

Baskets filled with all donated ornaments would be passed around to the residents, who each got to choose at least one to put on a branch. People were already gathering around the huge tree in the center. Ava Del Toro, president of the Chamber of Commerce, climbed up the temporary risers hauled over from the high school.

Meanwhile, this year's Santa walked through the crowd, handing candy canes out to kids as the ornament baskets made the rounds. Twyla glanced in the crowd for Noah, since he'd texted her that he'd be there early and she should come and find him. At first, she didn't see him at all, and then noticed him talking to Sabrina, one of his old girlfriends. Most of his life, Noah had never failed to get the attention of girls, and later, women. It was the whole bad boy thing. He'd surfed, driven fast cars and even had a motorcycle for a nanosecond. Twyla hated motorcycles but she loved those boots Noah got to wear when he rode one. Even teachers liked Noah. He wasn't a stellar student, but he was funny and kind.

When he'd been hospitalized after the accident, there had been so many flowers in his room that it resembled a botanical garden.

Twyla watched now as Sabrina leaned into Noah, touched his broad shoulder and tossed back her long red hair. The familiar and unwelcome pinch of jealousy, this time on Michelle's behalf, burned in Twyla's stomach. Then Noah turned, saw Twyla and his smile brightened. He gave a little "see ya later" wave to Sabrina.

He walked over to Twyla, hands stuck in the pockets of his blue denim jeans. "Hey, Peaches."

She grinned, ready to tease him. "Um, I'd be careful. You're going to make Michelle jealous."

A flash of guilt crossed his eyes. "Yeah, about that—"

But he was interrupted by a loud Ava nearly yelling through the bullhorn in her hands.

"Welcome, everyone! It's time for the lighting of the

tree! So! Fun! This year our tree is donated by Tree Growers of Bent, Oregon. Another Douglas fir. Before we hit the switch and light up the night sky, you'll each get to place an ornament on the tree. Just reach in the baskets we're all passing out. Find an ornament in there and put it on the tree! And don't forget the upcoming Snowflake Float Boat Parade, followed by the first annual literary costume event at Once Upon a Book. Come dressed as your favorite literary character and support the giving tree! One of you could win a gift card worth hundreds of dollars, which ought to help with all that holiday shopping."

Many turned to Twyla and smiled, giving her a thumbs-up. She'd love to claim the idea as her own, but it had been yet another one of Ava's creative brainstorms. The woman was a marketing genius when it came to town tourism and supporting local business. Before Noah's return, the costume event would have been the most excitement she'd have all year. She'd been planning for months, her own ideas swinging between Elizabeth Bennet and Hermione Granger. She hadn't yet decided, but she already had the long Jane Austen-style dress she'd found for a deep discount on eBay.

"Literary character." Noah winked and tipped back on his heels. "Does dragon slayer count?"

Her heart raced at the memory. Their favorite book. She'd misplaced *A Dragon's Heart* about a year ago, just before the move into a smaller rental to save money. Books tended to get swallowed whole in a bookstore and half the time she expected to come across it on a shelf. So far, she hadn't. Everyone, including Mr. Finch, was on the lookout. This particular copy was unlike any other, and even though the genre had grown out of popularity with most readers, Twyla liked to read the book once a year. She'd ordered another copy for that reason alone, but it could never take the place of the one she'd lost. Noah's handwriting was in the margins of that book, along with her own.

"You can come as anything you'd like. I'm just happy to have you."

She nearly corrected herself but then let it go. He knew what she meant. She didn't *have* him. Michelle had him. And though she wondered with every moment that passed what he'd meant when he said, "About that..." she refused to ask.

"I kind of look like a dragon slayer and I'm sure I can find a cool sword."

She chuckled. "You do *not* look like a dragon slayer and I'm fairly sure you already own a plastic toy sword."

"Are you calling me an overgrown child?" He narrowed his eyes, filled with humor and mischief.

"Maybe."

"Got to say, it's tough to hang out with someone who knows me so well." The basket came around to them and Noah dug for several long seconds, causing even Valerie to quirk a brow. "Ah, yeah. Here we go."

He held up the ornament depicting the cover of *Where the Wild Things Are*. "My favorite book. Still read it every night before bed."

"Bless your heart," Valerie said and waited while Twyla dug through the basket.

She picked out an elf from the Lazy Maisy store and together she and Noah went forward and placed the ornaments. Side by side like they'd done for years. Just like old times.

A few minutes later, the lights slowly went up the giant tree, starting from the lower half and scrolling slowly to the top until bright lights beckoned.

Noah turned to Twyla. "Let the wild rumpus start."

Chapter Four

The night was clear and bright, not socked in with fog like the Gulf Coast could get on some nights. Twyla and Noah strolled along the seawall. She should go home soon and feed Bonkers, even if he was the most antisocial cat on earth. Also, she looked forward to changing into her favorite jammies and curling up under the covers with her book.

But she kept hoping Noah would restart the conversation from earlier without any prompting.

About that...

"I'm signing the contract tomorrow morning."

Noah went on to explain how he'd managed to get Mr. Curry to agree to owner financing and then cashed out all of his savings to invest. He'd now be the proud owner of a catamaran, rental equipment and big plans to grow the business. Twyla swallowed hard at the thought of how fully invested Noah was in this new venture. Now she'd have no choice but to be his cheerleader or stand by as he lost…everything.

"I'm all in."

"Have you told your mother?"

Twyla could only imagine how that conversation would go over.

"Not yet."

She walked next to him as he ambled onto a pier and sat, his long legs swinging over the edge. It was on the tip of Twyla's tongue to ask how Michelle felt about him moving back to Charming and whether or not she'd be joining him. But she simply let Noah take the lead as he asked questions about the bookstore and drilled her on the finances until she asked him to drop it.

"But I'm worried," he said.

"Don't be. If we have to, we'll sell. It was a nice run."

He snorted, understanding her words betrayed how difficult it would be for her to let go. "And what will you do then?"

"Ganny always promised me a trip to New York City to introduce me to some of the booksellers she'd met over the years. Last night, I thought that was going to be my surprise."

"Sorry to disappoint."

She playfully slugged his shoulder. "You never could, Noah. Stop it. You are always the best surprise."

He turned to her then, so close she could breathe in his delicious scent. The moonlight made his dark eyes shimmer and her heart tugged with the familiar warmth. *Noah.* She didn't think she'd ever love anyone quite the same way she loved her best friend.

"Yeah. Something you should know about me and Michelle. We're not together."

Poor Noah. Weren't they a pair? He had about as much luck as she did in the relationship department. "What happened?"

"I told her the life she wants to lead is not my life. Then she accused me of having commitment issues. Commitment-phobe, I think she called me." He whistled. "It was ugly. It wasn't great to admit to myself that she's probably right. But I wasn't going to ask her to come along with me on this new adventure. This is my thing, my dream, and I won't answer to anyone."

She linked her arm through his. "When you're ready, the Almost Dead Poets Society likes to play matchmaker."

"Um, no thanks."

Twyla chuckled. "Last month they set me up with Tony."

"That would never work. For obvious reasons."

"It was better than Zoey, who fixed me up with Gus."

Noah's neck jerked back. "*That* loser?"

"He's a bit handsy but I wouldn't call him a loser."

"Did he *try* something with you?" Noah narrowed his eyes.

Her cheeks flushed. "No, and never mind."

They sat quietly for another few minutes as the waves lapped against the wood piles of the pier.

"Do you think you'll leave town if the bookstore closes?"

"I don't know, but I might need to leave. At least for a while."

"Why? I just got back."

"Noah, you're not the only one that thinks it might be nice to start over somewhere else." She swallowed hard. "Do you realize I still occasionally get referred to as Will's girlfriend?"

"You mean by someone other than my mother?" Noah shook his head. "If you want her to move on from your tragic love story, you need to give her something else to talk about. Give *everyone* something to talk about. Learn from my experience. Life is too short to please other people."

"You must really mean it this time. Breaking up with another girlfriend is going to make your mother pretty unhappy."

"Yeah, well, so is buying Nacho Boat."

"That one's going to worry a lot of people."

"Don't you be one of them. I'm going to stick around for a long while. Long enough to make sure you don't get fixed up on any lousy blind dates. Everyone is going through me from now on." He thumped his chest.

"Really? You're not going to find something wrong with every date I have? That's kind of your thing."

"It's only *been* my thing because of the men you've picked."

She bristled at the memories, because she had a truckload of them. "How was I supposed to know Jimmy Lee was engaged to be married?"

"You couldn't have known. That's why you have me."

But she also had him to stop her from dating some of the better-looking guys in town.

"Well...what about Finn?" she asked.

Noah blinked. *"Finn?"*

You would have thought she'd asked him to fix her up with Chris Hemsworth.

"Is that so crazy? Isn't he single again?"

"Finn is going to be busy. He's my partner and is helping me get this business off the ground. He won't have quality time to spend with you and that's what you deserve."

She hesitated from stating she wouldn't be that picky with the right man. For reasons she didn't quite understand, Noah did not want her dating his other best friend. To her, it was further confirmation that, in his mind, she'd never belong to anyone but Will.

"Fine." She stood, frustration spreading through her like a wildfire. "This lonely spinster is going home now."

"Hey." He followed her, coming within inches of her before he stopped and reached to slide a warm palm down her arm. "Don't be mad."

His touch, the warm timbre in his voice when he apologized, never failed to squeeze her heart with a powerful ache.

"I'm not *mad.* Just…tired of being lonely. I don't need forever but I refuse to spend another Christmas alone. This might be one of the few times when you're single at Christmas, but it's not new to me."

"Great. If that's really what you want, I'll ask Finn if he's interested in dating someone again." He grimaced, like the thought of the two of them together made him sick. "What's so great about Finn, anyway? I don't see it. He's tall, sure, but so am I."

She nearly rolled her eyes. *Tall* had never been on her list of qualities for the perfect man.

"What do you mean? He's a nice guy, and he's got one fantastic quality. He's available."

The next morning, Noah left the local bank as the proud owner of Nacho Boat Adventures. He drove the truck Mr. Curry had indeed thrown in as part of the deal straight to the docks. A few residents honked when they saw him driving down the road in the painted truck, giving him a thumbs-up.

Today, he'd called for a meeting of his staff to discuss the transition. Noah had a running list of things to do started on his phone app and he glanced at it now.

1. Staff meeting
2. Inventory
3. Boat inspection
4. Check the ledgers
5. Make plans for grand opening
6. Join the Chamber of Commerce
7. Talk to Finn about Twyla (maybe next week)
8. Call Mom

Nope, he hadn't called his mother yet. For all she knew, he was still on the job in Austin. No harm done. The fact that he'd listed talking to her below talking to Finn said it all. The problem was that Noah was like many men in his generation. He hesitated to disappoint women until the last possible second.

It was the primary reason his relationship with Michelle had gone way past its natural expiration date. He'd tried to fall in love with Michelle with everything he had, agreeing it was time to settle down and have a family. He wanted that, too—children and a wife to grow old with. Someone who made him feel good about himself every day, someone who loved him unconditionally. Someone he looked forward to *seeing* every day and not out of obligation. Someone who looked just as good without makeup and perfect hair.

Someone like Twyla, but...*not* Twyla.

Noah opened up shop, and as the morning progressed, he set up, pinning a scrolled red banner Ava had handed him this morning after his signing at the bank: *Under new ownership.*

The first staff member to arrive was Eddie Pierce. He had a Mohawk and wore board shorts, boat shoes and a black T-shirt that read: *I hate it when the voices inside my head go silent. I never know what they're planning.* According to Mr. Curry, he was the one working on his captain's license. Well, he'd be working on it for a while longer if Noah had anything to do with it. He intended to keep everyone on his staff safe.

"Call me Tee, Bossman." He fist bumped with Noah.

"Tee?"

"I like to wear T-shirts year-round. It's kinda my thing."

His other staff member, Diana, arrived just behind Tee, the girl who booked appointments and answered the phone.

When he greeted her and introduced himself, she barely looked at him.

"What do we call you?" Tee said. "Mr. Cahill? Can I call you Bossman? Head honcho? Captain? Nacho Man?"

"Nacho Man is my favorite of those, but just call me Noah."

"Chill. Dude, that's super easy. I had a lot of other great names but that one works, too."

The girl had still not looked at Noah, but she made an agreeable sound.

"I know Mr. Curry has given y'all a lot of freedom

here, but I'm a stickler for rules. Regulations. Safety first and foremost. Got me?"

Jesus, he sounded like a drill sergeant. Tee's neck jerked back slightly, and Diana continued to study her shoes.

He pulled back some, clearing his throat. "Of course, we're going to have fun here, too. No doubt about that. This is a great part-time job and I appreciate your dedication. I'll be hiring some others as time passes and we grow the business like I plan. But first things first. Let's take a look at the inventory. Today, I want a list of everything we own in this shop and how many we have."

"Um, we did inventory," Tee offered.

"A year ago," Noah said. "I have to believe there might be some changes."

"He's right," Diana said, looking up for a second. She caught Noah's gaze and blushed a thousand shades of crimson.

"Yeah, I guess." Tee shrugged.

"Inventory is not fun, I know, but it's necessary to a solid business plan. I'll start ordering right away if we're short on anything." He offered Tee one of the laptops he'd invested in to bring the business into the new millennium. "Everything has to reconcile with what we have listed on the master spreadsheet."

Tee not so discreetly passed the laptop to Diana.

"Also, all boating excursions are on hold until I personally inspect every inch of the catamaran. I have to prep it for the Snowflake Float Boat Parade."

"But—" Diana began.

"Shouldn't take me long." He pointed to Diana. "You can reschedule. Blame it on the switch in ownership and the fact that the new boss is a hard-ass."

She flushed an interesting shade of purple. "Um, yes."

Noah scrolled through his phone notes to see if he'd missed anything. "Any questions?"

"Can we have Pizza Party Saturdays?" Tee said, scratching the side of his Mohawk. "Mr. Curry said that'd be up to the new owners."

Far be it from him to ruin all the excitement around here. He remembered the fun of being a teenager far too well.

"Sure. Let's see how we do this week, and then we'll talk."

Chapter Five

"They're here!" Twyla ran to the shop door and threw it open for the delivery guy to come inside.

At Once Upon a Book, receiving day was a bit like celebrating Christmas once a month, all year long. For December, Twyla had ordered extra copies of the children's books on the giving tree wish list. But as usual, there was a mix of everything. The latest *New York Times* fiction bestsellers, a little bit of mystery, fantasy, romance and women's fiction. She'd also ordered several copies of the latest nonfiction number one bestseller in the country—a memoir from a cervical cancer survivor. And the special orders for poetry books, at the request of her staunchest supporters, were also arriving. They always sold out within a day.

"Look at you." Carlos, the UPS guy, grinned as he hauled one box in over his shoulder. "I love book day."

"Even if these boxes are the heaviest?"

"Nah, why do you think I work out?" He set the box down, then curled his arm, showing off biceps. "Months of weight lifting all to prepare for the holiday season."

He left, waving with a wink and a goofy smile. Twyla went to opening boxes and shelving. She had to remove some of the older books that hadn't sold, always causing a heavy ache to form in her throat. *Books without homes.* But though most of the publishers had a good return policy, Twyla usually donated them to organizations like the women's shelter and the local library, of course. Probably not the best business practice, come to think of it. Next year, if they made it through, she'd have to start returning unsold inventory.

Using her X-Acto knife, Twyla carefully sliced through the top of a box. The wonderful scent of paper and ink immediately filled her with memories. Twyla had an e-reader like everyone else, but there was nothing like the feel of a book in her hands. She turned it over and admired the cover, then read the synopsis on the back of the book and all the author endorsements.

Sliding a heavy box down the aisle, she moved over to the children's section. The same throw pillows Ganny had bought on a trip to India with her second husband years ago were scattered cozily in a nook. Twyla smiled at the *Where the Wild Things Are* tapestry that hung on the wall nearby. Leave it to Noah to mention Christmas as a wild rumpus. He wasn't wrong. But she wished she could have people knocking her doors down like they did at the big-box retailers in Houston.

Maybe instead of donating these books, she should line them up outside and offer a two-for-one discount.

Something to think about even if she hated discounting books. It seemed criminal, like she was somehow devaluing them. But every book deserved to find a home. She'd just finished making shelf space for new additions when the familiar bell chimed as someone swung open the doors. It was wrong to hope for Noah, of course, because he'd be busy all day. But she hoped for him anyway.

"Hey there, girlfriend!" Zoey Lambert, Twyla's good friend who ran Glamtique, walked inside.

The boutique was the perfect place for the always-fashion-conscious Zoey. Gorgeous and statuesque, she was often mistaken for a model. Her black corkscrew curls framed her flawless latte skin.

"I'm back here." Twyla waved from the children's section. "It's delivery day."

Zoey appeared around the corner, her eyes narrowed in concern. "Oh, no. That also means books-go-away day. You want to go have a drink after work? Drown your sorrows? Is there a book I can buy before it goes bye-bye?"

"It's just business. By now I should realize I order too many in anticipation of a book's success. But—"

"No one can guarantee any book's success." Zoey completed the sentence. She understood the book business nearly as much as Twyla did—the casualty of being the best friend of a bookseller.

"I don't want to go anywhere, but why don't you come over? We'll watch a movie and I'll make cupcakes."

It had been a while since they'd had a girl's night because Zoey was spending much of her spare time power dating a kickboxing trainer from Houston. She'd gone in for lessons and left with a boyfriend. This was always the way with Zoey, who never seemed to have any trouble in the romance department.

Zoey took her phone out and started swiping. "If you don't go out sometimes, you'll never meet anyone."

"Ugh. Yeah, I guess that's true. But I don't want any more of your fix-ups!" Twyla pointed her finger. "And I mean it!"

Zoey's face fell almost comically because apparently that was exactly her intention. "I was just texting Drew that I wouldn't be available for our usual, um, session tonight."

Twyla flushed when Zoey smiled wickedly. She unfortunately heard too much about their sexual "sessions" which seemed to verge on acrobatics.

If nothing else, they were both in fabulous shape.

Zoey followed behind Twyla, pushing boxes she could probably lift with one hand. "So, I heard about Noah. Your grandmother told me."

"Yes, that was my Christmas surprise."

"But did you hear he and Michelle broke up?"

"*Yes*. Of course, he told me."

"I heard from Betty that it was ugly."

"Ugly?" This didn't sound like Noah at all, and Twyla resented the implication.

She didn't want Betty floating around rumors that put Noah in a bad light. When he'd broken up with girls in the past, they'd always remained friends. Zoey was a perfect example. She'd also dated Noah for a time.

Really, who hadn't?

Twyla. Twyla hadn't. That would be a big fat no for her. But there were several benefits to that, one of which was that at least she'd never be one of his exes.

"I heard she accused him of being in love with someone else!" Zoey huffed in outrage.

"That doesn't sound like Noah at all. And if there was someone else, I would know!" She thumped her chest.

"That's what I thought, which is why I'm here."

Twyla paused shelving to plunk her hands on her hips. "You're *not* here to commiserate with me over 'the book has to go away' day?"

"I actually *forgot* that was today." Zoey grabbed a book from the children's section and flipped through the first pages. "I'll get this one for my nephew."

"If that's your guilt talking, get another one for the giving tree."

"Okay, *fine*." Zoey grabbed another one. "Are you just going to ignore this latest development?"

"I've actually reformed my vision around that. All positivity. There's probably no one better to take over Nacho Boat if Mr. Curry is set on retiring. Noah will be super safety conscious and I've seen the way Tee pushes limits. That won't happen anymore. Not under Noah." She drew an imaginary line in the air. "Poof! Another teen safe from his own stupidity."

"What? He bought Nacho Boat?" Zoey gaped.

"I'm surprised the news isn't everywhere by now."

"He just got back, didn't he?"

"Apparently he's been planning and talking to Mr. Curry about this for a while."

"Well, then that's probably the real reason those two broke up. Long distance wouldn't work."

"If you weren't talking about Nacho Boat, what development *were* you talking about?"

"Duh. Noah is single again, and so are you."

"Well, maybe not for long."

"You're not kidding. Sabrina is already moving in. She said she's all about second chances. You've got to work fast. Check me out with Drew. You have no idea how many women were swooning for him. I locked that down the first day." Zoey held up her fist in triumph.

"I meant *me*. I might not be single for long."

Zoey blinked. "Who is he? Why don't I know about this?"

"Because *Noah* is going to fix me up."

"Um what? With who? When? How? Why?"

"With Finn." Twyla smiled with satisfaction. "He's single, too."

Zoey clutched her chest. "Finn? Finn *Sheridan*?"

"The one and only."

"I've had a crush on him for ages." She fanned herself. "But Noah. He's even better than Finn. What about *Noah*?"

"Noah is unavailable—" When Zoey made an exasperated "I give up on you" face and threw her hands up, Twyla went on, "To me."

"Bull hockey! Why don't you just grab the bull by the horns and *tell him* already?"

"What is it with you and bulls?" Twyla shook her head.

She did not understand Zoey's obsession with getting her and Noah together. Twyla loved him, sure, but it was a different kind of love. A deep friendship. She just didn't feel that way about Noah.

"I'm serious now. All you have to do is stare at his lips and wait to see what happens."

"He'll just ask me if he's got something on his mouth."

"You're hopeless. Stare at his mouth while you lick

your lips. Like this." Zoey did just that and looked ridiculous, quite frankly.

Twyla gaped. "And men go for this?"

"Yes! You can't just wait for the man you want to show his interest. Sometimes they're waiting for you. I'm telling you. Noah has the hots for you."

"No, he *doesn't*."

"You're just scared to realize it, which is totally normal."

"You don't understand. We're close in a way no one else seems to understand." Only someone who had been through the grief she and Noah both shared would know. "We have a friendship that means everything to me."

So many things in life changed and evolved, and for someone that loved quiet, solitude and the comfort of routines, she loved what she had with Noah. After the accident, he'd been a shell of her friend. Recovering from the accident that had nearly killed both of them.

Dealing with his grief over losing Will, over feeling responsible because he'd been driving the boat when it hit a sandbar and threw both of them out. She'd simply been there for him, as his best friend and someone who also loved and missed Will. She'd sit and read to him, eventually finding *A Dragon's Heart*, which she read for the first time when he was in the hospital. He'd loved that book.

After leaving the hospital, Noah had gone out of town for some extensive rehab on the leg he'd injured in the accident. When he'd returned weeks later, they went back to their easy friendship. They moved on without changing a thing. And now that she'd seen

Noah through so many girlfriends, she'd grown accustomed to feeling nothing but friendship.

"I mean, how can he even know you're interested? You just asked him to fix you up with Finn!"

"You don't get it. That's just the thing. I'm not interested in Noah."

Zoey snorted. "Please, girl."

"Look, I can see why you and everyone else mix up our friendship with something else. But it is possible to simply be friends, and that's all we are. It's all we'll ever be. Now, if only *you* would understand this."

Twyla went to the register and rang Zoey up, then placed the two books in individual Once Upon a Book gift bags. It had always been their special touch.

"See you tonight?" Zoey handed over her plastic.

"Sure. What kind of cupcakes would you like?"

"No cupcakes. Come with me to the Salty Dog. Please."

"Oh, Zoey. I don't know. There will be people there."

"Exactly. And how are you supposed to get a date for New Year's Eve if you don't ever leave the house?"

"I leave the house all the time!" She made a sweeping motion around her shop.

"You know what I mean," Zoey said, hand on hip.

"Fine! But just one drink and then I'm going home."

Because Zoey did have a point. She wouldn't meet anyone unless she put herself out there.

For the next few days, Noah skillfully avoided everyone. He even managed to hold Twyla off, telling her he was "working" on Finn, that they were busy with inventory and a dozen other things, and he'd let her know when he had a free moment.

Right now, he had surrounded himself with seaworthy tasks and was settling into his new reality. If now and then he had flashbacks to the day of the accident, he was dealing with them.

He and Will had been on a motorboat when the accident happened. It had been such a bright, clear summer day and Noah had begged his older brother for a ride. Will, having just received his license, drove them at high speeds. They'd had an argument over, of all things, Twyla. Will had broken up with her and Noah pointed out he was an idiot.

You have a thing for my girlfriend, don't you? Will had winked.

No, of course not.

He'd never admitted that he pined away for Twyla. She was his brother's girlfriend and that was the end of it.

Now, Noah pulled his attentions back to the matter at hand. He'd been to the store to buy more lights for the parade tonight. He had Finn's help, which made this all go much faster. Finn, who was an expert diver, and one of his best friends. Finn, who Noah was supposed to fix up with Twyla.

He didn't want to, so he kept stalling.

Noah threw a strand of lights toward Finn, who stood at the stern. Tonight was the Snowflake Float Boat Parade, an annual Charming event.

"I still think this is a ridiculous custom." Finn grumbled as he picked up the lights and began to wrap them around the hull.

"Bah humbug. What's your beef? Electricity and water? C'mon, live a little." Noah chuckled.

They worked together in silence for several more

minutes. This would be the perfect time to suggest he ask Twyla out. But then, Diana came out with a light-up wreath, green garland and fake tree. She handed them over to Noah and indicated their placement. She tried directing them for a bit, coming out of her shell more than he'd seen so far. But then she had to head back inside when the phone rang.

Noah felt his heart race. This was so ridiculous. They weren't in eighth grade, were they? He should be able to fix Twyla up with a date. Even if he never had before, there was a first time for everything. If she didn't share the feelings Noah had for her, and she clearly did not, he'd rather see her with someone he approved of. Like Finn.

"So, I guess I should fix you up with a woman," Noah grumbled.

Finn snorted. "No, you *shouldn't*."

Yeah, he wasn't any good at this. "No, really. You'll like her and you already know her. She's super sweet with a good personality."

"Oh, Jesus." Finn groaned.

"Okay, never mind, that came out all wrong. It's *Twyla*, okay? Tell me now how you feel."

Finn blinked and dropped the strand of lights. Yeah, of course. Because this was Twyla. Gorgeous, smart, kind and, for reasons he'd never understand, still somehow available. It was the eternal mystery of the cosmos. Where do we go after we die, and why is Twyla still single?

"You know what? I *should*, just to shake you up." Finn crossed his arms and scowled.

"She asked me about you, okay? So that's why I'm going through with the insanity. Believe me, I know you can get your own dates without any help from me." Viciously, he wound the lights around the tree and strapped it tight to the mast.

"I'm never stepping into that mess of a triangle so forget it. Just go for it. Tell her how you feel and be done with it. You know you want to."

"I can't. It's complicated for us. She had a thing for my brother, or did you forget?"

"How could I forget? It's all anyone around here talks about. You're going to hate yourself when she winds up with some other guy who doesn't like you as much as I do. Who won't care what you think. Then, it's going to be too late."

"It's already too late."

Noah had fallen second best with his own mother, so to say he never wanted to be in that position again was an understatement. From the beginning, in their family the alliances had been Will and their parents. Noah the second child, feeling at times like an afterthought. He'd rather not wind up second best with Twyla, too. But it went far beyond pride.

After everything they'd been through and had invested in each other, he wouldn't cross the line. No matter how much he wanted her, no matter how deeply he needed her, he had to be smart about this. There was too much to lose.

"It isn't too *late* until one of you is married. Don't wait until she's finally happy with someone else to tell her how you feel. Don't be an idiot. I hate idiots."

And as if he wanted to confirm the state of his idiocy, Noah leaned over to tie a light on the bow and promptly fell overboard.

Even from under the water, Noah heard the deep

sound of Finn's laughter when he leaned over and offered a hand. It was like the universe giving Noah a hard slap. A heavy jolt. He was once again reminded that when it came to Twyla, he was indeed a one hundred percent, certified dummy.

Chapter Six

Twyla stood near the seawall where she could get the best view of the Snowflake Float Boat Parade. The evening was cold and brisk for Charming, the skies a bit cloudy, but she loved this time of the year. Though she'd never move anywhere where the weather suited her clothes, it had occasionally been a passing thought. In New York City, for instance, she could wear boots in autumn and all through spring. Oh, she understood she tended to romanticize New York. But after a steady diet of Nora Ephron books and movies, it was only natural to dream.

As usual, families had come out early and already staked the best places to view, setting folding chairs out hours in advance. Twyla didn't plan on staying too long, but because Ganny loved this kind of thing, she'd driven her out and scouted an available seat with a good view. Only one, but that was okay. Twyla would stand for the thirty or so minutes it would take for all the boats to glide by.

"I'll get you some hot chocolate," Twyla said to her grandmother. "Sit tight."

"Don't be gone too long, dear, or you might miss Noah."

On her way to the Salty Dog, supplying hot chocolate just outside their doors, she ran into at least a dozen people she knew. Ava and Max cuddling, Adam and Stacy walking with their little toddler, Valerie and Cole with their baby. And there was Zoey, too, cozy under a Dallas Cowboys blanket with Drew. Couples everywhere cozying up to each other on a brisk night. Sigh.

Zoey was right. She hadn't met anyone in her rental or at the bookstore. Two places, unless you wanted to count the grocery store, so the odds were low.

Two days ago, Twyla watched Finn walk by with barely a nod in her direction. So, it looked like yet another Christmas of being single. That was fine. She had so much to do when it came to work, and romance would only take her attention away from her real problems. Which was, of course, exactly what she'd wanted. An escape of sorts. A moment to know everything would be all right whether the bookstore survived or not.

She didn't want to be the Thompson forced to hang up a sign that said that after forty years, they would have to close their doors. Flashback to Meg Ryan, sadly closing the doors to her family bookstore in *You've Got Mail*. It didn't help that Twyla had remodeled the shop to resemble the one in the movie.

When Twyla got back with two hot chocolates, some members of the Almost Dead Poets Society were hovering over her grandmother. Every year at this time, they tried to talk Ganny into joining their poetry club.

"We can't lose our bookstore!" Patsy Villanueva fretted, obviously on another subject now.

"We won't," Mr. Finch assured her.

"Of course not! My granddaughter is on it," Ganny said. "She has so many wonderful ideas."

"The literary costume event!" Patsy clapped her hands. "I can't wait."

"How will you be dressing?" Susannah asked.

"Scarlett O'Hara, of course!" Patsy fanned herself and pretended to spin a parasol and hold it over her head.

The others were planning to be Jo March and Hester Prynne, "Lest anyone forget!"

"The poetry books y'all ordered arrived," Twyla interrupted. "I've got them behind the counter for you."

"I'll be in tomorrow for mine," Ella Mae said.

"Would you pick mine up, too?" Patsy asked. "I'll vemma you the money."

"What's a vemma?" Ella Mae wrinkled her nose.

"I don't know, but Valerie will do it for me." Patsy waved a hand dismissively. "She does this all the time and people never complain."

"Oh, thank the good Lord, here come the boats and not a moment too soon," Lois said. "I'm shivering."

"Why in the world didn't you say something, darlin'?" Mr. Finch removed his suit jacket and placed it over Lois's shoulders.

The night was cold by Gulf Coast standards and Twyla snuggled into her sweater. The boats sailed by, all decorated with colorful bright lights, which lit up the dark sky. First came the Santa boat hosted by the

Salty Dog Bar & Grill this year, with a chubby Santa dressed in full regalia, waving to the crowds. There were blinking patterns of fairy lights, boats filled with flashing stars, wrapped presents, a tiny sleigh, plastic reindeer and trees. Another was filled with characters from *The Nightmare Before Christmas.* A Texas-themed boat sailed by, complete with an inflatable horse and a large lone star blinking brightly enough to be seen from outer space.

And bringing up the rear came Noah's boat, decorated with wreaths, trees and plenty of twinkling multicolored lights. Nacho Boat Adventures, his sign read. He received the biggest cheers of the evening as Noah and Finn waved to the crowds.

"Yay, Noah!"

"Way to go, son!"

"We're here for you!"

On the way back to the car, Twyla did a double take. A woman looking very much like Michelle was strolling toward the Salty Dog Bar & Grill. But that couldn't be because she was in Austin, probably fuming over Noah's imagined interest in someone else. There were plenty of tall willowy women with long blond hair in Charming and this didn't have to be Michelle.

"Isn't that Michelle?" Ganny asked, still as sharp as ever.

Well, it looked like a distinct possibility now.

"No, maybe just someone who looks like her?"

"You're probably right." Ganny buckled into her seat belt. "What would she be doing here anyway?"

"Trying to get Noah back?" It was an obvious answer to Twyla.

Some days, she didn't honestly believe they were

done. Michelle was a practicing attorney and a smart woman. If she threw her support behind Noah and his new business, he might actually consider taking her back. After all, he never said he'd stopped *loving* her. He'd been, in fact, very vague about the whole breakup and she hadn't pressed for details. She attributed this to the fact that they didn't normally share all the gritty details of relationships and she'd like to keep it that way.

She'd never told Noah that her most recent ex-boyfriend of two months, Alex, had broken up with her because he was tired of coming in second to Noah. His timing couldn't have been worse. Shortly afterward, Noah had moved to Austin, and it became a nonissue. Still, she was so tired of needy and insecure men. If Alex had been worried about Noah, he could have upped the stakes and thought to also bring her chicken noodle soup when she was sick the way Noah always did. But no, all he wanted was for Twyla to be at *his* beck and call.

Twyla had pulled into the circular driveway leading to her grandmother's front door when her phone buzzed. An incoming text from Noah.

Movie night tomorrow? I'll bring the popcorn. We're watching Die Hard.

A smile came quickly to her lips because some things never changed. She and Noah would have the annual argument over whether *Die Hard* could be called a Christmas movie. He'd say he was bringing the popcorn but then forget. She'd make it and he'd complain the kernels were too brown, the way *she* liked them. Then, he'd *really* piss her off and proceed to hog the remote control. But in between all that there would be a lot of laughs. There would be touching because when wrapped up in a movie, that tended to happen. They'd sit on the floor, and she'd lean against him to get comfortable. They forgot themselves, too involved with the movie. She called it snuggle time and it had never been anything more than that.

She might not have a Hallmark movie romance, but she had Noah.

And sometimes he was all she really needed.

After the parade, Noah texted Twyla. Then he and Finn docked the boats and unstrung the lights. They headed out for a cold beer at the Salty Dog to celebrate the end of this particular holiday event. The way Noah looked at it, he only had obligations for one more. The literary costume event at Twyla's bookstore. Then maybe he could focus on the plans he had for the business and plan their grand opening after the first of the year.

He swung the door open to the sounds of cheers and waves from some of the locals. Obviously, many had made their way inside after the parade. In the year since Noah had been gone, the bar had undergone some changes. Mostly the staff. Bartenders and a few waitresses he didn't automatically recognize on sight. The former navy SEAL owners were hit and miss these days. Noah wanted to connect with Cole at some point and ask his advice on surfboards since the dude was an expert. He'd simply have to give him a call or drop by the renovated lighthouse where the lucky man lived.

"Noah," came a soft voice from behind.

Every muscle in him tensed. *No, no, no.* Not this again.

He whipped around to confirm his suspicions. Michelle stood behind his stool, wearing her barracuda "I'm going to win this argument if it kills me" smile. And to think he'd once found the smile wicked in a *good* way.

Noah exchanged a look with Finn. He shook his head and downed the rest of his beer.

"What are you doing here?"

She placed her hand on her hip. "Making sure you don't make the biggest mistake of your life."

"And on that note..." Finn stood and clapped Noah's back.

Michelle gave Finn a grateful, non-barracuda-like smile and took his place on the stool next to Noah's.

"You're wasting your time." Noah gripped the neck of his beer bottle.

"It's never a waste to try to salvage something real."

Something real. If that were true, he'd have never left Austin—even if a roof nearly fell on his head. Something real was worth fighting for. With something real, he'd have never walked away.

"It's time to face the truth. We can work this out, but you need to explain to Twyla that she should give up on you. Then we can try to put the pieces back together."

Noah nearly choked on his beer and swallowed, then thumped his chest. "Um, what?"

"Twyla has a thing for you and please don't be a stupid guy about this. I'm going to assume she was behind your decision to come home. I know you feel responsible for her because of Will, and it makes sense. She's safe. Familiar. Twyla won't ask anything more of you. She won't demand that you stretch and grow to become the best man you can be."

Noah groaned. "We've already talked about this, and I won't do it again for the hundredth time. That's a common misconception about me and Twyla. But she does *not* have a thing for me. You're one hundred percent wrong."

"I'm not, Noah. You're the one who refuses to see it."

It wasn't the first time one of his girlfriends had mentioned Twyla's obvious "crush" on him. At one time, it had reached such a fevered point that he'd been within two seconds of asking Twyla if any of that was true. He remembered the day and time because she'd told him about Alex, a guy she'd met at a book convention and was so happy to be dating.

No, Twyla had plenty of opportunities to tell him how she felt and never had.

"You have misled poor Twyla at every turn so of course she pines away for you. Every time she called, you would leave the room to talk to her. You've encouraged her. It's like you two have something going on that you won't let the rest of the world in on. When you had an issue at work, you confided in her. Not *me*."

"She's been my best friend for more than half of my life."

"And she would like to be so much more than that."

"You're wrong. She just asked me to fix her up with *Finn*."

Michelle blinked. "That's surprising."

"You don't know her. Stop trying to make excuses for what happened between us. It didn't work, even though we tried."

"Noah, what did happen?" Her hand rested on his forearm. "I thought we were doing okay."

"I'm sorry," he said, shaking his head. "I care about you, and I realize that I wasn't being fair."

He'd wanted to love her, desperately, but couldn't give her the words she wanted to hear. It was his deepest regret because he'd never intended to hurt her, and now he had.

"If you cared about me once, you can't turn it off that quickly. I'll be patient."

"No, I can't ask you to do that. It wouldn't be fair. Your life is in Austin."

"My life can be anywhere I want it to be. Law firms are everywhere. Even here in Charming."

The words shocked him, and he wouldn't be lying to admit she'd flattered him. He'd never expected this development. No one had ever given anything up for him. No one had ever rearranged their life for him. Michelle was an attorney at a prestigious law firm in Austin and now she was willing to forgive him for being an idiot. Willing to move here so they could work it out.

In the meantime, Twyla had asked him to fix her up with Finn. It was time for Noah to stop dreaming.

One woman wanted to fight for him. The other had loved his brother, and Noah could hardly compete with that.

"Okay. Good to know."

Michelle smiled and Noah's phone buzzed in his back pocket. "Excuse me. This could be important."

He was hoping for Twyla, but no. His mother's voice greeted him and the moment she spoke, Noah knew it wouldn't be an easy conversation.

"Noah Michael Cahill! You bought Nacho Boat? Are you *trying* to kill me?" his mother said.

He held up a finger to Michelle and walked outside for some privacy with his mother. "Who told you? I want names."

"Never mind who told me. Why didn't *you* tell me?"

Noah rubbed the spot between his eyes, feeling a headache coming on. "Listen, I planned on telling you everything when I came over for dinner."

"Well, in the future, if you could tell your own mother before everyone in town knows, I'd appreciate it!"

If he thought he'd catch his mother at the Snowflake Float Boat Parade, he would have told her by now, but she hadn't attended for years. Hadn't even stepped foot near the docks since the accident.

"Sure. Yeah, and I'm sorry."

"Fine, I'll see you at dinner and don't be late this time."

"I was late once—"

But he didn't get to finish that sentence as his mother insisted on the last word.

Noah went back inside to see that Michelle was already being hit on by one of the men at the bar. A beautiful blonde, she never failed to get attention from the opposite sex. Noah didn't know if he should feel jealous or relieved. At the moment, he was a mix of the two.

Unfortunately, he fell far more on the side of relieved that he should.

Chapter Seven

When Noah came to movie night this time, he actually brought the popcorn.

Twyla clapped her hands. "Oh, my God, you remembered!"

"What do you mean?" He shrugged off his windbreaker after he handed her the bag of kettle corn. "I said I would bring it."

"But you always forget." When he gave her a blank stare, she waved her hand in the air to jog his memory. "And then I make some in the microwave and burn it a little?"

"Glad we're avoiding that." He scowled.

He seemed to be in a mood, but Twyla's spirits were buoyed the moment she'd spied the big bag of salted caramel kettle corn from the boardwalk. In the kitchen, she grabbed a big bowl and poured some from the two-foot-long bag. He'd brought her the extra large one. This could last all week if she rationed, but she'd bring in some for Mr. Finch tomorrow. It was good to feel almost as if she had a real coworker. It brought back the times both she, her mother and Ganny ran the bookstore together.

Bonkers slunk out of the bedroom and gave Twyla his usual disgusted look.

"Hang on, I have to feed Bonkers."

"You still have that cat?"

"I sure do, and you know what? I think he's really starting to like me."

Noah groaned. "You're way too good to him."

But Noah was a dog person so what could she expect? She had originally adopted Bonkers in hopes he'd also make a good bookstore cat. Customers could pet him as he sat calmly in his box near the register. Sadly, on the first day she'd taken Bonkers to work, he'd hissed at a child who'd made the unfortunate mistake of petting him.

And that was the end of Take Your Cat To Work Day.

Bonkers tended to look at her as if she was a five-foot can opener, but hey, things were getting better. He'd even let her pet him without hissing.

"There you go."

Twyla set his bowl down and backed away because Bonkers didn't like to be watched while eating. It was one of his many quirks.

On the couch, Noah had already spread out his long legs and taken control of the remote. Little cat, big cat.

She sighed. "It's on the DVR. I recorded it."

Twyla placed the bowl between them. Noah worked the remote, all the while grinding his jaw like something, or someone, had royally pissed him off.

"Okay, tell me what's wrong."

"What makes you think something's wrong?"

"Um, the clenched jaw?"

"Someone told my mother about Nacho Boat before I could."

"It wasn't me!" She brought her hand to her chest.

"I know." He slowly shook his head. "Anyway, I got read the riot act. She's not happy, but what else is new? I never fail to disappoint her."

Twyla tried to put herself in Katherine's position. Were Twyla a mother who'd already lost one son, she'd feel the same kind of fierce protectiveness over her only remaining child. She'd worry every day that something would go wrong somehow. Just as it had for Will. How could Katherine simply trust that the universe would allow her to keep Noah? Twyla thought for many years that Katherine needed the type of grief counseling they'd given all students after the accident.

"It must have been a tough conversation."

"Yeah." Noah ran a hand over his jaw. "Not much of a conversation, though. Pretty one-sided."

While Noah always wore a well-trimmed beard, tonight he looked almost…unkempt. The guilt had to weigh on him because he'd always felt as though he owed his mother something. He claimed he'd never been her favorite but was the only son she had left. Twyla didn't disagree that in those early years, Will had clearly been Katherine's favorite. He had been the people pleaser, the one who toed the line with her authority. Noah never had.

Too many times, Twyla had wanted to step in and say what everyone else was thinking out loud: *Noah lost a brother, too. He could use your attention as the only son you have left. He might not be a straight-A student headed for medical school, but he deserves your love.* Still, over the years, no one had the guts to tell Katherine that she had to be strong for Noah and not the other way around.

She took the opportunity to grab the remote. "Well, let's fast forward and watch evil Hans fall off the Nakatomi building. That's your favorite part."

"*Great* special effects. He actually looks like he's falling."

"I know. He was such a great actor."

"But we're starting from the beginning." Noah reached for the remote and lowered himself to the floor with his back leaning against the couch, then pressed play. "Hey, do I…um…"

There was a pause. Too long of a pause. "Do you what?"

"Confide in you too much?"

"What's too much? We're best friends. I've known you for over half my life."

"Okay. So, it doesn't bother you?"

"Why would it *bother* me?"

There were already lines they wouldn't cross. She and Noah were both private about stuff you wouldn't necessarily share. They had achieved, in her opinion, the perfect balance. Were there times when she shared more with him than a partner? Sure, yes, but that was only reasonable given their closeness.

"I had a feeling I was wrong about this."

But rather than seem happy, he looked disappointed.

"Wrong?"

Twyla felt a pinch of dread squeeze between her ribs. Since the moment he'd returned, she understood on a bone-deep level that he wasn't telling her something. This thing, whatever it was, was bigger than his breakup. Bigger than a decision to go after his dream.

And every time she saw him it felt like that tiny thing had grown larger between them.

"Don't worry." Noah patted the empty space next to him. "Some people are trying to mess with me."

The movie had started, and Bruce Willis now carried an enormous teddy bear off the plane and met his driver. It was difficult for Twyla to focus.

Something had rattled Noah.

She plopped down and grabbed a handful of popcorn. "Who's messing with you? Finn?"

"No." Noah scowled. "Why are we talking about him?"

"Did he say you and I are too close? I shouldn't have asked you to fix me up with Finn. That was stupid."

"You're right. That *was* stupid."

"Why was it *stupid*?"

He cocked his head, observing her as if studying a strange phenomenon. "You just said so."

"Well, I can say that. But why would *you* say it?"

He closed his eyes and rubbed the middle of his forehead. "God, help me."

"Honestly, is there something fundamentally wrong with me? Why is it so stupid that me and Finn could be a thing? He's single. I'm also single."

"It's because..." Noah's eyes were strangely focused on her now, as if there was nothing else in the room. No TV on in the background with Bruce Willis making his way into his screen wife's boisterous office Christmas party. "Well, Finn...is... He's still hung up on someone."

"Oh."

"Yeah, so it wouldn't work because he can't stop thinking about this other woman."

"Well, that's a good reason."

"He thinks about her all the time. Day and night. It's…ridiculous." Noah rubbed between his eyebrows and looked genuinely worried for Finn.

"Gosh, don't be so hard on him," Twyla whispered. "It happens."

"Yeah. Okay. I won't be." Noah squeezed her hand, like he always did. A little pat of reassurance.

But this time, his hand lingered on hers even as he put his attention toward watching the movie.

Twyla lost what little focus she had, though she tried to follow along. Easy to do since they'd watched this movie dozens of times.

She was afraid to speak or even breathe.

Noah practically recited certain lines verbatim. Twyla winced when the elevator doors opened, and a dead man appeared wrapped in lights and wearing a Santa hat.

"This is not a Christmas movie," she said, shaking her head.

Noah smiled, but even after she spoke, he didn't seem to notice they were basically still holding hands. The popcorn bowl sat between them, and she took handfuls with her left hand though she was right-handed. Letting go of his hand to take some might be easier, but if she let go there were no guarantees they'd get back to this moment.

Which was…nice. This didn't mean anything. It didn't have to. She was with her best friend, and he needed extra comfort tonight. But she could almost see Zoey's deadpan expression if Twyla told her about this.

After the movie ended, she walked him to the door and this was different, too. *Awkward* different. Instead of casually giving her a quick hug before leaving like he always did, he gave her a long look. He behaved like he'd never even *seen* her before.

Oh, hello, nice to meet you. Who are you again? Have we met? I feel like we've met before.

Honestly, it was surreal.

She leaned on the door frame while he lingered just outside, checking his pockets, finding his phone, then pulling out his keys. He seemed so…out of sorts.

"Well…call me tomorrow?"

"Yeah. Okay, good night."

Then he was gone, concluding their strangest movie night in history.

Twyla was helping a third grader find the perfect book just after the incident happened. Valerie had brought her class in for a field trip right before the long holiday break and she was in the middle of breaking up a disagreement between two boys.

"Apologize to Jackson," Valerie ordered.

"I'm sorry I shoved you, but you called my sister dumb. She's not *dumb*. She's smarter than you'll ever be!"

Valerie rolled her eyes and pointed to the other kid. "Jackson, apologize for calling Naomi dumb."

"I loved this one when I was a girl," Twyla said louder, to distract the girl the boys were fighting about. She handed her *A Wrinkle in Time*. "My mother used to read it to me every night before bed."

Naomi sweetly cradled the book to her chest. "Reading is my favorite thing in the world."

"Me, too."

She was so cute, dressed in the school's uniform—a blue skirt and tan top with matching windbreaker. Her dark hair was coiffed into two perfect braids, and she wore wire-rimmed glasses. It was like Twyla going back in time and helping little Twyla. She'd been the bookworm that had never been cool. Later, both Will and Noah became her pseudobrothers, ready to punch anyone out that called her an ugly name.

"I bet you fall asleep reading, too."

She pushed her glasses up her nose the same way Twyla did at least once a day. "My mom won't let me. It gets past my bedtime, and she says, 'Lights out.'"

"I bet you would if you could."

She nodded. "Yeah."

Twyla bent low and met her eyes with a conspiratorial smile. "When you're a grown-up, no one can stop you. I do it all the time."

Of course, that often meant staying up until two o'clock because the book was too good to put down. Adulting 101: you have to pay for your mistakes by getting up and going to work anyway.

A few minutes later, Valerie was gathering the class and, with the assistance of her parent chaperones, herding the kids into the line to pay for their chosen book.

Thirty-five sales later, Twyla wished every teacher brought in the children for a field trip. As an independent bookstore, her prices were steeper than ordering online, or from a big chain store, so she appreciated every sale.

"Thanks, Valerie," Twyla called out as they were leaving.

"See you soon." Valerie waved.

And at that moment, Michelle held the door open for the class as they followed their teacher outside.

Michelle.

So, she hadn't been a mirage. She was here and Twyla had no idea why. But if she was going to accuse Noah of cheating, Twyla would set her straight. That could never happen. Noah was too loyal of a person. She'd defend him till the last breath left her body.

"Hi, Michelle."

Twyla waved from behind the counter and tried to plaster something resembling a smile on her face. Now, with the children gone, she and Michelle were alone. Completely.

"Hey there," Michelle said, sauntering up to the counter. "We need to talk."

"Well, I'm working right now. Can I help you find a book?"

Relationship Rescue?

Moving On After Heartache?

"Gosh, I wish I had the time to read *fiction.* You must have such fun. Meanwhile, I have legal briefs to read. Very boring intellectual stuff. If I had enough time, I'd give my brain a break."

"Uh-huh."

Twyla wished she had a smart-aleck reply to the obvious dumbing down of fiction books. She could explain that she both read and sold nonfiction but that wouldn't be snappy and snarky. She'd likely think of the perfect comment lying in bed tonight when it was far too late.

"Well, you've probably heard all about Noah and me by now. He tells you everything."

"Not *everything.*"

"Right. Would you do me a giant favor and meet me for lunch at the Salty Dog? My treat. I have something to discuss with you."

"I brought my lunch." She fished under the counter and held up her paper sack. PB&J for the win.

"Adorable. Bring it with you if you insist."

"It will all depend on if Mr. Finch gets here before noon. Otherwise, I can't leave the store."

"Surely you can afford to close up for an *hour*."

"I really *can't*. Not at this time of the year. My busiest season."

She glanced around the empty shop. "I don't see the crowds. You'll miss one sale, if that."

"And I really can't afford to miss a single sale."

Only a moment later, with the timing of a metronome, Mr. Finch arrived. "Good morning, ladies."

"Perfect timing." Michelle greeted Mr. Finch with a smile and strolled toward the door. "See you at noon."

"You have a lunch date?" Mr. Finch came behind the counter and made himself at home.

"I suppose I do." She sighed. Then as soon as the door shut, she thought of the perfect snarky comeback to Michelle needing to give her "brain a break."

Well, it sure sounds like you could use one.

"Ha!" Twyla snort laughed. "Good one."

"You all right, dear?" Mr. Finch said.

"Yep!"

Twyla pulled out her phone and texted Noah:

Your ex is here and wants to take me to lunch.

She waited for the bubbles to appear indicating he was composing a reply. Nothing.

Hello? Noah? A little help here?

With Mr. Finch here to take care of customers, Twyla busied herself in the back, folding up cardboard boxes. Her mind drifted back to last night and all the hand holding with Noah. She hadn't actually held hands with a guy since possibly seventh grade. But there was such a sweetness to holding hands simply to keep the connection. The whole thing had also been so confusing, so unexpected. It was likely because Noah was lonely after his breakup, seeking some kind of comfort. She wouldn't make too much out of it.

Twyla glanced at her phone. Still no reply from Noah. As the hours wore on, Twyla cleaned and dusted every nook and cranny. She rearranged shelves and stocked some of the new educational toys. Finally, she could avoid it no longer.

Lunchtime.

"Don't rush," Mr. Finch said, as he read a book behind the counter. "I brought a sandwich."

"I won't be gone even thirty minutes. You and I need to go over the plans for Literary Character Day when I get back."

It helped to put her mind to something far more pleasant and with less of a root-canal-like appeal. She drove her sedan to the boardwalk and found a parking space close to the Salty Dog. Inside, she found the usual holiday frivolity and spotted Michelle almost immediately. She waved from a booth near the back. Okay, so this is how they were going to do it. Privacy, so Michelle could trash talk Noah without any judgment. Uh-uh. Not going to happen on Twyla's watch.

"Thank you for coming." Michelle set down the menu. "I've lost my appetite, but please, you go ahead and eat. I'm still treating."

"Um, I'm not hungry, either." She *was* hungry but damned if she would eat while Michelle stared at her chewing.

Debbie dropped by, and they both ordered diet sodas.

"What's going on?" Twyla made a show of glancing at the clock above the bar to send a message. "I only have thirty minutes."

"I'll get right to it. I want Noah back and I'm wondering if you can help me."

Chapter Eight

"Help Noah see that he will never have a chance with you as more than just a friend."

"Huh? What?"

"I'm sure you see that on some level he feels responsible for you because of Will. But I talked to him the other night and I know we can make things work. I'm willing to move to Charming to do it."

"You…you are?"

This shouldn't surprise Twyla. She wasn't sure how Noah was still single, frankly. Over the years, he'd had plenty of women fall for him. Hard. Many had come to cry on Twyla's shoulders afterward, in fact:

I miss him so much. You're so lucky, Twyla. He'll always be a part of your life.

And Twyla had listened, agreed and commiserated, knowing they were right. Noah would always be in her life. She couldn't imagine life without him. Eventually, his exes had moved on. But now here was Michelle, back to fight for Noah. She wanted Twyla to help. How could she say no? She would have to consider this because there had to be a way to say no without being mean.

"I'd like to help, but I don't know what I can do. We're best friends, but Noah hardly takes relationship advice from me. Not that I've ever tried giving it."

"Maybe it's a good time to start."

"I wouldn't know what to say." Twyla studied her hands. She'd never been in this position before.

"As I told him, feelings like the ones *we* had for each other aren't ones a person can just turn off like a light switch. There's still something there, a little spark, and I'm willing to work on it."

"That's…amazing. I know he must appreciate it."

Michelle smiled and Twyla noted that she really was a beautiful woman.

"Sometimes, in order to get what you want, you have to swallow your pride, take a risk and put yourself out there. That's what I'm doing. Noah means a lot to me. Listen. I apologize for hitting you with this now. Especially during the holidays with how busy you are. But Noah is quite obviously struggling after the accident, and I'm concerned he's making a mistake leaving everything he built in Austin behind."

"Wait. What *accident*?"

Twyla's hands shook. An accident he hadn't told her about. Maybe this was the thing between them.

Michelle's neck jerked. "He didn't tell you?"

"I told you that he doesn't tell me *everything*."

"Probably because of how protective he still is over you. This is exactly what I mean. He's still thinking of *your* feelings when a roof nearly collapsed on him in a fire. And that's when everything really changed. He said he needed time, but we were trying to work things out. After the accident, everything got much worse. The secret phone calls to you increased. The plans to move to Charming and buy the business formulated, and nothing I said could talk him out of it."

"I didn't know about those plans, either, until he showed up. It was a surprise to me, and I thought he was just visiting for Christmas, not that he'd moved back."

"It's a confusing time for him. Anyone who cares about Noah should be concerned. He could be making a big mistake."

But all Twyla could think about was one more accident in which Noah came close to death or injury. It had to have brought back some of those old memories and nightmares. Maybe Michelle was right and he'd had a knee-jerk reaction when he'd broken up with Michelle.

"I didn't like the idea of the charter business, but I trust Noah. He'll be safe. The dream means too much to him to treat any part of this recklessly."

"Here's what I think." Michelle folded her hands together as if preparing for closing arguments. "Noah moved back for more than one reason. You need him. After all this time, Noah feels responsible for you and *your* happiness. That's why we had zero chance of success from the start. I know you're a strong woman and don't want his pity, but until you let him go, he won't be free to have a serious relationship."

Twyla ground her teeth and fisted her hands. "I am not stopping him from having a serious relationship."

"I'm sure you're not one hundred percent aware that you are, but he and I could still have a chance at something real. Something lasting. It will be up to you to cut the unhealthy ties he still has to you. You were Will's girl, and on some level, now that he's gone, he feels responsible for you."

Unhealthy ties. Feeling responsible for Will's girl.

Noah, thinking he owed her something because of Will. All of it hit Twyla at once, making her stomach burn. She did not want to accept that Noah felt *obligated* to her. She would not accept that his relationships with other women had never worked because he was reluctantly tied to her. She got enough of the "poor, sad Twyla" comments from other people, and she expected Noah to know better.

But maybe…maybe her heart and mind had overreacted to this suggestion because on some level, she knew it to be true.

A saltwater fishing expedition had already been scheduled with a group of folks that Noah hated to disappoint, so after he passed the USCG test, he chose not to cancel. Mr. Curry would have pitched in if he'd asked, because he and his wife were still trying to decide where in Arizona they would move. But Noah didn't want to bother him. Retirement should be enjoyed fully and without feeling any leftover obligations. Finn was otherwise busy at his current place of employment since Noah couldn't offer him a salary yet. Of course, he had Tee who was on a school break and looking for all the hours he could get. Today Noah's assistant wore a T-shirt that said, *In my defense, I was left unsupervised.*

Note to self: never leave Tee unsupervised.

"Hey, Noah. Should we call you Captain?"

Terry, the organizer of the group of avid fishermen and an old friend of Noah's father, climbed aboard. There were three of them on the hunt for flounder. Since fishing was good year-round in the Gulf Coast of Mexico, they were bound to catch something.

"Call me Noah, Terry. I've known you all my life."

"You got it, son. Hey, Rick? Have you met Noah Cahill?" Terry made the introductions.

"Are you the one on the plaque?"

Noah was bound to come across this and he was prepared. He simply nodded and gave a hand to the next fisherman. This man seemed older than the others and a little wobbly on his feet. Noah would keep a close eye on him, because Terry had the whole story regarding the plaque that hung on a spot on the dock, and was retelling it now. Noah readied the boat with Tee and half listened as Terry rehashed the story.

Boat capsized on the bay…young driver…little experience…heroic rescue…nearly drowned. Of course, the way everyone told the story, Noah had been driving the boat. That's what he'd told everyone when the coast guard rescued him after several hours of treading water. No one ever questioned the story because it made sense. Noah was the wild card. Will was the good son. He'd screwed up once. Once. And Noah would not let him be remembered as anything other than the good brother he'd been. It had been a small price to pay. The people who loved him before still loved him afterward.

If anything, they understood he'd paid the ultimate price and sympathy for him grew and never waned. He hadn't been charged since there had been no drinking. Simply a terrible unforeseen accident when they hit a sandbar at high speeds and lost control. And Noah did feel responsible because he'd been the one to beg Will to go on a ride on that late summer day.

He understood the residents of Charming wanted to remember. On some core level, they *needed* to remember. A few years ago, he'd felt differently. Now, he realized with the benefit of some maturity that their discussion of the accident was no different than the remembrance of historical events in the larger scope. They couldn't forget, lest they risk repeating.

The only thing Noah wanted to forget was the constant reminders that he hadn't saved his brother. It didn't matter that he'd tried. He'd *failed.* That was the point no one but him seemed to fixate on. Him and his mother, that is. He doubted she'd ever forget only one son had walked away from that disaster. Probably not the right one.

For a while, every news media outlet in Texas covered the story of the two Cahill brothers. Photos of the capsized boat graced the covers of the local paper, *The Charming Times*. Pictures of Noah being airlifted to Houston for his injuries. In later weeks, a photo of him and Twyla had been on the cover. He'd been holding her tightly in his arms, his head lowered to her head.

Surviving brother and girlfriend united together in grief.

Tragic and dramatic. Will would have hated every part of the attention and coverage. Especially the tragedy of it all. He'd had an almost gallows-like sense of humor and would have hated the tragic tone.

Noah accepted the role of a cautionary tale. The part he'd chosen for himself. He'd never wanted Will's memory to be reduced down to an eighteen-year-old who'd made one stupid mistake.

Finally, they arrived at the fishing spot on the bay. Tee anchored the boat, and everyone cast their lines. He and Tee went around helping the others and Noah constantly checked their navigation and reports of any weather changes. But after a while there was nothing to do but kick back and wait. Sooner or later, someone would get a bite and Noah and Tee would render assistance if needed.

"I didn't know that was you with the rescue," Tee said, cracking open a soda.

"It was a long time ago."

"Yeah." Tee shook his head. And then, quite unexpectedly, he threw his arms around Noah in a bear hug. "My dude."

Noah shook him off, suppressing a chuckle. "I'm your *Captain*."

"Oh, Captain, my Captain." Tee saluted.

"Got a live one!" Terry called out and Noah and Tee went to offer encouragement and stand by for help if needed.

By the time they headed back, after all fishermen had a catch, the sky had turned a striking yellow with hints of blue and deep purple. The figure of a woman stood at the pier and as they drew closer Noah saw Twyla. Dressed in her usual skirt with thick stockings, boots and a sweater, she had a hand cupped to her forehead. For a moment, she looked like a figure from the past, watching and waiting for her sailor to return.

A lump formed in his throat at even the thought that he could be the one she waited for.

He waved to her as they drew closer to the boat slip.

Noah docked the boat. Tee hopped out to tie the ropes. After a fishing expedition, there was much to do, and

Noah first busied himself helping the men with their catch.

"I'll be a minute," Noah called out to Twyla. "Anything wrong?"

"Nothing," she said in a tone that meant, *everything.*

Fantastic. Maybe Mom had put a bug in Twyla's ear to get him to stop this nonsense. They were still close, and Twyla dropped by from time to time.

He took his time unloading the boat, not wanting to face another argument, but it all went a lot faster with Tee there to help.

Finally, Tee took off. "See ya tomorrow, Captain!"

Noah hopped off and briefly balanced between the stem of the boat and the dock, and Twyla slid him a look he couldn't quite decipher. A moment later, he read it clearly enough. He almost heard her thoughts, the way he did when she couldn't hide them. She was…hurt. Had Finn said something to her? Turned her down? Embarrassed her in some way? That didn't sound like Finn. He'd let her down easy and he had enough experience turning down eager women.

He walked to meet her at the edge. "Got your text but couldn't reply. We were on the boat all day."

"I couldn't get out of it, so I went to lunch with Michelle."

"She shouldn't involve you in what's going on with us. Yeah, she wants to get back together. I have to admit, I'm surprised she would move here. She'll have to find another job if she leaves her law firm."

"I think you really hurt her when you left."

"I never meant to."

"No, you never mean to hurt any of them, but you just do."

The words were quiet, but they hit him like little bombs.

Guilt spiked through him, because he thought he might know exactly why he'd hurt so many people, thanks in large part to Michelle's words. She was right that he felt responsible for Twyla, but not entirely because of Will. He'd taken this on himself, wanting to keep her close even if she'd never return his deeper feelings, and keeping her safe the way he hadn't managed with Will.

It didn't matter. She would never love him like she'd loved Will and he wasn't about to compete with the ghost of a first love. Either way, Noah had been careless and he'd hurt enough people for a lifetime. From now on, he would be the perfect angel. He'd stay single and work on the business until he made it the successful venture he envisioned. That would require all his focus and energy. After all that was in place for his future, if there was time for romance, well, he'd *think* about it. For now, he felt done with women and all the expectations. He would answer only to himself.

Michelle would either have to wait for him, or just give up.

"Did you have an accident at work?"

He shut his eyes, anger piercing him. "She had no business telling you any of that."

"You're right because *you* should have been the one to tell me."

"I didn't want to worry you. Since I was okay anyway, it was a nonissue."

"That's not a nonissue. It must have been terrifying for you."

How could he explain? No one but the people who

were in that fire with him would understand. The hard crackling sounds consuming everything in its way, the darkness of the moment filled with smoke, the sounds of the building falling all around them. The sense that something or someone had shoved him out of the way.

"It *was* terrifying. Want to know the scariest thing about that roof nearly falling on me? The fact that I might have lived the rest of my life worrying what other people thought of me. Yeah, the fire changed me. I realized that I don't care anymore whether people blame me for the boating accident."

Her eyes were wide like she'd never considered this. "Noah! No one blames you."

"Well, maybe you don't. The residents see me as the hero of this story which is dead wrong. You don't know how many times I've wanted to pull that plaque off the wall and throw it in the ocean. And my mother? That's a different story. My father left us because he couldn't stand looking at me anymore."

This was the truth and something he hadn't even spoken out loud until this moment. It was as if he thought if he didn't say it, maybe it wasn't true. But it was. He'd heard his parents arguing late at night after the accident, their despair mixed with anger. They'd blamed Noah and how couldn't they? He blamed himself.

"That's not true."

He hated the sorrowful and pitying look in her eyes. She'd been the one person who also loved Will but didn't blame Noah. And this was even though she still believed he'd been driving the boat.

"Yeah, don't feel sorry for me, Peaches. I don't deserve that or want it."

"Do you feel sorry for *me*?" she interrupted him, her voice nearly a whisper under the sound of the waves.

"What? No, I don't. What's this about?"

The sun set over the horizon and seemed to frame Twyla's form. "I thought we were friends because we love each other but I never thought it's because you feel *sorry* for me."

"Why would I feel sorry for you?"

"The same reason everyone else does." Her lower lip quivered, and she didn't have to say more. "Like I had my chance and now I'm going to wind up like old Mrs. Havisham living in her wedding dress."

He quirked a brow. "No, I do *not* feel sorry for you."

Instead, he fought the overwhelming urge to take her in his arms, pull her against him and take all the hurt away. But especially now, he couldn't afford any more risks. He'd already lost a brother, and somehow come back from that.

He'd never survive losing Twyla.

"Michelle thinks you feel obligated to take care of me, to watch over me because of Will, and that's why none of your relationships have ever worked."

"Victim blaming?" He snorted. "That's all on me and not on anyone I've ever dated. She's looking to blame someone else because she can't accept my decision."

"She must really love you." Twyla twisted her hands together.

He shook his head because he no longer believed this to be true.

"No, she doesn't. She just can't stand losing."

"You tend to underestimate the way people feel about you. Nobody likes the idea of losing you."

He tapped her nose. "You're not going to lose me."

"Is this…is this why you were being weird on movie night?"

He hesitated a beat. The oddity of movie night had been Noah forgetting himself. He'd allowed that door between them to open a small crack, because of the shock when he realized Twyla wasn't going to shake off his hand and tease him about it. Honestly, he hadn't watched much of the damn movie and simply stared at the screen, wondering when she would finally notice he wasn't letting go.

He hadn't replied and Twyla wanted an answer.

"I can stand a lot of things, but I can't stand your pity."

"You don't have it," he said slowly.

"Good. Please be honest with me. Because…I don't want to hold you back from being happy. Whatever it takes. I'll help Michelle understand, maybe give you some more time and space so you can eventually… I don't know. Get back together with her if that's what you want. You know I'd do anything for you."

She met his eyes and gave him her sweet, heart-stopping smile. Something inside him cracked open and slid into place like a key.

But then, she took a step closer, running her hand down his arm. "Okay?"

He swallowed and only his willpower kept him from crushing her in his arms and kissing her fiercely.

"Peaches, you and I are *always* okay."

Chapter Nine

Both Twyla and Ava had determined the rules of the literary character costume contest months ago. The costume itself would be each person's entry. The give-away, for one lucky person, was five hundred dollars in gift cards donated by local vendors. The entire point of the contest was a fun way to get more customers inside her brick-and-mortar store. People were far more likely to buy a book when they actually stepped inside.

Twyla's grandmother, dressed as Jessica Fletcher from the mystery series, brought her famous peppermint squares. Others had contributed candy canes, hot chocolate and cookies in the shapes of stars, trees and reindeers. "All I Want for Christmas" by Mariah Carey piped through the speakers, and the room was filled with the spirit of the holidays.

In the end, Twyla went with the classic Elizabeth

Bennet costume. Wearing a long brown dress with pockets, she'd drawn her hair up into a historically appropriate bun. The dress was a little long for her frame and she hadn't taken the time to hem it. She should have worn heels but considering she expected to be on her feet for hours, that hadn't made sense. All night long she'd had to raise her hem slightly in order not to step on her own dress. In addition, in order to remain a purist to the character, she'd set her glasses behind the register. This made her squint a lot, but she'd put them back on when she had to drive home.

"Good evening, Sherlock." Twyla greeted Mr. Finch, wearing a tweed trench coat and carrying a large magnifying glass.

Next to him, Lois had dressed as Mrs. Marple from the Agatha Christie mysteries, complete with a gray blazer and hat.

"You two are adorable." She pointed to the table with the clipboard. "Make sure you enter your names into the giveaway."

She could always count on her senior citizens. Patsy dressed as Scarlett O'Hara as promised, Susannah as Daisy Buchanan and Ella Mae as the accused Hester Prynne, with a huge scarlet *A* stitched over her modest period dress. Books had come alive tonight with people dressed as everyone from the Cat in the Hat to Harry Potter. Max and Ava had coordinated their costumes to be Peeta and Katniss and looked intriguingly dangerous. Valerie was another Elizabeth Bennet, this one with her own Mr. Darcy. Stacy had on an obscure costume no one recognized, and she promised to give the first person who guessed a second entry. Adam, dressed like Eeyore, carried his daughter on his shoulders, dressed as Winnie the Pooh.

And a few minutes later, Zoey and Drew walked in as Bonnie and Clyde.

"Give me all your money and nobody gets hurt," Zoey said.

Twyla put her hands up. "You look great, but that wasn't a *book*. So, it can't be a *literary* character."

"They made a movie from the book," Drew said.

"They were real-life people." Twyla studied the ceiling to locate her misplaced patience. "Nonfiction."

"Such a stickler for detail! Did someone write a book *about* them?" Zoey placed a hand on the hip of her flapper-style dress.

She wasn't fooling anyone. Zoey wanted to look dangerous and sexy for Drew. She very much doubted this was her favorite literary character from a book she'd actually *read*.

"Um...well..."

"I rest my case."

Zoey had her. She'd found a loophole. Quite a stretch. Nonfiction, yes, but Twyla would allow it.

"Fine. Go ahead and enter your names for the giveaway."

All night, she searched for Noah, turning and squinting every time the door opened and more characters stepped inside. None of them disguised enough to be unrecognizable. And still no Noah. After the other night and learning how responsible he still felt for Will's death, she hadn't slept more than four hours a night.

She'd tossed and turned, reliving the day she'd learned from a classmate that both Will and Noah had been in a terrible accident. One brother had died, but no one was sure which one. To her shame, for a brief moment, Twyla had prayed it wasn't Noah. *Please not Noah, with his sweet smile, and lock of hair that perpetually fell over one eye.* In the midst of one of her nightmares, she'd jerked awake, bathed in a heavy sweat, certain Noah was gone and she'd lost them both.

She hadn't been able to get back to sleep until it was late enough in the morning to text him and wait for his reply.

The event had given her a good excuse. She'd already told him she was dressed as Elizabeth Bennet, but he still hadn't made up his mind.

You are coming tonight? she texted.

Try and stop me.

Now, she grabbed her phone, squinted and texted him again, Are you here and hiding in plain sight? Who are you? Where are you?

On my way. Be there in five, he answered.

This meant he had to be close since the boat docks were a good fifteen minutes or more from the boardwalk. Twyla busied herself with matching books to their owners. Someone wanted to read a particular book but could only remember the cover was blue. A few months ago, after the third time Twyla had a similar request, she'd created an entire display of blue books. They ranged from romance to science fiction, but hey, they were blue. She'd put up a display sign that read, *The cover was blue.*

"If it's not here, I probably don't have it." Twyla pointed to the sign. "But I can order it!"

The children were always her favorite. Their eyes widened when she told them about dragons, magic and sorcerers. The twins, Naomi and David, were here with their mother. Amy was dressed as Glenda the good witch from *The Wizard of Oz*. Of course, Naomi was Dorothy, complete with red and shiny shoes. David was the scarecrow. What an adorable family. Their father traveled for work, so he wasn't here with them tonight.

"I'm afraid I'm going to hate you after tonight," Amy said. "Or at least my wallet will."

"This one, too, Mommy!" Naomi put another book on the pile her mother carried.

Twyla bit back a smile. There had to be close to a hundred dollars' worth of books in their pile.

"She is probably my best customer." Twyla patted Naomi's head.

"Either way, I'd rather buy books than video games," Amy said with a sigh. "C'mon, kids, let's get out of here, go home and read these books."

"Have a peppermint square or two before you go," Twyla said. "I'm not taking those home with me."

She helped others find books and made more recommendations. By her calculations, it had been more than five minutes and Noah was still not here. Something must have gone wrong. Maybe Michelle had intercepted him. Either way, she couldn't dwell on Noah. He showed up or he didn't. The bookstore was having a great night and Twyla began to think they might pull out of this slump. She'd ask Ganny to see the ledgers after tonight. Maybe she wouldn't have to give the speech at the Chamber of Commerce that had her in an almost constant state of panic. They wouldn't need the angel investor loan, after all. Leave it to the citizens of Charming to save the bookstore and prevent Twyla from public speaking. She was one of those people that would rather die.

When someone dressed as Professor Dumbledore, completely with cape and long beard asked for a rare special edition, Twyla couldn't turn him down. She pulled out her rickety ladder and pushed it to the back of the store. It was old but still did the job.

"Are you sure you have it? I don't want to bother you if you don't," the customer said. "I can always order online and have it shipped home."

But that's precisely what Twyla wanted to avoid. People could always buy books at home, but what she wanted with Once Upon a Book was a sense of community. A place to belong. Everyone spent far too much time behind their screens. It wasn't healthy. She wanted the days back when kids hung out after school like she had, when avid readers haunted the bookstore or came in just for that unique book smell. You couldn't bottle the scent of a freshly printed book or one with weathered pages. And like so many other small-town places, the bookstore brought people together. That's why she was still here and not giving up. This place still meant something to her that went far beyond books or making a living. It was about people.

She made a note to put some of these thoughts into her speech if she was forced to make it. So far, she'd struggled to put her ideas into a structure that made sense. She worked on it every day behind the counter but frankly, she'd rather be reading.

"I'm sure I have it. Sometimes I send books back if they're returnable, but I kept a few copies of this one. It's the reissue of a classic for a reason."

She climbed up a few steps to the top shelf. Here, she had a somewhat blurry bird's-eye view of the entire store and as she found the book and pulled it out, she took a moment to soak this in. Characters from all the books she'd enjoyed as a child and adult were crowding her little store. The sensation was one of books literally coming to life, the way she'd always hoped for as a child. She saw Valerie, the other Elizabeth Bennet, holding her baby boy. She was standing between what appeared to be two Mr. Darcy's. Twyla hadn't seen the second one come in. They both had their backs to her, but then Valerie handed Wade to the Mr. Darcy on her left. The other one turned, and it was…Noah. Or was it? She squinted hard.

Noah—or whoever—smiled, then held up his walking cane and bowed. The regency tailcoat, the Victorian ascot necktie with a white shirt…this guy was the image of a classic romantic hero. When the errant hair fell over one eye and he pushed it back, she knew. This was her Noah. Noah, like she'd never seen him before.

Her pulse quickened and a sharp sting of awareness slammed into her. Prickles of desire sliced through her, blood rushing too fast to her head. In that moment, a blindfold was removed. The mask that said "friend and not lover." The one that refused to see what had maybe always been there. A weight pressed on her, heavy and warm like a blanket. All those tender emotions for him over the years. The longing. She'd told herself all those feelings were normal for someone she knew so well. Understood and, yes, loved.

Now, for the first time, the thought came fully formed:

I'm in love with Noah.

Dear *God.* She wobbled on the ladder and had to right herself. No. No, it couldn't be true.

Noah headed toward her now, with a determined gait. Mr. Darcy, wielding his cane, made his way through the crowd.

"So…you have the book?"

Oh, yes. She was up here to find a book.

In a somewhat stupefied daze, Twyla bent to the customer's outreached hand and handed him the book.

"I knew I had it."

"Super." The customer turned it over to glance at the back cover copy.

Twyla headed back down, picking up her dress as she went down every rung, careful not to step on it. Then, for reasons she could not explain, the next rung on the ladder disappeared beneath her. She heard a loud crack, then a gasp, before everything went dark.

When Twyla opened her eyes again, the faces of characters from books surrounded her. She was in a dream. Sherlock Holmes fanned her with a book while Eeyore ordered everyone circling her to back up and give her some breathing room. Bonnie was crying into Clyde's chest.

And her aching head…was in *Mr. Darcy's* lap. He had his fingers wrapped around her wrist yelling at everyone to stand back. His haunted expression made her wonder if somehow, in the past few seconds, she'd been told she only had months to live.

The last thing she remembered was Noah, in his collared shirt, looking so handsome that her equilibrium had been upset.

Had she literally *fainted* over Noah dressed like Mr. Darcy? Really, how embarrassing.

"W-what happened?"

"I've told you to stop using that ladder," Ganny said. "It's older than I am, and my brittle bones creak every morning. What on *earth* were you thinking climbing that ladder?"

"It's not her fault," Noah said, but it sounded more like he'd yelled.

"Of course, it's not," Scarlett O'Hara said.

Oh, it was Patsy. Next to her was Rhett Butler, who Twyla assumed was her husband. What a cute couple they made.

"It's *my* fault," Professor Dumbledore said, hand to his chest. He was the customer she'd been helping before she fell. "I should have waited for the book. I could have ordered it online and had it delivered right to my house. Then none of this would have happened. She climbed the ladder to get my book!"

"It's not your fault, either. It's nobody's." Twyla sat up, loosening Noah's grip around her wrist and wiggled her hands, to demonstrate she still had control and possession over all of her limbs. "Look, I'm fine. I just lost my balance. And it's an old ladder."

"You were out for a few seconds," Noah said. "The longest seconds of my life."

"It rather seemed like hours," Sherlock Homes said. Oh, Mr. Finch. That's right.

"You of all people know how clumsy I can be," Twyla said to Noah.

Someone handed him a pillow and his hand gently pushed her back down. "You need to get checked out."

"I agree," Mr. Finch said. "There's no mystery here."

"Very funny, Mr. Finch."

Former paramedic Noah would naturally want to put her through the paces and make sure she wasn't dying. She had started to argue her case again when the EMTs arrived.

"Who called the ambulance?" But she didn't really have to ask, did she?

Twyla groaned. "Oh, Mr. Darcy. What have you done?"

He smiled and flashed a single dimple. "Be quiet, Miss Bennet. You swooned."

Noah got a few strange looks in the Houston emergency room waiting area.

"Costume party?" a lady sitting nearby asked.

Noah nodded.

"Who are you supposed to be?" the kid next to her asked. "You look like an old-timey guy. And…kind of *weird*."

"Damon!" his mother chided. "Don't be rude."

Noah swirled his walking stick. "I was going to be a dragon slayer, but then…well, Mr. Darcy is a character from *Pride and Prejudice*. You know that book?"

Damon wrinkled his nose. "You should have been the dragon slayer."

"Tell me about it."

After all, Twyla had expected him in the dragon slayer costume. Maybe if he'd worn it, she wouldn't have looked at him with such surprise in her eyes right before the ladder rung broke. He'd wanted to impress her—that was the ridiculous truth of it all—wanted to see her eyes widen, the brightness of her smile show the colors only he saw in her. But he hadn't wanted to *stun* her.

She fell, and for one moment, it was *his* life that flashed before his eyes. Enough. He was tired of losing people he loved.

He stood and walked over to check in with the receptionist. "How much longer?"

"Five less minutes than the last time you asked me."

He couldn't sit any longer, so he paced the hallway, occasionally getting too close to the automatic doors so they swung open when nobody was ready to leave. Except for him. He'd been ready hours ago and he resented being kept away from all of the medical information he would understand. Possibly yeah, he had too much knowledge, and it had forever been an issue with his loved ones. One year, his mother complained of a slight pressure in her chest after a large dinner. He'd rushed her to the ER worrying about full cardiac arrest. She'd had a bad case of gas, but one could never be too careful.

Finally, eons later, an orderly wheeled Twyla out. She sent him a scowl.

"Hospital procedure," Noah answered her unasked question. *Why am I in this wheelchair when I can walk?*

Funny how in some instances he could hear her thoughts. He'd parked nearby, so he ran outside and pulled up his truck within seconds. The orderly wheeled her to the passenger-side door.

"Thank you, good sir," Twyla said in full character. "I am forever indebted to your kindness."

"What's the name of that book again?" the orderly said.

"I'll write it down for you." He handed Twyla a pen

and she ripped off a piece of what must be her discharge instructions. Great. "You're going to love it."

Always the bookseller.

Noah leaned over and clicked her seat belt into place. This was quite possibly overkill, and his suspicions were confirmed when she slid him a look that said, *I'm not a child.* Unless he got that one wrong. She might also be thinking, *Not how I planned to spend my evening.* Sometimes hearing her thoughts wasn't much fun. It seemed at the moment that she might be quietly listing how many ways she could hurt him without killing him.

"What did the doctor say?" He took the papers from her. "Let me see."

"He said I'm fine, but he understands how I would want to be checked."

Reading over the discharge instructions, he saw the usual warnings of watching for symptoms of extreme headache, nausea or dizziness. There was the standard recommendation for observation and quick action if anything changed. Call 911, in other words, and don't wait.

"You have a mild concussion."

This was fairly standard and what nearly everyone who arrived at the hospital with a bump on their head was told, but if he said that she'd shrug it off as nothing.

"I should get back to the store now. This was definitely not on the schedule tonight."

"Don't worry. Ava chose the giveaway winner, and your grandmother closed the bookstore."

"And I missed it all." She slumped down in her seat.

"You were busy getting your brain checked." He turned onto the highway and headed for Charming.

"Wasn't it wonderful tonight?"

She'd moved on to earlier in the evening. Good deal for him.

"It was a great turnout."

He'd been late, having spent too much time on the accounting ledgers, and then been irritated to find the entrance blocked. People were packed in too tightly. After a brief discussion with others as to why the doorway had to remain clear for fire safety, he told himself not to worry about whether they were exceeding capacity. He wasn't an employed firefighter any longer. His new modus operandi was to stop saving people.

Then Twyla fell and everything stopped. The world just…froze.

"I might not even have to make my speech now. We should do it every year." She leaned back in the seat now, relaxing. "You make a very handsome Mr. Darcy, by the way. But why Mr. Darcy? I thought you were coming as a dragon slayer."

"Too predictable. I wanted to surprise you, and I did."

"You don't think I…? That's *not* why I fell."

"I know. One of the ladder rungs broke because you're still using one from the regency period apparently. I'll get you a new ladder, the highest-rated one for safety. The old one is going to be scrap."

He swung by his rental to grab a change of clothes. A few minutes later he'd pulled in front of Twyla's small cottage downtown not far from the bookstore. She'd moved to this neighborhood sometime last year to save money. The area was a mix of business and residential zones, with all the homes from the post–World War II era. Charming didn't have a dicey or questionable part of town, but if they did, this would be it. He hated the fact that she'd been forced to move here to save money but had no say in the matter.

Tonight, at least, he had a voice. He shut off his truck. "I'm staying with you tonight."

She met his gaze, eyes cool and assessing.

"No, you're not. I know this is you feeling that you should have done something to stop me from falling off that ladder. But listen carefully—it was an *accident* and I'm fine. You can go home now. You've done your duty."

"You think this is about *duty*?"

"Because this is what you do. You try to fix things and rescue people. Well, I'm here to tell you I don't need to be rescued."

"Who said that? I didn't." He reached for the discharge instructions and read the section about observing slips out of consciousness and having someone wake the patient every few hours.

"I'll set an alarm clock."

"Which would work well as long as everything is fine. And defeats the entire purpose of when something is suddenly *not* fine."

"You want to stay here all night dressed as Mr. Darcy? What if I ask you to walk around the living room?"

He hadn't read *Pride and Prejudice*, granted, so he was a bit confused. "Why would we walk around the living room?"

"Well, because I don't have a garden."

"This is something from the book, isn't it?" He narrowed his eyes.

"You should have read it years ago, when I first

suggested it, and then you'd know what I'm talking about now."

"I prefer *A Dragon's Heart.* At least it's not written in old English." He snorted.

The mention of the book spiked his anxiety. He still had the damn book, packed away in a box, and at some point, he should really confess. Confess and give it back to her. Okay, but maybe later.

"Honestly, Noah, you can stay with me if you insist. But don't be surprised if I force you to dance the Boulanger with me. It's a circle dance with other couples but we'll fake it."

"I don't dance."

"The tango? Waltz?"

"No."

"Slow foxtrot? Quick step?"

"No dancing."

She drew her hand over her forehead, as if she'd swoon again.

"With me as Elizabeth and you as Mr. Darcy it will be inevitable, I fear. We must dance or die."

"You're such a smart-ass sometimes."

He chuckled, the joy of the moment almost unrecognizable. But Twyla never failed to make him laugh. Twyla, who always had his back, whether he was in Charming or Austin.

Too many times, he'd failed to be there when she needed him.

Tonight would not be one.

Chapter Ten

Best friends were annoying sometimes. Particularly when they were over-the-top alpha dogs like Noah. The way he dressed tonight, as the genteel and well-heeled Mr. Darcy, was totally incongruous with the real Noah. No wonder she'd been so surprised that she fell. The real Noah Cahill occasionally wore motorcycle boots and leather and had often run into burning buildings.

But damn he looked fine as a regency-era gentleman. Fine enough to knock her off a ladder, apparently.

"This isn't up for discussion." He climbed out of the truck.

All she wanted now was to go inside and put an ice pack on her head. It still hurt, not that she would tell him that. He'd probably phone 911 again when all she needed was some Tylenol and a little sleep. She also wanted to change out of this dress which, while it had pockets, wasn't exactly her style. The next time she wound up at the ER, she would not be dressed as Elizabeth Bennet. In the bay, the nurses' teasing over Mr. Darcy driving Elizabeth to the hospital seemed to never end. At least she'd introduced one new reader to *Pride and Prejudice*. Everyone else had seen the movie, and not read the book, and said Noah was better looking than the actor.

She didn't disagree. Not for the first time, she felt the pinch of having a gorgeous looker for a best friend. She supposed it was better than having a girlfriend who continually outshined her, but then again, she had one of those, too. And speaking of Zoey…

"I should really call Zoey, or should I say 'Bonnie'? She seemed really upset."

"And call your grandmother. She made me promise."

Bonkers met them at the door and greeted her with his usual mix of disgust and apathy. He hissed his welcome, then turned his back to her as if he couldn't be bothered.

"Hey, Bonkers." Noah bent to pet him before Twyla could warn him.

"Don't tou—"

Bonkers made the guttural sound of a cat possessed, baring teeth, and arching his back.

Noah straightened and frowned. "I thought you said he was doing better."

"And he is doing better, but still a little temperamental. We understand each other. See, I have to act like I don't care. As soon as he relaxes, and sees I'm not terribly needy, he'll curl up at my feet or jump in my lap, purring away. But the trick is he has to *think* I'm not interested." She tapped a finger to her temple.

"So…you play hard to get. With your cat." He sent her a look from under hooded lids.

"You wouldn't understand. You're a dog person."

"I'll pretend I don't care. See how that works for me."

Noah ambled into the kitchen, and Twyla went to her landline to call Ganny. She reassured her that she'd been thoroughly checked out, and that Noah was doing his usual over-the-top thing and staying with her tonight.

"Thank God for Noah," Ganny said. "You do as he says, young lady. He's a professional."

"Yes, he is. A professional pain in the neck. How do you think we did tonight?"

"I'd say it could be a record December if we go by tonight's extraordinary sales."

"Fantastic!"

"But."

"There's a but?"

"I still think you should still try to get the angel investor. Do the speech and see what happens. It won't kill you."

"Won't it? I don't like people, much less a room full of them staring at me. I don't know if I can do this."

"You *can* do it. You're a Thompson through and through, made of strong stuff."

"I haven't got a clue what makes you think that. I'm a reader and I have a big imagination but even I can't imagine myself making a speech to all those people."

"Practice with Noah."

"No way. He'll throw spitballs at me and make me laugh."

"Oh, you two act like you're still in third grade."

Except that the feelings she'd had for him tonight were not at all childlike. Watching Noah tonight made her body do things. Almost unrecognizable things. She'd never been one to have bursting, hot sexual chemistry or attraction with any man, but tonight her body seemed to house a furnace.

Twyla said her goodbyes, then went into her bedroom to change out of her frock. She found her standard uniform of black yoga pants paired with a long-sleeved T-shirt. With some welcome privacy from Noah, she phoned Zoey to assure her she only had a mild concussion. With only a smidge of sarcasm, she told Zoey she would live to read for another day.

"It happened so fast," Zoey said. "What do you remember?"

"Not much. I was coming down the ladder when I saw Mr. Darcy. I mean Noah. He smiled and..."

She recalled the sweaty palms, the racing pulse. Heart pounding against her rib cage. But that had to have been excitement at the success of the evening and the surprise at seeing Noah in a whole new way.

"I guess I did hear the crack of the ladder rung and felt myself slipping."

"Noah tried to catch you. He ran so fast, like a cheetah or some other wild animal. Just one second quicker and he might have broken your fall. He was kind of amazing, even if he yelled at everyone to get away from you, which startled me so much I started crying. Then Adam and Max got everyone to back up and give you some air. After that, you woke up and told us you were fine. Thank you. It was quite the end to a dramatic evening."

"I honestly think calling 911 was a little over-the-top but what do I know."

"Well, it was the first thing Noah yelled at us and he sounded so scary. No one was going to argue with him. I think at least three people called."

"Something happened and I haven't had a chance to tell you."

"Oh, my gosh, spill the tea!"

"Michelle wanted to talk. She came to the bookstore and wanted to take me to lunch. Which I thought was so mean because then she wouldn't eat. So, of course, I couldn't eat."

"What did she want, anyway?"

"She wants me to help her get Noah back and she thinks all I have to do is tell him I don't need him anymore. She says he feels sorry for me and feels an unnatural attachment because of Will." Twyla took a breath. "Do you…think that's true?"

"No. But what did Noah say? I assume you asked him."

"He said no, of course. But even if it's true, I mean, he wouldn't want me to feel bad."

"I don't think it's true if it helps. You and Noah have your own relationship now."

"Sure, but I…" Twyla couldn't say it out loud.

Surely she was wrong about this. She couldn't be in love with Noah.

"What happened with Finn, anyway?"

"Noah said he's hung up on someone else. He can't stop thinking about her."

"What a shame. I mean, if you and Finn could get together, that would make sense. Then you and Finn can double date with Noah and Michelle. That will cure her of thinking he needs to take care of you."

The thought made Twyla sick, which was plain weird. Since when did the thought of Noah with someone else make her sick?

Maybe since the moment she realized she'd started to fall for him.

Oh, this was impossible!

"Unless…that bothers you."

"She said Noah always leaves the room to talk to me."

"Wait. He does? Just to take your call? I mean, why? That's really suspicious behavior."

"I don't know why, but maybe he wouldn't have done it had he known the way it bothered her."

"Maybe. But honestly, c'mon, I thought Noah was smarter than that."

"With any other woman he would be. But it's *me*."

"Yes, you. A very attractive single woman his age. I can understand why anyone who had her sights on Noah would feel threatened. Can't you?"

"But…Noah doesn't think of me that way."

"Before tonight I might have agreed with you. Now, and with this brand-new information, hmm. I'm not so sure."

"You just think that way because you've never had a man be a close friend."

"Noah is pretty unique. I don't think many men can keep those relationships completely separate." She called out to Drew. "Hey, babe, do you think a man and a woman can be good friends and nothing more?"

"Zoey!" Twyla hissed. "Do not bring him into this."

"If they're not attracted to each other," Drew could

be heard responding, "then of course, it's totally possible."

"Did you hear that?" Zoey said.

"Yes, and I'm worried Noah heard it in the next room."

"What? He's still there?"

"He's staying the night. Because of the concussion thing."

Zoey whistled. "Oh, my God."

"It's nothing, just Noah's over-the-top concern. He'd do it for anyone."

"Well, I doubt he'd shove people out of his way to get to *me* if I was falling." Zoey paused and it sounded as if she'd moved into another room when TV sounds faded into the background.

"You might ask him why he always left the room to talk to you. Keeping your conversations private was not a good way for him to reassure her, you have to admit."

"This is something I should stay out of. Bringing it up now sounds like asking for trouble."

"Maybe trouble is what you need right now." She hesitated a beat. "Trouble of the fun kind. I mean, how off base is she? Aren't you even the slightest bit attracted to Noah?"

"No, I—"

"You're not being honest, Twy. I mean, hell, even *I'm* attracted to him. He's a good-looking man, charming, fun. If you're not attracted to him, I guess I can't understand why."

"You know me. Sexual magnetism, the stuff that happens to you daily, almost never happens to me. And...I've repressed it."

"Oh, okay. Kind of like me and my college calculus

teacher. Man, that guy was hotter than a jalapeño pepper. And married. It was never going to happen." She sighed. "But Noah isn't married or too old for you. You two would actually be kind of perfect together. I'm not sure why it never happened."

"You know why."

"Honey, you haven't been Will's girl in over a decade."

"He still thinks of me that way. Maybe he always will. You know how loyal Noah can be."

"So, that's it? *Will* is the reason you two have stayed apart? That's getting old. If that's all, it's not enough."

"Look, even if he's interested, which I highly doubt, maybe I don't want to take the risk. Noah has a lot of ex-girlfriends in his past. I don't ever want to be one of them. Ganny adores him and he's like part of my family already. And Noah needs family."

She peeked into the living room to see Noah had plopped down on the couch. He'd changed into a pair of jeans that were hung loose on his hips and a faded blue T-shirt that read, *Surf's Up*.

"Anyway, I'm fine. I'll talk to you tomorrow."

"Be sure to thank Noah for me. He didn't just save his best friend, he also saved mine."

Twyla hung up and the first thing she saw as she walked into the living room shook her to the core.

Noah sat stretched out on her couch, a purring Bonkers in his lap. And Twyla could tell he was there by choice.

"I did what you said and played hard to get. He's half in love with me now."

Twyla plopped down on the couch beside Noah and gaped.

"He's a Benedict Arnold. I should change his name. Do you know it took me *two months* to get him to jump on my lap? Some days I had to pretend he wasn't even in the room. I'd put his food dish down and leave."

She reached to nuzzle Bonkers between his gray ears and noticed something else entirely. She and Noah sat close together, hip to hip, knees brushing against each other. They'd sat close before, but it was only that now this felt…*different.* Something had indeed shifted for her in the store when, for one moment, she'd seen Noah in a different light. She saw him as she had the very first time. This time it wasn't the crush that she'd suppressed for so long from the moment she'd met both brothers and only one of them had stolen her heart. This felt like falling in love. The feeling was so rare that she might be mixing it up with some other deep emotion. This *had* to be wrong.

She *couldn't* fall in love with Noah Cahill. It would be the dumbest thing she'd ever done. When she glanced up, he'd cocked his head and continued to study her with…what? Concern? Yes, of course, worry that she'd hit her head. Nothing to see here.

"*What?* I'm fine, don't give me that look." Self-consciously, she touched her head.

"What look?"

"The one that says you're concerned. It's the same look the doctor gave me and I'd appreciate it if you didn't."

"And how *is* your head?"

"My head is fine. Let's talk about something else, shall we?"

He continued to pet Bonkers, who may have actually sighed, but didn't offer up a subject change, so she did.

“It looks like I’m going to have to make that speech for the Chamber of Commerce, after all.”

“You said you’d rather walk barefoot over hot coals.”

“And that’s still true, but no one is going to give me an angel investor loan for walking over hot coals. I wish they would.”

“Okay, let me hear it. Give me the speech.”

“You? What for? You’ll only make fun of me.”

He sent her an easy smile. “Nah. I promise to be good. No spitballs.”

“Well…”

“C’mon, be brave. It’s just me. I’m a good person to practice with.”

He might be right. At least she was comfortable with Noah. But it would also be different because she was here in the comfort of her home, the place where she felt safest. She went to her notebook and the speech she’d been working on about books and community. It was pretty good, though she wished she had the nerve to ask Stacy to write it for her. Though that would probably be cheating.

Speech in her hands, she read the first few lines she’d memorized to herself, then faced Noah. His earnest dark gaze pinned her, and all thoughts seeped out of her like wind through an open window.

“Stop looking at me! I’ll lose my place.” She pointed, hoping to look threatening. “Just…turn around and face the other way.”

“You might as well get used to it the way you’ll have to do it.” He hooked a thumb to his chest. “It’s just me.”

“And you’re a person.”

“A man waits his whole life to hear those words.” He quirked a brow. “Just picture me naked.”

She swallowed hard, nearly choking on her own saliva.

"I...I don't think that will help me."

Picturing Noah naked might send her into cardiac arrest. Which might help, because then everyone would give her a pass on the speech.

"It's what they tell everyone who's giving a speech for the first time. You're supposed to picture everyone in your audience naked. You never heard of that?"

"Maybe. But why? What's the point?"

"To make you laugh and realize you shouldn't take it all so seriously." He shrugged. "People are all the same."

"I don't think that's going to work for me." She very much doubted that any man would look the way Noah did naked. Which meant, again, she had a fantastic imagination.

"Look, let's go slow with this. You're a novice. Think of me in my underwear."

But that was almost worse. She thought Noah wore boxer briefs because once, his shirt rode up as he stretched and revealed a taut and tanned hint of bare skin. It was just the small peek at the elastic band of his underwear. Black. Picturing him wearing those now tantalized her and would not accomplish anything but making it hard to sleep tonight.

Now she couldn't *stop* thinking about Noah naked!

He sat up straighter and Bonkers hissed, disgusted that anyone would move his current resting place.

"What's wrong? Is it your head? You look a little pale."

Maybe because all the blood had drained from her face.

She threw her notepad on the couch and covered

her face. "At this rate, you won't have to wake me up, because I won't be able to sleep tonight thinking about this stupid speech."

Yes, that was her story, and she was sticking to it. It wasn't because she'd suddenly developed a keen awareness of Noah. And it couldn't be because her cheeks warmed when he said *naked.* He'd always been handsome but now she noticed it a lot more. Noticed the stubble that darkened his cheeks and chin. The long, hard body. For almost as long as she'd known him, Noah hadn't grown a beard—and as a firefighter, he hadn't been allowed to. He'd had to remain clean shaven and now…he was not. It gave him a roguish, almost dangerous air about him.

But she wasn't *attracted* to Noah because she one hundred percent refused to be.

Nope. None of that.

If Twyla bit on her lower lip one more time, Noah would lose his ever-loving mind. She was already dressed in a white nightshirt so thin he could see through the cotton to her plunging pink bra. He wasn't trying to, honestly, but he couldn't look away. Or wouldn't. Whatever.

"Let me show you how it's done." He picked up the notebook she'd thrown down and took her place.

"Now you're good at giving speeches, too?" Her eyes widened. "Perfect."

"I'm not going to do it *for* you, so stop looking at me that way."

She shook her head sadly, pouted and curled up on the couch. "No, they wouldn't allow it."

"At least once a year, it was my turn to give the fire safety speech at the local elementary school, so

I got used to it." He glanced at the few sentences she had written down. Not long enough to be a speech, but they'd worry about that later. Knowing Twyla, the writing was the easy part.

"Just picture me naked," she said, coming up on one elbow.

"I don't need to do that."

Besides, he already had. Countless times. Both naked and wearing sexy lingerie, which is why he knew it would not help him.

"Eyes on me," Noah began.

"Why do I feel like you're about to tell me where I can find all the fire extinguishers and exits in the building?"

He snorted but ignored that. "This is how you do this— Good morning, everyone. I'm Twyla Thompson and—"

She burst into laughter and threw a pillow at him. "No, you're not. You're not *Twyla*."

"C'mon, Peaches, you gotta suspend disbelief. That's what you told me about the dragon books. Yes, there's a shaman who can chant a few words and turn a dragon's fire into ice. I totally buy it. So, here we go." He glanced down at her notes, then straightened. "The trick is not to read it all but to try to look up and make eye contact every few seconds. Bookstores are important to a community."

Noah read a few lines, then glanced up. And was promptly hit in the head with another pillow.

"Hey!" But he couldn't help but laugh with her as she threw every pillow and hit her mark each time.

"It's not fair that you're good at everything! I have to stop the insanity! You must pay!"

He could protest that he wasn't good at everything. Far from it. That had been Will. But instead of arguing, he returned fire. That was a hell of a lot more fun. The pillows became missiles and he showed zero mercy, but neither did she. Her glasses fell off and she scrambled to both put them down and get another pillow. Bonkers, who had been hanging out, hissed and arched his back.

When Noah ran out of pillows, he chased her around the couch, ducking shots. God, it felt good to laugh like this again. To play. His mother once accused him of never wanting to grow up, and that had been true at one time. But no one ever saw this side of him anymore. Just Twyla. Reaching her, he grabbed her from behind, his arms around her waist and lifted her. She squealed and continued to laugh when he threw her on the couch. It might have all stopped there but then she reached to tug at him, and he not-so-accidentally fell on top of her.

Then all the laughter abruptly stopped, and they simply stared at each other for one excruciating moment. He fixated on her full bottom lip and wondered if she would taste like caramel. Her blue eyes widened and appeared larger with her glasses removed. She was a woman who wore little makeup and her lashes were still dark and long. But more than anything, holy God, she felt good under him. Soft and sweet. He wanted her so badly that he couldn't think straight. The last time they'd been in this compromising position they'd been fourteen, joking around, and back then Noah had quickly jumped off her. *Will's girl.* He'd told Noah countless times that he had a thing for her, that he'd ask her out when he got the courage. Will hadn't asked

Noah to stay away from her, but of course he had. Of course. Will was his older brother and he looked up to him. Adored him as much as a teenage boy could adore anything or anyone.

But there was really nothing keeping them apart right now other than the status quo. Which could change. Maybe he only had to make the first move.

Bonkers suddenly hissed and pounced on Noah's back. The timing was impeccable because only an interruption like this would have stopped Noah from kissing Twyla.

"Ouch!" He stood, censoring himself. There were a few other choice words rolling on his tongue.

"Bonkers! You bad, bad cat!" Twyla chased him out of the room. "Noah, I'm so, so, *so* sorry. I should have him declawed. Are you okay?"

The cat's claws were the least of his problems. "Yeah, I'm good. I'm good."

"Let me see. Did he take some skin?" She came closer and he really should let her check but for the first time in longer than he could ever recall, Noah felt…vulnerable.

And not because of the cat's claws.

"No, I'm good. He barely touched me." That wasn't quite true, but he was having second thoughts about everything. He'd just decided he would stay away from romantic entanglements and what had he almost done? "I think you need to actually work on the speech. It's not long enough yet."

"Yes, I just started writing it."

"That's what I thought. Once you have it all written down, you can practice on me." He faked a yawn. "I'm tired. Think I'll hit the sack."

"Oh. Yeah, okay. You must be tired, getting up so early." She left the room and came back with a spare pillow and blanket for him. "I'm only doing this because you insist on staying here and I want you to be comfortable."

"And don't worry about the speech. You've got this."

Chapter Eleven

Twyla tossed and turned until midnight. Noah was *sleeping* in the next room. On *her* couch. He wasn't naked, but he didn't have to be. Thanks to a few glimpses and her active imagination, she almost *knew* what he looked like. *Stupid imagination.*

Despite what had to be scratches on his back, he'd simply gone to bed as if this was any other day. Now, she glanced in the living room and saw him curled up on the couch, an arm slung over his face. Carefully, she tiptoed close and pulled the blanket to cover him up to the neck. She could deal with a lot of things in life, but tonight she did not want to deal with noticing Noah's naked, perfectly sculpted chest. It was practically a work of art. Not that she was all that familiar with said works of art, but she watched Netflix, after all. And, one day, a little bored at the store, she'd created an entire display she'd labeled, *guys missing their shirts.* Some of the best books she'd ever read. And, well, let's just say that Noah could easily model for one of those covers.

She really needed to get her head screwed on straight. Slipping into the kitchen in the dark, she was careful not to wake Noah. What she really needed was a shot of whiskey to knock her out cold so she could endure this torturous night. But she could almost hear paramedic Noah's voice in her ear: *Um, no. Bad idea. Mixing alcohol with a concussion?* Well, even she realized that could be risky. She went for the milk since she was probably the least exciting person on the planet. Milk was boring. She poured some into a cup and warmed it up in the microwave.

Funny new things to note? Noah didn't even snore. And apparently, Bonkers didn't hate him. He sat at the edge of the couch like a sentry, guarding Noah's feet. Occasionally he took a swipe but always missed. Bonkers never missed. He didn't hate Noah!

Right now, Twyla desperately needed to think of one thing that was very wrong with Noah. Just one thing, please, other than the fact that he hadn't even let her attend to his cat scratches. That was irritating, sure, but it could be said he didn't want to bother her. She was at a loss, other than his often unnerving need to rescue everyone. And she could be more irritated by that if she didn't realize exactly what had caused it.

She turned and blinked when Noah's chest appeared in her line of sight.

"Hey," he said from under hooded lids. "I was just coming to wake you."

She tried to ignore the way he rubbed his eye with

the back of his palm. And suddenly, she had it. The one thing that irritated the hell out of her about Noah.

She pointed her finger at him. “That’s it! I have it now. Want to know what your problem is? You’re stealthy and sneaky. It’s no wonder Bonkers doesn’t hate you like he hates everyone else.”

“Huh? He attacked me.”

Right. He had, in fact, pounced on Noah’s back, which was the kindest thing he’d ever done to a guest.

“I didn’t hear you there, right behind me.”

“Sorry, I wasn’t trying to sneak up on you.”

No, of course he wasn’t. Regret pulsed through her. He wouldn’t understand why she suddenly had to come up with something awful about him.

“You look tired. Do you want some coffee?”

He slid her a blank stare. “It’s after midnight.”

“Oh, so you’re going back to sleep?”

“I was planning on it. You seem to be firing on all cylinders. Can’t say I’m worried.” He scrubbed a hand across the beard bristles on his jaw.

“Good. Nothing to see here.”

Except her suddenly wild and raging crush on Noah Cahill. All those years spent quietly pushing her emotions down and one Mr. Darcy costume had them roaring back to life.

The timer to the microwave dinged and Noah reached past her, brushing his hand against her waist when he did so. He pushed the button to the microwave, and it clicked open.

“You’re having warm milk?” He sent her a slow smile. “What a classic.”

For several long seconds, she simply stared into his eyes. “That’s me. Boring and classic.”

Twyla Thompson, bookworm and faux Elizabeth Bennet. Not even the real thing. Even for her time, Twyla could probably take lessons from the regency-era lady. The woman had loved books and reading, but she had chutzpah, too. Then again, *her* Mr. Darcy was rude and a complete stranger.

"You're not boring, Peaches. Far from it."

Twyla was locked in a staring contest with the only man she'd ever truly loved. Of course, theirs was a philia type of love—a deep friendship. Except at the moment, with the darkness surrounding them and the utter quiet of the night, they were like two different people. They weren't Twyla and Noah who had known each other for years. And now she wondered what it would be like to meet him for the first time. What it might have been if she hadn't said yes to Will about that first date. If she'd have waited for Noah to ask. Would she have waited forever, or would he have eventually asked her to be more than friends? It was long ago, and she'd never know. They had all this history buried between them, and it would require a wide and sturdy bridge to get across all the years.

His eyes were the deepest shade of brown she'd ever seen. Like dark chocolate. Like melt-in-your-mouth brownies.

Okay, stop this right now.

"Guess I'm going back to bed now that you say I'm okay." She turned but then stopped midway out of the kitchen.

Maybe she *would* like to change everything. It wasn't like her love life was something to be envied. But changes like this couldn't be made on a one-way street.

"I think…I'll go." It was almost as if he'd read her mind. "You definitely are okay."

"I tried to tell you that, but thanks for listening." Twyla might not want Noah to go, but she did not want him to stay with her out of obligation. As her caretaker. Given that, it was best to say good-night now and not wait until the sunrise.

She followed him into the living room where he pulled his shirt over his head in about two seconds flat.

"If you feel nauseous, if anything happens at all, you call me. I'm as close as the phone."

"What if I see a spider?"

"Yes, smart-ass. Even a spider."

"Thank you, Noah, I'll be fine."

She walked him to the front door where he hesitated for a moment and turned as if to do one last triage on her.

Eyes? Check. Color? Check. Alertness scale? Double check. They'd done the same thing to her in the ER.

"I'm *fine.*"

Then with little warning other than the sudden shine in his eyes, he hauled her by the neck to him and kissed her, square on the lips. It was a deep and long kiss that didn't seem to have a beginning. Nor did it have an end. He pulled her tight and they were hip to hip, belly to belly. Even through the shock of the totally unexpected, she kissed him back. She sunk her fingers into his hair and kissed him with everything she had in her. With every last inch of longing wrapped up in her, saved over the years and packed away where the raw intensity of the emotion couldn't destroy her.

She fisted his shirt. She ran her hands up and down his back, feeling the muscles tense and bunch.

It was over just as quickly and then they were both panting, staring at each other.

"I'm sorry." Noah took a step back, leaving a healthy distance between them. "Yeah, I shouldn't have done that. That's wrong."

Wrong?

"It's okay," she stammered because she didn't know what else to say in the moment.

Yes, it was wonderful, please kiss me again, because I think maybe I've always loved you?

"It's just...that was wrong of me. I don't feel that way about you."

Oh, God. There went her heart, pierced and sliced into tiny bits.

I don't feel that way about you.

No, he was right. This *was* wrong. And if he had regrets then damn it, so did she.

"Me, neither. I don't feel that way about you."

"I know."

The certainty in his voice broke her heart a little. How could he be so sure she wasn't straight-out lying, trying to save her pride?

She chewed on her lower lip. "So, let's just forget it. Pretend the kiss never happened."

"But...we're okay?"

Worry and regret filled those dark puppy dog eyes. Not long ago, she would have understood. But now she knew what it was like to be kissed by Noah and her heart shattered to think it would never happen again.

"We're okay. You're probably right, huh? Bad idea."

"Yeah, I just don't want to...you know..." He ran a hand through his hair, looking desperately vulnerable, like a man searching for a lifeline.

And what kind of friend would she be not to throw one to him?

"It was just, well, okay, maybe we're both lonely. And it's after midnight. I...got um, confused." She had no idea what she was saying but it sounded good, and he seemed to be receptive.

"Yeah, so did I."

"And I've got a date tomorrow night so that could be awkward."

Now she'd lied to her best friend, but she'd also kissed him within an inch of his life, so either way she was in brand new territory here.

He quirked a brow. "You have a date? Who is he?"

"Some guy."

"Some guy? Does 'some guy' have a name?"

"Of course he has a *name*, Noah. He's some guy I just met." She crossed her arms. "Weren't you leaving?"

He scowled. "Yeah. I have an early day tomorrow."

"Bye." She closed the door before he could say another word.

Now she was going to have to find herself a date.

Noah spent the rest of the day irritated with everyone. It wasn't fair to Tee or Finn, who had dropped by to help with inventory, otherwise known as the job that never seemed to end. Every time he thought they'd finished, they found another box of ropes or T-shirts or boat shoes.

Last night, once again, Noah had taken what he wanted without thinking or caring what anyone else thought. Not thinking of what he could risk. Of what he could lose.

He'd kissed Twyla and felt an intense pull that tugged him under.

I'm sorry, he'd said to Twyla, like he'd accidentally stepped on her foot.

Now he'd probably screwed up his friendship with Twyla, and he didn't know how to move forward. Worse, he'd lied to her when he said he didn't feel anything more. But this was one lie that would stay in place. She deserved someone better. Noah couldn't give her everything she deserved. And whether right or wrong, he did not want to come in second.

And besides, Twyla had a *date* tomorrow night.

"Are you going out tomorrow night?" he now asked Finn.

Were Finn to have asked Twyla out, he would have surely said something to Noah first. Considering Finn knew Noah had a thing for Twyla, he'd sounded pretty negative about the whole thing.

Finn glanced up. "Why? You want to hit up the bar for a cold beer or two?"

"I meant whether you have a date with a…a lady."

"I'm taking a break from 'the ladies.'" Finn held up air quotes. "But hey, thanks for caring."

"Hey, boss," Tee said. "I'm not seeing anyone."

"So?" Noah barked.

"In case you've got someone you're trying to fix up. I'm available." He held his arms out. "Just sayin'."

Finn chuckled and shook his head.

"A cold beer actually sounds like a good idea," Noah said.

It was highly likely someone there would know Some Guy. He couldn't believe she wouldn't even give him the name of the dude. All he could say was Some

Guy better be a saint. A man just as good as Will would be today. Nothing less than Twyla deserved.

Later that night, Noah headed to his mother's house for dinner as promised. It was nothing less than he'd earned after the stunt he'd pulled. He'd once more be reminded of Will, the perfect son, and Twyla's first love. Just in case being in his mother's house wouldn't remind him enough, there were the photos she still displayed. Photos of Twyla and Will, even if their romance had been a short-lived one.

His mother's oldest friend, Ella Mae, answered the door with a huge smile.

"Is that my son?"

Noah could hear his mother's voice calling from the kitchen.

"Yeah, it's me, Ma. The prodigal son returns."

"It's so good to see you, Noah," Ella Mae said. "Please talk to your mother about joining us at the Almost Dead Poets Society meetings. I think it would be so good for her. Poetry is an escape for me, as you know. There's so much to say and now I have a chance to say it. I think Katherine would greatly benefit from the creative expression."

He followed Ella Mae into the kitchen. "Absolutely. I couldn't agree more."

"We have a lot to talk about, young man!"

Despite the fact that he never seemed able to please her, Mom still greeted him with an all-encompassing hug. She held him a little longer than normal this time, almost as if she was remembering. She seemed to do a lot of that these days.

Even though she was barely in her sixties, her life had changed so dramatically that to Noah, she'd aged twenty years in a decade. Her once red hair was now completely white, and she'd never regained the weight she lost ten years ago when she wouldn't eat and rarely left her bedroom. She looked feeble and felt small in his arms as he squeezed her tight.

Dinner, it appeared, was the usual tuna fish casserole, which Noah detested. She never seemed to remember that it had been Will's favorite and never Noah's. Either way, some days it gave him some comfort to indulge her in these small rituals.

"I'm on my way out the door," Ella Mae said. "But I brought dessert. Please enjoy it even if you don't eat anything else."

She said the last words in a half whisper as even she remembered that Noah was not fond of tuna casserole.

"Thanks, Ella Mae." Noah bent down to buss her cheek.

The senior citizen had acted as a pseudo-older sister to his mother for all these years, doting on her and checking in on her frequently. He had particularly appreciated this after his father left them. And during the year Noah had been gone, he could relax knowing that his mother always had a friend even if she didn't particularly do anything to encourage Ella Mae's devotion.

Katherine did not have many friends because she'd chosen to isolate herself. Her oldest friends remained the women she'd known as a Dallas cheerleader. Yes, his mother had been a cheerleader in her twenties. She'd returned to Charming after college but despite the years and distance, the Dallas connection used to mean that she'd visit the city. She hadn't in at least a decade.

"I don't understand, Noah. What happened with Michelle? She's such a great girl, such a wonderful girl."

"I know she's great. She really is. Just not for me."

"But why Noah, *why* won't you settle down? No one is going to be perfect."

And neither were Will and Twyla a perfect couple. What would his mother say if she knew what he'd done with Twyla last night? He'd kissed her and felt an ache grow and spread in his chest. For one sweet and carefree moment he had lost control and taken what he'd wanted for so long.

"I know I won't ever find anyone perfect. You're going to have to understand that when the time is right it will happen and you'll accept the woman I love, no matter who she is."

She bustled around the kitchen, then leaned over and served him a huge helping of tuna casserole. Noah tried not to gag.

"I *would* like some grandchildren before I'm too old to enjoy them."

"It's going to be a bit longer for that." He helped himself to dessert first—an apple pie.

Silently, he thanked Ella Mae as he took a bite.

"I know what the problem is. You're just frightened. And I can't say that I blame you when you look at what happened between your father and me. But what you have to understand, honey, is that sometimes tragedy brings people together and they're even closer than before. It's an unbreakable bond. Maybe that didn't happen for us, but God forbid if you go through something tragic and terrible again in the future, you and your wife should be able to work through it. Stay together."

Funny thing, he did understand this far better than

she realized. He supposed his mother could not see that he *had* already bonded with someone in tragedy and that connection never seemed to wane. It was Twyla, of course, the one girl who knew him almost better than he knew himself. And if he didn't do something to stop the insanity of last night from happening again, he supposed he'd risk losing her friendship, too. And that was one thing he could never bear. Almost unconsciously, he glanced at the framed photo nearby of Will and Twyla on their first date.

Next to that were plenty of photos of Will and Noah, and also of the three of them in earlier years. One was taken at the boardwalk at the Fourth of July celebration. Twyla was sandwiched between them and both he and Will had an arm slung around her. Noah swallowed hard at the photos of him and Will fishing and boating. The pit in his stomach grew.

Mom noticed him glancing at the photos and smiled.

"How *is* Twyla doing, the precious girl? I'm sure you've checked in with her. I think of her all the time. I keep meaning to invite her over to dinner."

"She'd love that."

But Noah wasn't sure Twyla liked coming here anymore, even though she was very fond of his mother. She'd once told him she felt like the daughter-in-law that never was. That would never be.

"Mom, you do remember Will broke up with Twyla because he wanted to be free to date whoever he wanted and whoever he met in college?"

"Yes, of course, but I believe he would have quickly changed his mind. Don't you think? He would have never found someone better than Twyla. There's just something about first love, I guess..."

"Yeah."

Noah felt the familiar pinch in his chest. That feeling that no matter how hard he tried or how well he did he would never be good enough.

He pointed his fork at her. "Hey. Think about the poetry group. I think it would be good for you."

"That group is scandalous." She plopped in the seat across from him and helped herself to some tuna casserole. "I heard Patsy Villanueva's poetry is verging on erotica."

"I'm sure that's not true." He shook his head, biting back a laugh. "And anyway, what's a little erotica between friends?"

"Noah Cahill! I am your mother, young man. Do not mention that word at my table again."

"You brought it up." He scowled.

It wasn't like he relished the word mentioned anywhere near his mother, which said something about how much he wanted her to join the club. She'd get out of the house once a week.

"Mr. Finch's poems are about the history of Texas. And I know how you love Texas. Besides, they meet at Twyla's bookstore. Two birds, one stone." He made a shooting motion with his thumb and finger.

"I support my sweet girl's bookstore. I order my books online through a system that lets me assign the sale to Once Upon a Book."

"That's great, but Twyla mentioned something about community. People can get their books anywhere now, but a bookstore is a lot more than a place to buy books. It's a place to get together and talk about important things. Check in with each other."

"I've been so busy organizing. There are still piles and piles of papers to go through." She sighed.

After ten years, she still hadn't adjusted to life in the much smaller house she'd moved to after his father left. Donating or recycling was a four-letter word to her. She'd had a difficult time letting go of anything that belonged to Will, naturally. Anything from kindergarten drawings to book reports. She kept Noah's cards, drawings and homework, too. Even if he'd begged her to get rid of it all. Who in the world cared that he'd drawn a red fire truck when he was five? He'd rather she care more about what he was doing *now.*

"I'll help you. Anytime you'd like. We can go through it all and make piles. Stuff to donate, stuff to keep."

"I tackle a little bit every day."

Noah knew the subject was a touchy one but he would ask anyway. "What about a tree this year?"

"I...don't think I'm ready for that. Besides, it's so much work for such a short time."

"Some people get started earlier for that reason."

"Well, it's too late now."

"No, it's not. What if I do it for you?"

She quirked a brow. "Do you even have a tree of your own?"

"No, but I will." The other night at Twyla's house, his spirits were lifted considerably by all the decorations.

"Well, maybe when you get a tree, I will, too."

Yeah, she didn't believe him. Noah got it. Christmas was a tough time for the Cahill family and had been for a while.

"I'm not kidding," Noah said. "I'm *getting* a tree."

His mother glanced at him, quirking a brow, shaking her head. She had her doubts. But finally, it was time to move on and it was up to Noah to lead by example. Will would want it. He would hate that they'd stop celebrations because of him.

Now, Noah would simply have to prove that he meant it.

Chapter Twelve

As it worked out, it had been much easier to find a date in one day than Twyla had ever thought possible. The trick? One couldn't be too picky. So, she'd agreed to let Zoey fix her up. This wasn't always a great idea. In the past, Zoey had introduced Twyla to a drug dealer, a gorgeous actor with an anger management problem and a man clearly not over his ex. He'd sobbed through the bruschetta appetizers because they'd reminded him of her.

"I hope tonight will be different," Twyla had said over the phone just before she grabbed a seat at the bar inside the Salty Dog Bar & Grill.

She'd given Zoey a small list not long ago: no drug dealers, no anger management problems and no criers. But she was already way out of her comfort zone among all these…people in the bar.

"His name is Paul. He's Drew's cousin and they look like they could be brothers."

Drew was a good-looking guy, so this filled Twyla with some hope. Either way, she wasn't really interested in a long-term relationship. She just wanted someone for the holidays. It would be nice if she could tell Noah about a new relationship so he wouldn't think she was pining away for him and another kiss. Even if she was. Whatever. All she wanted was someone to kiss at midnight on the thirty-first. If the guy wasn't a face-sucker or a drooler, she'd be happy. Clearly, she wasn't asking for the moon.

"Are you sure about this? I mean, Noah kissed you! He *kissed* you," Zoey said.

"And regretted it the moment that he did."

"That's only because you've crossed a boundary. He must feel weird about that. I mean, don't you feel weird?"

"Yeah, sure, of course."

But she didn't.

It hadn't felt strange at all, which should be disturbing on some level. How long had she secretly fantasized about him and ignored her feelings? Or was this something new? If this was new, she couldn't afford for it to be transient. Maybe Noah was right in that it would be best to forget about their kiss. If she could manage to do that.

"He said it was a mistake and he doesn't feel that way about me."

"Liar."

"It doesn't matter because I have to forget about it. I don't like him as anything more than a friend, either. So, we're even." An extremely handsome man walked inside and waved in her direction. "I should go. He's here."

Now, this was more like it. He was, if possible, even better looking than Drew. Clean-cut and clean-shaven and dressed in a double-breasted suit, for crying out loud. He was taking this seriously, or maybe he worked as the VP of a company. Maybe they'd marry, have beautiful children and he'd help her run the bookstore in all his free time.

"Hello, Twyla. What a pleasure." He reached for her hand and kissed it.

"Oh." Gosh, was this guy royalty? Nobody kissed hands anymore. "It's nice to meet you, too."

They ordered appetizers and drinks and within minutes, Twyla learned that Paul was a great conversationalist. Most of the conversation had to do with him, of course, but she was here to get to know him. They'd never met before so it was only natural that he would discuss all of his many achievements at length. She simply nodded in places, trying to look interested when he recited his college football stats. Currently, he worked as a car salesman. That seemed to be a bit of a jump in careers, and she asked the question.

"What made you settle into sales after your college career?"

"Good question. Mostly, I'd have to say it's the money. And fast cars. I love fast cars. And fast women." His gaze slipped down and admired what little cleavage she was showing tonight.

Okay, he was coming on a little strong but nothing she couldn't work with. Maybe he was nervous. She shifted the conversation away from fast *anything* and toward her own life. The bookstore, how much it meant to her and her family for generations, and books. She, of course, tended to ask men what they were reading. She felt it told a lot about a man.

"What would you say is your favorite book of all time?"

"The Bible." He nodded.

That seemed to be a bit of a canned response, especially after the comment about fast women. He might be trying to form a different connection with her.

"How about fiction?"

"I don't have time to read fiction. But I do love bookstores. They're actually a great place to meet women." He put an arm around her shoulder. "So, tell me. Is this bookworm-sexy-teacher thing something that works for you?"

"I'm sorry?" Twyla pushed her glasses up her nose.

He slid her a knowing look. "The moment I walked in here, I knew you were someone I wanted to get to know a *whole* lot better. What's your favorite fantasy?"

"Oh, definitely a house with a floor to ceiling library—kind of like Belle has in Beauty and the Beast. Have you ever seen the movie? I assume you have."

His neck jerked back a little in surprise and he gave her a strange look. "That's not the kind of fantasy I was referring to. I mean, do you like to be tied up? Handcuffs?"

She blinked. "You know what? You're coming on a little strong. I'm not interested in either of those two things."

"You mean this whole Little Miss Perfect vanilla thing isn't an act?" He circled his hand around her.

The doors to the Salty Dog swung open and in walked Finn, followed by Noah. Both were dressed like they'd just come off the water, wearing their windbreakers and well-worn jeans. They strolled in casually, shaking hands with some of the regulars and going up to the bar.

Twyla stared longingly at the man who had never once mentioned ropes and handcuffs to her, nor lost his temper, cried over a former girlfriend or tried to sell her a bag of weed.

And she'd bet he never would.

"You know what? I don't think this is going to work out. Maybe we could just be friends."

"Me?" He snorted. "Friends? With a woman? It's not possible. Not possible because I'm always thinking about how I can—"

"You don't need to finish that sentence."

Looked like she had one more item to add to her list for Zoey. No more men like Paul, Drew's cousin.

"Hey, I'm sorry. Why don't we just start over? Let me order you another drink. What do you say?"

"Well, I suppose it couldn't hurt."

At least, in this way, Noah might notice her here with someone else. It didn't hurt that Paul was definitely handsome even if he was a little icky. But Noah didn't have to know that, did he? All he had to know was that she was here with a date, as promised. No lie.

Paul ordered their drinks, then turned to her with an apologetic expression on his face.

"Look, I'm sorry. I didn't mean to come on so strong. I can go slow if you'd like. I mean, I have a sister, so I understand."

How nice. Maybe she could reform him. Stranger things had happened. She smiled and accidentally met Noah's eyes. He'd been looking in their direction. She didn't know for how long. He smiled back, then went back to chatting with Finn.

"I'm sorry for the misunderstanding, too. You see, I really haven't been out with anyone for a while. I have to confess I'm kind of a homebody. My perfect night is a good book, a bag of salted caramel popcorn and my cat. If he's being nice."

"Hmm," Paul said, and took a pull of his beer.

"It's not easy to get back into the dating scene. Don't you think?"

"No, I kind of love it. I love the adventure. I love the start of something new each time. Endless possibilities ahead."

"I wish I could feel that way."

"Maybe you just need to loosen up a little."

"No, I doubt that's the problem."

It happened so fast that Twyla almost didn't see it coming until it was too late. Like a slithering snake, Paul's hand slid under her skirt, up to her behind. Her eyes widened as she stood in a state of semishock and then met Noah's gaze. *Help*, she said via mental telepathy.

Noah's eyes narrowed and his brow furrowed. And then without words he understood. A few things happened in quick succession. She slapped Paul and Noah stood right behind him.

"Do we have a problem here?"

"Apparently, we do. Look, Twyla, you're very nice but I'm really not into violence. At least not this kind. This isn't going to work out." With that, he threw a few bills on the bar and stomped out.

Noah's gaze followed him out the door, his jaw tense. "Was that Some Guy?"

"Yeah, and I won't be seeing him again."

"Do I want to know?"

"No, you don't. I guess I'll get myself home. Hey, at least he paid for drinks. I'm still going to have words with Zoey. That's the last time I let her set me up, so help me God!"

"I'm going to hold you to that, Peaches. And you deserve a lot better than a guy who pays for *drinks*."

"I don't know what I deserve anymore." Twyla glanced in Finn's direction, who now chatted amiably with a beautiful brunette.

"Is that her? Is that the woman Finn has a thing for?" Twyla didn't automatically recognize her. But she might be a tourist or possibly new in town. They were very cute together. She'd have to say that.

"Yeah, I don't know. I guess… I think she's… That might be. I don't know." He lifted a shoulder.

"Tell him I think it's sweet that he can't stop thinking about her. I'm rooting for them." She slid off the stool. "And now, I'm going home to change into my pj's and read."

It was supposed to have been a carefree night, but for Noah it had quickly segued into the seventh circle of hell when he saw Twyla with Some Guy. Irritation and something resembling jealousy spiked through him, and he slammed the first beer down.

He met Twyla's gaze and she smiled back, looking happy. Happy with that jerk? What was *wrong* with her?

Noah jutted his chin in their direction and snorted. "Check out that loser."

Finn followed his gaze. "You mean the one wearing

the double-breasted suit? Yeah, he looks like he just crawled out of his tent."

"Ha! I see right through that whole presentation. He's trying to *prove* something."

"By dressing nicely for a date with a beautiful woman?"

"Overcompensating." Noah actually sounded like he knew what he was talking about.

He'd read a lot over the years, a casualty of having a best friend who wanted him to read a book so they could discuss it later.

"His mother probably didn't love him enough." Umma, the new part-time bartender, set another beer in front of Noah. "He might be handsome, but he lacks character."

"Exactly. I don't think he's handsome, but you know what I'm talking about!" Noah said, finding an ally. "She could do so much better."

Finn moved his hand to Umma in the universal "cut it out" gesture. "Don't get involved in this. It's a whole thing he does."

"What thing?" Umma said.

"He acts like he doesn't care who she goes out with, but nobody ever seems to be good enough."

"Especially not this guy." Noah nudged Finn's elbow. "Check out the way he's looking at her, like she's a piece of meat."

"I wouldn't know." Finn rolled his eyes. "I've never done that."

Umma threw a look in their direction, then wiped the bar. "The guy *might* be a vegetarian and you're wrong about the piece of meat thing. Maybe she looks like a tasty avocado."

"You don't understand. Twyla isn't the kind of

woman you treat casually. And that guy has 'temporary' written all over him."

"Here we go," Finn said.

"Am I boring you?" Noah turned on Finn.

Finn shook his head slowly. "I wish you'd get on with it. Just get over yourself and admit you're in love with her. Save us all a bunch of time."

Umma gasped and held a hand to her chest. "Oh, my God. I didn't see that coming."

"You didn't see it coming because it's not true. She's my best friend."

And it was precisely at that moment when he glanced over to find Twyla, eyes wide, and Some Guy busy groping her so blatantly that Noah could see it from where he stood. He didn't process any other thoughts but moved to their side of the bar so fast it was like he'd been beamed over there. He stood behind the guy at the moment Twyla slapped him, and Some Guy reared back, taking his filthy hand with him. Twyla quickly smoothed down her skirt.

Noah's hands had curled into fists, and he heard himself growling in a voice he barely recognized.

Less than a minute later, Some Guy was gone with his ridiculous excuse of not condoning violence. Good riddance. Noah hated that Twyla was desperate enough to date someone clearly not good enough for her.

Is there anyone good enough?

Finn would say that Noah didn't believe anyone could be.

Before she could go, too, he grabbed her elbow. "If you really want to go out with someone, I'll find a decent guy worthy of you."

She cocked her head. “No *thanks*. I don’t want to date the reverend.”

There went his best idea, the closest he would ever get to a real-life saint. “Fine. Not a reverend. I promise.”

He walked her to her car and tapped the hood before she drove off. Then he headed back inside where Umma, Finn and the brunette he’d started chatting up turned to him.

“You’re going to fix her up?” Umma deadpanned.

“I don’t want to talk about it,” Noah said, throwing his hands up.

“What a mess,” Finn chuckled.

Noah hated to admit it, but in this case, Finn was right.

Chapter Thirteen

The next day at work, Twyla decided that if Noah ever found anyone he believed was good enough for her, she'd turn the guy down flat. It didn't matter if he was the Second Coming of Henry Cavill. She was done. Done! Maybe she'd become a nun. Nuns could own bookstores, right? First, she'd have to convert to Catholicism but that sounded a whole lot easier than her love life these days.

Zoey had apologized profusely about Paul, excusing his behavior by the fact that he'd mixed alcohol with over-the-counter medication. Really? This was going to be his excuse. At least she had the Almost Dead Poets Society coming in today. They were all such a breath of fresh air. Ironically. Old as the hills and still bright with fresh, new ideas. She hoped she'd be that way in her old age, still running the bookstore, encouraging her young grandchildren to read. *Grandchildren.*

For that, she'd need some children first. Plus, a husband would be nice.

Mr. Finch had already been working a shift today so as the time approached, he helped Twyla set up the chairs in a circle. First to arrive was Lois, early so that she, too, could help. Susannah arrived with Patsy and bringing up the rear was Ella Mae. But utter surprise hit Twyla when Katherine Cahill came through the door behind Ella Mae.

"Look who I found," Ella Mae said. "We have a new member, folks."

Katherine shook her head. "Let's not get ahead of ourselves. I'm here tonight and I'm not promising anything. Y'all know that I don't like *clubs*."

"Oh, we're not a club." Lois waved her hand dismissively. "We're a *society*."

Twyla went into Katherine's arms because she hadn't seen one of her favorite people in months. Her always slender figure was even more so now. Katherine Cahill had once been a knockout, a former cheerleader, and still had those great legs.

"How are you, my darling girl? I want to have you over for dinner sometime. I think the last time you were over was with Noah."

"Has it been that long?"

"Noah was just over a couple of nights ago." She turned to the senior citizens. "I'm actually here tonight for *him*. For reasons I don't understand, my son is worried about me. He thinks I should get a hobby." She held up air quotes.

A few of them laughed. Patsy elbowed Lois, seated next to her now. "And my granddaughter would love nothing more than for me to stop this particular hobby."

"If I'm joining this society, then your grandmother should as well," Katherine said to Twyla.

"I've been saying that!" Ella Mae called out.

"You know her. She prefers people come to her and she loves to entertain. But I'll keep bugging her."

"We need to talk later." Katherine patted Twyla's hand and went to find a seat.

As the senior citizens read their poetry, Twyla stood in the back, their eager audience. Here and there, customers would stroll in and listen. The seniors always brought in their fans. Twyla would then lead prospective customers to the shelf they needed. Even if they hadn't heard them before, customers naturally gravitated to listening to the old folks. As usual, Mr. Finch spoke of Texas, and everyone clapped at the end of his poem, which today fixated on the rolling hills of San Antonio.

Susannah had a new poem about Doodle, her poodle, now getting older and far less active. As she spoke about growing old together, Ella Mae wiped away a tear.

Ella Mae's poem was about the power of friendship, and several times she met Katherine's eyes. Katherine observed all of them curiously as if they were a strange lab experiment. But she nodded and clapped in places until Patsy came up. Tonight's poem wasn't nearly as seductive as many in the past, but she still discussed the special romantic love between two people.

"Some of us are done with romance." Katherine clapped politely at the end of Patsy's poem.

"Oh, no," Patsy said. "You must never be done with romance, not until they put you in the ground."

The whole "put you in the ground" comment seemed

to freeze Ella Mae's face. She reached to pat Katherine's hand.

Patsy covered her mouth. "Oh, I'm sorry. I didn't mean—"

"No, we know you didn't," said Mr. Finch. And he turned to Katherine, his very old-school stately demeanor dripping compassion. "We're so happy to have you here tonight, dear."

"Thank you."

Now and again, Twyla believed they all tiptoed around Katherine's grief in an unhealthy way. All the books she'd read on grief claimed there were stages. Katherine had been through all five of them in the past decade, maybe even twice. In some ways, she seemed stuck in the depression cycle. She had a wonderful son in Noah, who she had never failed to compare to Will. Noah, somehow, seemed to come up short. As a friend, it had been painful to watch. It wasn't anything Katherine did with intention, but now she did not seem able to move on and Twyla wondered if, somehow, they all were enabling her.

She could not imagine the pain of losing a child, but Katherine had another son who needed her, too. He needed her to love him unconditionally and without judgment.

At the end of their poetry session, everyone wandered around the bookstore as they tended to do, looking for something new to read.

Katherine found Twyla. "I think our boy is in trouble. You know how he struggles sometimes. He's making some bad decisions."

Twyla remembered the other night with Noah and the kiss. Perhaps she was also a bad decision.

"The boating worried me, too, but we have to trust in Noah. He grew up on the water. And I think being back there again must remind him of Will. It could be a good thing. Maybe he feels closer to him."

"I'm not actually talking about any of that right now. My concern is that he's ended things with Michelle. She was his best chance to be happy—finally settled down—and have children."

"I'm sorry to hear that," Twyla said, pretending she didn't already know.

"He won't listen to me, of course, but you're his best friend. When you talk, it's almost as if Will is talking to him."

It wasn't anything like that. But Twyla stayed quiet, simply nodding.

"Maybe you could talk to him? Help him reconsider things with Michelle."

From somewhere deep inside her Twyla found the courage to say something she'd waited a long time to say.

"I think people need to make their own decisions about relationships and, if things don't work out, move on without them. Life goes on. Even when we love someone, if it doesn't work out, we have to accept this."

Katherine did not seem to read between the lines.

"Noah has always had a very strong head, always the most stubborn child. If he'd just listened to me long ago and understood he couldn't have everything he wanted right when he wanted it…well. Maybe things would have been different."

Twyla prayed Katherine wasn't going to bring up the boating accident. Not now. She really could not stay silent if she did or deal with that tonight. Inside her shop, fairy lights were blinking and her little artificial tree in the corner was finally decorated. Outside, she could hear Christmas carols as people walked by, carrying their purchases. Life went on.

People made mistakes, but they should not have to pay for them for the rest of their lives.

Yes, Noah had asked Will if he could drive the boat on that awful day. But he hadn't seen the sandbar they hit. He'd been the one to try to pull Will out of the water but hadn't been strong enough to do it. Still, he'd nearly died trying.

And all Katherine had seemed to focus on was that it was Noah who had wanted to drive. Noah who had begged his older brother.

"I don't think Noah…"

"Just talk to him, please. I want him to be sure before he moves on that this is truly what he wants."

"Of course, Katherine. You know I will."

"All I want is for him to be happy and finally settled. He's the boy that survived. He can't throw his life away."

So now he was throwing his life away if he didn't reunite with Michelle?

Ella Mae came to the rescue with a book she placed in Katherine's line of vision. "You need to read this book. One of my all-time favorites this year. A wonderful escape. It's about a woman who starts over in her sixties. She buys a ranch in Wyoming and falls in love with a local beekeeper."

Katherine rolled her eyes. "Well, *that* sounds realistic."

"And there's always this one." Ella Mae held up another, far less exciting book. The book was titled, *Moving on from an Endless Cycle of Grief.*

Twyla stiffened over the absolute and direct honesty coming from Ella Mae. But wasn't that what friends were for? Someone who could tell you when you were screwing up because you were too wrapped up in yourself to see it? Twyla had once told Zoey that she had to stop going after unavailable men. She found and bought her a book and forced her to read it. They even did the exercises together in a workbook. And shortly after, Zoey went into therapy and discovered she was going after unavailable men because she was dealing with abandonment issues with her father. Problem solved. Well, maybe not completely, but at least she was aware of it.

Should Twyla really be forced to do this kind of thing for Noah? Should she get him a book on commitment issues? She couldn't help but think that he'd laugh. He'd make light of it, but that was his go to response when faced with the uncomfortable.

"If I had to pick between those books, I'll take the ranch." Katherine grabbed the book from Ella Mae. "I'm fine, and I wish you would all stop worrying about me."

"I would, but what are friends for?" Ella Mae winked.

After everyone had left, Twyla took in the cozy stillness of the shop. She had the best job on earth, one in which she could almost be paid to read. Last week, she'd finished another rom-com on the *New York Times* bestseller list. And now, unable to resist another moment, she went to her copy of *A Dragon's Heart* and pulled it from under the register where she kept it hidden. To think that once she'd thought a man could slay her dragons. But that was fiction. A myth. She'd learned to slay her own dragons. So, yes, this meant she'd been lonely for years, but she'd undergone a lot of personal growth during that time. She'd learned she wasn't responsible for other people's happiness. And she'd learned, through the fog of grief, that happiness was a choice. One she made every day because the other option was unthinkable.

Her heroines—those in the pages of the books she'd loved so long that they'd become a part of her—never gave up. Neither would she.

Flipping off the lights as she went, Twyla took her book, and locked up the shop.

Noah began to feel the pinch of loneliness like he did every Christmas. It always hit him late in the evening when it was time for bed, the feeling large and crowding. Suffocating. Christmas in the Cahill home used to be an event. The biggest tree they could cut down. Decorations galore, both on the lawn and anywhere they had an empty space indoors. Not anymore. Not for years.

He drove to the boardwalk and wandered up and down the stores. The only gift he had so far was Twyla's. Like most men, he wondered what to buy the women in his life. His mother claimed every year since he and Will were ten that she wanted something handmade with love. He didn't draw stick figures and hearts anymore, so he'd pressed her for something else that he didn't have to make.

"A framed picture of you."

"Ma, I'm not going to get you a picture of *me*. Who am I, Narcissus?"

He hated to cheat with a gift card so usually he tortured himself doing the shopping thing twenty-four hours before Christmas Day. This meant he used to wind up with batteries and car air fresheners. Practical gifts.

One Christmas, he'd given Twyla AAA batteries and a car air freshener that he thought smelled like her. Like fresh apples, though he'd never told her this. He'd given the same to his girlfriend at the time, and she'd yelled and broken up with him. Not that he blamed her now. The gift was lame and showed the little thought he'd put behind it.

But Twyla laughed so hard she nearly fell off her chair.

What? he had said, laughing, too.

He loved how they always laughed together. It was the best part of being with her and always had been.

Oh, my god, Noah. You're so bad. Was this all they had left at the gasoline station?

How did you know? I waited too late, as usual.

Just so you know, for me, chocolate is always a good choice. How hard is it to find chocolate?

He'd pulled a bag of M&M's from the drugstore out of his pocket and handed them over. This time she laughed so hard she had to run to the bathroom.

When he was smart, he remembered to buy the women in his life chocolate.

Tonight, he couldn't face going home to his unfurnished, barely decorated cottage. He didn't have to be alone. Michelle kept calling, inviting him to a party with a law firm interested in her. It sounded like she was staying, and he wasn't any more excited about it. He'd never moved past the flattery that someone, anyone, would rearrange their life for him. Even though he'd refused her invites, she just wasn't getting the message.

Now it was ten days before Christmas, and Noah suddenly wanted a tree. A tree, and possibly some lights. Although he had no idea if he could find anything at this stage of the game. What he did know for certain was Twyla would help because she loved the holiday. And this might be a way to get over the awkwardness between them.

He texted her:

Need help. Now. Christmas emergency.

Rather than text, she phoned him.

"Noah! What's wrong?"

Damn, he hadn't intended to *spook* her.

"What's wrong is that I'm completely clueless about decorating and I really don't want to sit in this place another day without having a tree or some tinsel inside."

"*That's* your emergency?"

"Yeah, I figure all the decorations have to be gone by now. Where am I supposed to find a tree? I checked and the lot only has Charlie Brown trees left."

"There's nothing wrong with that, but I actually have an artificial one you can have. It was too big for my new place once I moved, and I already have one for the bookstore so I'm not using it. You can have it."

She had an *extra* Christmas tree. He was not surprised.

"When should I pick it up?"

"I'll be over in a little bit."

This was far better than he'd hoped. They were

going to get over this little bump in the road and things would go back to normal. Whatever that meant. If it was *normal* to pine away for your best friend, that is. This was the kind of normalcy he'd come to live with, however, and he'd like it back thank you very much.

Twyla arrived a few minutes later with not only a tree in a box but several bags filled with string lights, ornaments and decorations. She wore an elf hat, and a long-sleeved blouse that said *Merry and Bright*.

"Hey there!"

"What in the hell is all this? Did you buy out the store? I don't think I need all *this*."

She gazed at him from under hooded lids. "You *said* it was an emergency and I took you at your word so don't even think you're going to back out now."

She was right, of course, as usual. He'd asked for all *this*. So, he hauled a huge box inside and all the rest.

"Tell me you didn't buy all this."

"No these are just some of the things I had left over. I got some new decorations donated to the bookstore, so I decided to switch things up a little. But there's still some good stuff in here."

It was his job to unbox the tree and put it together, which he did, linking the pieces easily. The mechanics of it were easy and in his wheelhouse. But then Twyla glanced in his direction and brought her hands to her hips.

"That's sad. You think that looks okay?"

He cocked his head and viewed it from another angle. "What's wrong? All the pieces fit together."

She walked over and began to spread out the fake branches and pine needles. "It's not going to look like a real tree unless we do this to every single branch."

"Jesus, we're going to be here all night!"

"I thought you wanted your house to look like Christmas."

"Fine, okay. Let's do this thing."

The best thing about having a task like this was that they avoided talking about anything else. And he mostly avoided looking at her in that cute getup—the skirt with red leggings. He worked on one side of the tree, and she worked on the other. After what seemed like hours, she finally stepped back to observe it, like a judge at a contest looking for the best in show. She walked around it, inspecting.

Noah snorted. "Does it meet with your approval?"

"I think it will do. Now, time for the ornaments."

"Right, can't forget the ornaments." And then an idea occurred. A way he could make this night last longer and do some good in the process. "After we're done here I have an idea. What if…what if we take Christmas to my mother's house?"

Twyla gaped. "She hasn't had a tree in years."

Not since his father left them but even before that. The holidays hadn't been enjoyable for years. All three would simply sit staring at each other, not knowing how to do this without Will. Noah had waited for his father to lead, which in hindsight was a mistake.

"But if *we* do the work…"

"Maybe you're right. There's something about the colorful lights that have a way of cheering a person up. It does seem sometimes like she's still, I don't know, depressed. But she did come over last night to the poet society meeting."

"Great, I asked her to just try it out."

"Don't get too excited. I'm not at all sure she'll be back but I'm proud of her for trying."

"She isn't getting out of the house much these days. Even less than before I left for Austin."

They were both quiet for a moment, knowing this wasn't anything new.

"She did ask me something. She wants me to talk you into giving Michelle another chance."

"I'm sorry she bothered you. I know it's that she just wants me to be happy and she doesn't see that I already am. Why do I have to be married?"

"No, you don't. But, let's face it, it comes down to the fact that she'd like grandchildren."

"Yeah, and I'm the only way she's going to get any." He reached to place the star on top of the tree. "I guess by now Will would have a whole gaggle of kids. He always did whatever she asked."

The quiet between them stretched, tight and strong. It was still tough to talk about him.

"And you never have," Twyla said, breaking the thick silence and turning it around. "You're stubborn."

"Look in the mirror sometime."

"I'm *not* as stubborn as you are. You take the prize."

"As long as it's first place." He chuckled.

"I think we're done here." Twyla rubbed her hands together. "Now, on to your mother's house. We're bringing Christmas to her!"

Noah attempted a smile, but emotions were swirling through him, heavy and raw.

He only wished this would go over as well as they both hoped.

Chapter Fourteen

"This one!" Twyla pulled out the last fresh tree on the lot not under three feet tall. "It was hiding all the way in the back."

Noah hauled it out. "From now on, I need you with me when I go shopping."

"I'll be goldarned! Women find all the things. I didn't even know this was back here," said the tree lot guy.

They paid and, within minutes, were on the road to Katherine's house. Once, she'd lived in a much larger home, the place where she'd raised her family. But after the divorce, Katherine had been forced to downsize. To say that downsizing had been difficult for the former Dallas cheerleader was an understatement. The last time Twyla had been over, there were still boxes of mementos that she struggled to find a place to display. It no longer seemed possible for her to get rid of anything.

For the first time since they'd had the idea, Twyla worried this could be a mistake. Katherine might resist the idea or be upset by the realization that yet another holiday had arrived, and she still hadn't unpacked. It was as if she thought maybe if she waited long enough, her situation would magically get better, and she'd be able to afford to move to a larger place. It wasn't optimism so much as delusion.

"Are we doing the right thing?" Twyla turned to Noah when he pulled into the driveway of the small residential home.

"We're cheering her up and this is what she needs whether she realized it or not."

"Christmas is always hard for her." But Twyla wanted, more than anything, for Katherine to start celebrating again.

She'd privately told Twyla once, *It doesn't feel right to be happy.*

And while her depression wouldn't be lifted in one swoop with decorations, or in one holiday celebration, maybe she'd at least enjoy their company. It would take her mind off her latest disappointment in Noah at the least. Maybe it would remind her she had a wonderful son who might have at least partially moved back to be near her.

When Katherine threw open the door, she glanced first at the tree, then Noah. Finally, Twyla. "What's all this?"

"We brought you Christmas." Noah brushed by her, then bent to kiss her cheek. "You said it's too much work to set up so we're doing it for you."

"But I don't have the room." She waved around the cluttered living space.

Surrounding them were unopened boxes still stacked one on top of another—labeled *office*, and *den*—stacks of paper both loose and in an accordion-style file. After they dragged the tree and decorations inside, Twyla set about moving boxes around almost immediately. With Noah's help, she simply moved them, giving them more space.

"This is just temporary," Twyla said.

"I'm *not* getting rid of anything. I still have to go through these boxes. I'm not quite ready to let them go," Katherine said, setting her hand on a box labeled *Boys' homework.*

"I understand," Twyla said. "And we're not throwing anything away. We're just making a little room."

Without Noah here, Twyla doubted she'd have ever had the nerve to take the initiative, but somehow the three of them being here together gave her added strength. Surprisingly, Katherine went along with it for the most part, admiring the fresh tree's scent.

"You know what? It's been years since we had a fresh tree for Christmas. Somewhere, possibly in the garage, I have an artificial tree."

"Sometimes you just need a fresh tree, right?" Noah said.

"I'll go get you two some eggnog."

"Spike mine with some rum and we've got a deal," Noah muttered under his breath as his mother walked away. "I'm sorry I suggested this. This is a lot of work, and I didn't mean to drag you into this mess."

"You didn't drag me. I love Christmas, remember? I'm happy to be here." Twyla elbowed him. "Let's get to work."

Meanwhile, Katherine observed, directed and gave

some input while they carefully set up the tree in the stand they'd bought. She would chip in now and then, bringing them the eggnog, then a pitcher of water for the tree.

Noah pointed to the basin. "Remember to water this tree every day. Otherwise, it's a fire hazard."

"I'm surprised you're even letting her have a fresh tree."

"Living dangerously. You have a way of doing that to me, Peaches. If the guys at the station could see me now."

Still, Noah had made certain they placed the tree nowhere near any vents or sources of heat. They'd placed the tree in front of the picture window so that it faced the street and when the curtains were open, it would be a bright display.

After they were done, not only did Katherine bring eggnog—the unspiked version—and cookies, she also brought out a photo album. This was not surprising, as nearly every time Twyla visited Katherine, the albums made an appearance.

"I don't think I've seen this one before," Twyla said, admiring the cover of a happy family of four. *The Cahills*, established 1989.

"This is why I don't throw anything away until I can go through it. I found this one in a box I had yet to unpack."

Katherine sat wedged between them and turned the pages, admiring the family photos, many of which included Twyla. Will, Noah and Twyla. Photos of them when they were children, on the first day of school. Then later, in their teenage years. Twyla had seen photos like these dozens of times in the past, but tonight, she caught something she'd never noticed before. There—in a photo of all three of them, Will with his arm over her shoulder—she caught a look in Noah's eyes she'd never seen before. Unless she was imagining it, it was a kind of wistfulness and longing as he looked at Twyla.

She glanced over to Noah but if he'd noticed this, too, he gave her no clue.

How had she ever missed this? Noah, his eyes on her as if *she* were the prize. The prize he'd lost to his older brother. How was that even possible? She'd never even seen a clue of it in those years. But now, she saw it in nearly every photo where there were three of them. In one photo of her and Will on the beach in which he was playfully giving her a piggyback ride, Noah stood in the background. With a gaggle of girls behind him, his gaze followed Will and Twyla.

Later, after the eggnog had been finished and the photo albums put away, Katherine hugged both of them tight.

"You were right. I needed this, and I feel much better now."

"That's great," Noah said, bussing her cheek.

"You two are all that's left of my favorite trio in the world. You're both very special to me."

Katherine cupped Twyla's chin in her small hand. "And you, my dear, brought both of my boys such happiness. But especially Will. Oh, how he loved you. Who knows? You might have been my daughter-in-law."

Twyla swallowed the raw pain in her throat. This was the opposite of moving on.

On the way back to Noah's place to get her car, Twyla sat huddled in the passenger seat, resentment and guilt filling her. Her thoughts were sprinkled with a heavy dose of sadness so complete that she nearly couldn't carry the weight. Some time ago, she'd relegated Will to good memories and happier times. But his mother would never let him go. It made sense. As a mother, Twyla never would, either, and sympathy carved another hole in her heart.

"That was tough."

"But necessary. Thanks for agreeing to it."

"I'll do anything for you. Nothing has changed." She reached and squeezed his hand briefly.

These tender and affectionate gestures no longer felt as friendly and chaste as they once had. At least, on her part. Noah had said that he didn't feel anything more than friendship for her. But those photos she noticed tonight showed her that at least at one time Noah might have felt more. Either way, they were both possibly better off forgetting.

"You want to come inside for a minute?" Noah asked.

"No, I should really get home. Tomorrow morning is the Chamber of Commerce breakfast where I'm giving the speech."

"You've written the whole thing?"

"I don't know if it's any good but yes."

"It's probably fantastic."

She smiled. "It's our only chance to get the angel investor. I never like to miss the holiday meeting anyway. Ava goes all out as you know. I heard the gift bags have a Tiffany item in them this year."

"I won't keep you. Just come in for a few minutes."

"Why, Noah?"

"Why?" He tipped back on his heels. "I wasn't aware I needed a reason. Never did before."

"Sure," Twyla said. Never let it be said that she wouldn't give in to Noah. "For a minute or two."

Noah got her a bottle of Cheerwine, turned the switch on for the lights and together they stood quietly admiring the twinkling lights on his tree.

"We did good tonight," Noah said.

"We spread the cheer." Twyla held up her bottle to his and they clinked. "So, any luck finding me a date for New Year's Eve?"

"I have until New Year's Eve?" Noah scowled.

"Or sooner but you're running out of time." She sighed. "Or, you could just forget all about it. I've been thinking maybe it's not a good idea to allow you to select a date for me."

"Why, since you've already explained the reverend is off the table? I understand that." Then he turned to her and there was a gentle softness in his gaze. "But you're right, I don't think I should fix you up with anyone."

"Why bother? Everyone is taken. Some Guy was a dud and Finn is pining away for a woman."

And you're still not available, even after that smoldering kiss.

"I have to confess. Finn doesn't have anyone." He took a step toward her, closing the tiny distance between them.

"Why would you make that up?"

"It was easy to do. I know what it's like to think about one woman all the time."

"Michelle?"

“No.” He shook his head. “I think if there’s any man in your life, it should be me.”

She blinked at the shocking words. He’d already said he didn’t feel that way about her.

“What are you saying?”

He set his bottle on the nearby table, then took hers out of her hand and set it down next. “I mean, you and *me*.”

The words didn’t sound real. She had to be imagining this. It was too perfect. Too wonderful. Maybe she hadn’t imagined seeing all those longing glances in the photos. Noah was the kind of brother who would have stepped aside, after all, no matter how he felt about Twyla.

“You and me? You and me. Y-you?” She stammered. “But you *said*—”

“Don’t listen to me, or anything else I said that night. I lied to you because I was terrified. But look, after being forced to go through that album tonight, I’m reminded of how much you loved Will. It’s in every photo we took. And that’s okay, I get it. I would have never interfered with that. But a lot of time has passed. Tonight, I thought maybe, just maybe, now there’s a chance for you and me—”

She didn’t let him finish the sentence but met his tender gaze. Simply the thought that Noah saw himself as second best, even with her, made her ache.

Slowly, she slid her hand down the slight scrape of razor stubble on his cheek.

“I did love Will. But I never loved him the way I love you.”

Noah tugged her the rest of the way to him, flush against his rigid body. He took her hand from his face and pressed a kiss on the palm of her hand. Then they were kissing, their mouths moving against each other in a crazy and fierce moment. They weren't tender or slow. Their kisses were desperate and deep, filled with explosive emotion. Her skin was too tight, her heart too full. She slid her hands down his back, feeling the taut and firm muscles bunching under her touch, the heat spiraling from his skin and emanating through his shirt.

They broke the kiss, his hand still cradling the back of her neck, warm and strong.

She pressed one finger gently to the hollow of his neck and sensed the steady thrum of his heart. "It's almost…too much. I'm going to explode."

He chuckled. "Good."

She reached for him and fisted his shirt in her hands to tug him close. Kissing and panting. Losing herself. It was freeing, the only kind of release that mattered. She was his and he was hers. Finally.

She wanted and needed his hands touching her everywhere, tenderly and with amazing skill. He moved from her sensitive earlobes to the column of her neck, taking his time with every nibble of her skin, every touch of tender flesh.

In one skilled swoop, Noah removed her top and it fell to the ground.

"You, too," she said, not wanting to be alone, and helped him remove his shirt.

His chest was a thing of beauty—soft, dark chest hair and sculpted muscles like those of a man who did physical work. His skin was taut and tanned and a little windburned in places. He kissed her bare shoulder, and the feel of his stubble against her skin gave her a full-body tingle. When he lowered his mouth to her nipple and drew her into his mouth, she moaned.

"Let's go," he said, cupping her ass and lifting her.

They rolled onto the bed, clothes discarded like flower petals. His warm bare skin pressed to hers, he slid her a slow smile. He threaded his fingers through hers and then braced her hands above her.

"I got you. You're mine."

"I'm not going anywhere."

She heard the sound of a condom packet ripping open and he slid into her, making them both gasp. He moved inside her with firm and unrelenting thrusts, as if certain of what he did to her. How he slayed her with every single touch and every single hot kiss. She could never trust anyone else the way she trusted Noah. Would never love anyone like she loved him. He had her heart. Always. This was it, finally, all she'd ever wanted.

Noah Cahill. Her person.

There had never really been anyone else. Not for her. There never could be.

"Twyla." Noah groaned and dropped his forehead to hers. "So good."

She wrapped her legs around him and arched her back, taking him deeper. Good was an understatement. Great didn't quite get there. Fantastic. Terrific. Nothing fit.

Maybe, just maybe, there was no one word big enough for this feeling.

Chapter Fifteen

Noah had dreamed of this moment once or twice before. Okay, many times. But the reality, as it turned out, had been far better than any of his horny teenage fantasies about Twyla. She was incredible and worth waiting for. Soft, tender and all the best kinds of wild. Their kisses were slow and lazy. Like making up for lost time. They'd languished and rolled around in bed for hours, napping briefly, then waking to reach for each other again and again.

"We should have been doing this all along. All that wasted time." He pressed a kiss to her temple. "What have we been waiting for?"

He'd waited for a guilt he hadn't deserved to subside. He'd waited to believe the lie he'd told everyone else about who'd been driving the boat.

Waited for the longing for her to go away but it never had.

"I was waiting for you." She whispered this softly into his neck. "I was hoping for you."

"Funny, because I was waiting for you. I mean, how could you not know?"

"Know what?"

"That I was crazy about you from the moment we met." He threaded his fingers through her silky hair.

"Easy. You never said anything. And I was too afraid to think it could be true." She hesitated. "Until I saw us in the photo albums tonight."

"That was my well-kept secret. I wanted you for myself."

He kissed her again and again and made love to her.

Later, he slept fitfully, waking only when rays of light gave way to the sunrise. Still, he didn't wake her as she lay quietly in his arms. *Just a little bit longer*, he told himself, feeling selfish for the first time in a decade and allowing himself to be okay with that.

He'd dozed off again when Twyla woke with a start and sat ramrod straight.

"Oh, my God! What time is it?" She rolled out of his arms, off the bed and bent to reach for her clothes. "The Chamber breakfast. My speech!"

"Oh, crap."

She rubbed her face and widened her eyes when she read the numbers on his digital clock. "I have to be there in half an hour."

Damn. He knew there was something she was supposed to do this morning. Of course, he also liked an early start at the wharf, but there were some benefits to being your own boss. With no scheduled tours today, he could go in whenever. But Twyla didn't have the same luxuries with a floundering business that depended on the community. That reminded him, he should probably join the Chamber of Commerce. This was something Mr. Curry had encouraged Noah to renew under his new ownership.

Noah flew into action, pulling on his jeans and rushing to the coffee maker. When Twyla hopped out after a quick shower, then dressed, he had a cup ready for her. Just the way she liked it with cream, no sugar. Never let it be said that he wanted her to regret a moment of last night. She would be at this meeting on time, or he'd die trying to get her there.

"Thank you." She met his eyes, then almost shyly glanced away. She seemed to really see him for the first time this morning. "Okay. I'm off."

"I think you'll be there on time. Don't drive too fast. Promise me." He tugged on her elbow.

"Of course. Please don't worry."

She turned, then stopped herself midway. Setting the coffee down, she threw herself into his arms. He gave her a long, deep and warm kiss that he hoped encouraged her to be back in his bed soon. Maybe happiness was really this simple. It came down to taking a risk at the right time.

"I can't believe this. We… Is this really happening to us?"

"It is. We crossed the friend zone."

"And it was glorious. I wish I could—"

"No. You told me about this last night, and I should have remembered to wake you. I don't want to be the reason you miss this meeting."

"If it wasn't for the angel investor and my speech, I'd forget the whole thing even with the Tiffany gift bags."

"That's high praise. Are you saying I'm better than a Tiffany bag?"

"You're better than one thousand of them." She then picked her coffee up and strolled to her car.

And he caught her smiling the whole way.

Noah got himself ready for work in record time and had just pulled into the harbor's lot when he had a call on his cell. Glancing at the ID, he saw the caller was Tate, his old crewmate at Station 80 in Austin. The bonding that happened at a fire station was real and lasting but the bonding after a near disaster was in another category. This crew would be with him and have his back for life. Since he'd retired and moved here, they checked in on him at least once a week.

"Miss me yet?" Tate said.

Noah would be lying to say he didn't miss the constant adrenaline rushes and the camaraderie. Mostly the camaraderie. For someone who'd lost a brother, the attachments had meant everything. He considered he now had roughly five brothers for life. It didn't make up for Will, nothing ever would, but it was something.

"Can't say that I miss your ugly mug," Noah chuckled.

"You doing okay, though?"

"Yeah. It's all good here. Things are going just like I planned. Better than I could have even hoped."

"No reminders?"

"Plenty of those, but it's okay now."

"If you need to talk…"

"I know, I know."

After their accident, the rotation crew that had narrowly missed devastating injury was assigned to therapy. Noah had sailed through his, because after what he'd been through as a teenager, the roof collapse was a blip on his radar. A blip that had him making some important changes, but still…a blip in the overall scheme of things.

"Man, what I wouldn't do to get up every morning and go fish."

"You're welcome anytime. Get yourself down here on your next vacay."

"I think I will. And what about Twyla? How's she doing?"

"Yeah." Noah sighed. "She's great."

Unfortunately, Noah had a bad habit. Dangerous. He talked in his sleep. He was really going to have to do something about that. Fortunately, he no longer had to bunk with men. One night, Tate had heard him calling out Twyla's name. When he tried to tell Tate she was his best friend back home and his brother's first girlfriend, he'd simply quirked a brow.

I don't believe you. It was the way you were calling out to her.

Noah remembered the dream, or rather, the nightmare. Instead of being unable to save Will, it was Twyla this time. Twyla whom he'd lost forever.

He'd endured some relentless teasing, but for the most part he didn't talk about Twyla. She was a part of him that he protected. And until the day he had impulsively kissed her, and she'd kissed him back, he'd never been sure she felt the same way about him. The day of the costume event at the bookstore, when she'd met his eyes and given him a look like she'd never seen him before. Well, now she had seen *all* of him. If he was lucky, really lucky, he'd be able to hang on to her.

After pushing the subject off to Tate's romantic woes, Noah eventually managed to hang up.

He had work to do, even if some days it did not feel like work.

"And in conclusion," Twyla said. "I want to thank the Charming business community for supporting your local bookstore. My family has long believed that bookstores serve communities. And communities serve bookstores. Books mean love and learning, and bookstores are yet another place to gather and express ideas. We're like a town watercooler. And I want to welcome you all to my watercooler, and to the irreplaceable beauty and importance of books. Thank you for your support."

With a round of applause, Twyla headed back to her table. She could no longer feel her legs, but she somehow made it back anyway.

The most wonderful part was she'd been too busy last night to stress about the speech. Then, she'd been too focused on making it to the meeting on time to worry about the actual speech. But the moment she'd stepped up to the podium after Ava's heartfelt introduction, her anxiety returned. A pebble lodged itself in her throat and her palms were sweaty. She adjusted and readjusted her glasses—a nervous habit pushed into overdrive. Faces of local business owners were trained on her and she swallowed. Zoey waved to her from the back, giving her a thumbs-up. So did Ava, then Max.

When all was said and done, she'd given a speech even she could be proud of. Plus, she'd walked back and forth to the podium and hadn't once tripped. The fact that she wore yesterday's clothes, her *Merry and*

Bright blouse, red skirt and green tights didn't seem to bother anyone here at all. Apparently, she was "festive."

"That was amazing, girl," said Zoey. "I thought you were going to be nervous and shy."

"I *was* nervous and shy. You couldn't tell? I kept staring at my notes and thought I'd lost my place once."

Reading, and even writing, was so much easier than talking.

"Nobody could tell and wow, va-va-voom. It's like you've got this whole new look about you. You practically strutted up to the microphone." Zoey leaned forward, squinted and examined Twyla's pores. "What kind of skin product are you using? Something new?"

It wasn't skin product. It had to be love. But this wasn't exactly the right place to mention this, especially when Twyla caught Michelle coming in her direction. Twyla could not deal with this right now. What on earth was Michelle doing here?

"Um, okay. I have to go to the restroom." When Michelle turned to greet someone, Twyla stood and practically ran all the way to the ladies' room praying Michelle hadn't noticed.

She shut the stall door and put her back against it. Maybe she could stay in there awhile before anyone noticed. But it wasn't long before she heard the distinctive high-heeled clicking steps of Michelle coming to the sink and turning it on. A moment later, she shut it off. But she wasn't going anywhere. To her utter shame, Twyla dipped under the door and spied Michelle's black stilettos pointing in her direction, crossed at the ankles, as if she intended to stay awhile.

Okay, this is it. Just face her. It's not going to kill you. Honesty is always the best policy. Really, was it her fault that she loved Noah? How was she ever to know he felt the same way? She hadn't a clue until the first impulsive kiss. And he'd asked her to forget about the kiss. Told her he didn't have those kinds of feelings for her. Liar, liar, pants on fire.

Look who's talking.

Twyla threw open the door and pretended she'd just noticed Michelle. She blinked a couple of times for good measure. "Oh, hey there. It's you. I didn't see you."

She went to the sink next to Michelle's and turned on the faucet to wash her hands.

"That's funny, because I'm pretty sure you did when you ran in the other direction."

"You thought that was for you? Listen, I drank a lot of water while I waited for my speech. What are you doing here? Joining the Chamber of Commerce?"

"I'm thinking of opening up my own law firm and wrangled an invite."

"You're officially moving here?"

"Yes, this way when it doesn't work out for you and Noah, I can consider taking him back. *If* he grovels." She crossed her arms. "Is there something you want to tell me?"

Damn, did she have surveillance on them? Otherwise, how would she know?

Twyla stalled for time and checked herself out in the mirror, pretending to dot her lips. Because she hadn't taken her makeup bag with her this morning, she wasn't wearing a stitch. Not that she wore much on any day—usually just a hint of mascara, a little lipstick and some blush. Interestingly, she didn't have her usual ghostly washed-out look. She noticed the pink cheeks Zoey had referred to. Twyla did look rather fresh and new today.

"I guess I haven't been completely honest with you."

"Yes? Go on."

She tossed her hands up. "I'm in love with Noah. I probably have been for a very long time, but I swear to you, nothing *ever* happened between us while you two were together. I wouldn't have done that, and neither would he."

"An affair of the heart is just as important." She quirked her perfect brow.

"I don't know if it could be called that when I wasn't aware I felt this way. I tried not to love him. I swear. I've always just wanted him to be happy, and I still do. No matter what happens."

Michelle simply stared at her for several long seconds from under those incredibly long lashes. Her expression was fairly blank.

"Besides, weren't you the one that told me love is worth taking a risk?"

Michelle's eyes narrowed, and she turned to the mirror to fluff her hair. "Thank you for being honest with me. I wish you both the best and I hope it works out for you. Even if Noah has a commitment phobia, you never know. You might get lucky."

Michelle turned and strutted out of the bathroom. Zoey was wrong. Twyla didn't strut. She'd never strutted a day in her life.

Now Michelle? *That* girl had a strut.

For a few minutes, Twyla imitated the walk. She gauged her progress in the mirror as she walked by, swinging her hips. Nope. Not happening.

When she got back to her table, Zoey had already opened her gift bag.

"It's a Tiffany headband which, if I put it on, looks a little bit like a tiara."

Twyla dug through her bag to find a similar gift. Ava had excellent taste. "Me, too."

"So, what happened? I saw Michelle following you into the restroom."

"She just wanted to make me feel guilty."

"About what?"

"Now please don't gloat."

"Who, me?" Zoey held her hand to her chest.

"You're right and I don't know why it took me so long to realize."

Zoey's eyes widened. "Oh, my God, are you finally going to start wearing heels?"

Twyla had to laugh. "No, I'm on my feet all day. Zoey, how many times do we have to discuss this?"

"Well, what is it then?"

"It's Noah."

"What about him?"

"It's *me*, and Noah." She slid Zoey a significant look until she gaped.

"You mean, finally? Finally! Really?"

And then Twyla told Zoey everything, censoring the more intimate details.

Zoey squealed and held up her palm for a high five. "Way to cross boundaries, girl. I wonder how many were technically crossed in one night?"

Twyla explained how she and Noah had brought Christmas to his mother's house. How they'd put up the tree and spent some time looking through old albums. And what she'd seen in those photos that rocked her to the core.

"Oh, my gosh. Come on. All that time pining over

you. But of course he felt guilty. He wanted what his big brother had, and then he failed to save him."

But the thing of it was, Twyla had loved Noah first.

She remembered the first time she had ever seen him—his wavy dark hair falling over one eye as it never failed to do. A smile that always brought one out of her. She wouldn't have called it love then, but what she felt for him had always been more intense than what she'd felt for Will. Her personality had been far better suited to Will, who was also the quiet type. Not quite as handsome or charming as Noah, he was still a good-looking kid. Twyla had been flattered when he asked her out. She'd said yes because Noah would never ask.

After the Chamber breakfast, and finally disentangling from Zoey's many questions, Twyla headed home to change and feed Bonkers. She opened the door to the sounds of mewing. If a cat could give the finger, Bonkers would. His eyes were tiny slits of utter disgust. His human servant hadn't been home to feed him last night.

"I'm so sorry, but it's not like you're going to starve." Her cat, according to the vet, was overweight.

She opened up a can of wet food and set his bowl down.

Tonight was the regular meeting of the poet society, and since even Katherine had attended once, Twyla thought her grandmother should make an appearance as well. She brought it up after the last poetry meeting, pointing out that even Katherine had now attended, so surely Ganny could as well.

"Poetry has never been my thing, and you know it."

"You could at least show up and support your friends. Be their audience. Art is a medium that needs an audience, after all. Poems are not meant to be spoken into the void. They just want to be heard."

"Well, you can do that. I did go to a meeting *once*, about a year ago."

"Then I think you're due."

"I don't have anything to wear."

"That's a lousy excuse. I'll find something for you to wear. Just watch me."

"Okay, okay! I'll go. Unless I feel sick that day."

Twyla had been checking on her daily just to make sure she couldn't fake it at the last minute.

Later that afternoon, Ganny, who got a ride with Mr. Finch and Lois, strolled through the doors of Once Upon a Book for the first time since the costume event.

"I'm just here to support y'all," she said. "My granddaughter doesn't think I spend enough time at the place where I worked all my life."

"Don't you miss it?" asked Lois.

"I do sometimes, but the world is a different place now. What with the e-readers and audiobooks, too many people have forgotten print."

"Not us!" the seniors said in unison.

"Print is actually making a comeback, Ganny," Twyla said. "And among young people, believe it or not."

Earlier today, she'd arranged a new display of print books that were bestsellers thanks to a new popular social media site. *As seen on...* the sign read. At least two teens had picked up one of those books.

"I'd love publishers to carry more large print books." Patsy sniffed. "If anything, the print gets smaller."

"And who wants to read with a magnifying glass?" Susannah said. "If you would tell the publishers, Twyla, that would be so helpful."

Yes, because publishers did exactly what Twyla said they should.

"I'll give it a try."

Finally, they were all settled in their circle and began to share their poems. Twyla applauded after each one, because honestly, they were all getting so much better. Mr. Finch's poems were verging on literary fiction, especially with the one tonight he'd titled, "When Texas was Young." But Twyla was suddenly quite partial to Patsy's romantic poetry.

Noah had texted her earlier today that he wanted to grab dinner, and he'd be by later. She already missed him in new ways that had her both giddy and anxious. It occurred to her that if they were able to save the bookstore as it looked like they were doing, and she could be with Noah, she might actually be too lucky. Did she deserve this much happiness? She wanted to believe so, but good people who meant well and worked hard did not often get what they deserved.

The poetry reading over, a few seniors were standing in a corner discussing the latest memoir on the *New York Times* bestseller list. In another corner, a couple of people were trying to understand a plot point in a book where the ending seemed to be in flux. Did she kill him or not? And if she did do it, then *how*?

Twyla usually eagerly added to the conversation, but as she stood back and listened in, warmth spread through her at the community they'd created here. Maybe it had taken selling educational toys, too, so a person could buy a toy for their nephew's birthday and the latest bestseller in the same place. Even the yoga classes meant someone lingering. The teacher had recommended many books in the health and wellness section. They had something special here and weren't going to lose it. It wasn't just a line in her speech, it was the dream, and it was here. Maybe not always bright and shiny and glowing, but nonetheless precious in the way the best things in life are. Not perfect, but real.

Force of habit had her glancing up when she heard the ding of the shop's bell and her heart tugged with sweetness when Noah walked in. He sent her a slow smile, then quirked a brow when she beckoned him to the back of the store. It took him a few minutes, but he finally joined her in the fantasy section. *Their* section. She wanted to pull the book out and read with him just like old times, this time knowing he had tender feelings for her.

"I got here as soon as I could, but the old folks sure know how to talk an ear off."

She went into his arms, threading her fingers through his soft wavy hair. "I thought you were going to meet me for dinner."

He pulled her flush against him. "I was, but I couldn't wait."

She loved hearing those words. They'd waited long enough.

"I forgot to say something earlier today. I hope you'll forgive me."

Oh, boy, here it comes. The one thing that might ruin everything. She almost didn't want to hear it because this moment was too perfect.

And the world tended to take perfection and squash it to bits.

"I don't want any more misunderstanding between us. I'm going to be one hundred percent honest with you."

She tensed. "Do I want to hear this?"

"I hope so." His voice was soft. "Last night? This morning? I forgot to tell you that I love you. And I have for as long as I can remember."

"Oh, Noah."

Her heart was too full. It was going to spring a leak any minute because it wasn't big enough yet, but it was already changing. Growing and stretching to let everything new inside.

"Is that okay with you?" He smiled, like he knew.

Then he pulled her in by the nape of her neck and kissed her. Like all his kisses, it was intense, long and deep. She almost forgot where she was, until the rather pronounced voice of Patsy Villanueva spoke, or rather squealed, right behind them.

"Oh, my God it's happening again! How long has *this* been going on?"

Before long, the fantasy nook filled with the senior citizens, elbow to elbow.

"Was it Patsy's poem or mine?" Ella Mae asked, hand to chest.

"Well, both were truly wonderful," Twyla said, lowering her hand from Noah's chest to his abs.

"Well, my poem was about kissing, and Ella's was about a garden. So..." Patsy said.

"Love grows in a garden! Remember the seed I mentioned? What do you think I was talking about?"

"A seed," Patsy said with a straight face.

"It's a *metaphor*." Ella Mae sniffed.

"I didn't hear either one of your poems but I'm sure both poems were great." Noah nodded.

"Of course, all of our poems are wonderful and that's not news," Susannah said. "But if you could give us some direction, we would love to be a little more hands-on with our matchmaking."

"That's true," Patsy said. "I want to know if I should get spicier or tone it down some."

"Do you young folks get the seed metaphor, or should I perhaps be more direct?"

"Ladies." Mr. Finch cleared his throat. "Time to admit a few things. We're lousy matchmakers. It's all been accidental. We've simply been lucky."

"Maybe we should rename ourselves the Accidental Love Poet Society," Patsy said. "It's a better fit. I don't plan on dying soon so I hate the 'almost dead' part."

"It is kind of morbid," Lois agreed.

There was some argument about renaming the society until Susannah reminded everyone the name was tongue-in-cheek and not to be taken too seriously. And also, they had already ordered business cards and it was too late to change now.

"I'm sorry, ladies, but Mr. Finch is right. At least about these two." Ganny muscled her way to the front and now waved her hand between Twyla and Noah. "*This* isn't new."

Twyla glanced up at Noah.

They were both brand new and old.

"What do you mean? She was Will's girl." This from Lois. "Wasn't she?"

Twyla wasn't imagining Noah tense beside her. His grip on her tightened.

Ganny shook her head. "A long time ago. But in my opinion, she's loved Noah for just as long, if not longer. And I for one, couldn't be happier for them."

Chapter Sixteen

Noah believed his own mother would be just as happy about them as Twyla's grandmother. If he got lucky, Twyla would one day soon be his mother's daughter-in-law. But he better not get ahead of himself. He already felt like someone who'd won the lottery—lucky and possibly undeserving. Even if his privacy had been violated, the knowledge these "accidentally matchmaking" senior citizens approved of him filled him with hope.

Instead of taking Twyla to a restaurant for dinner, Noah drove to his favorite stand by the wharf and picked up bread bowls of clam chowder, fried calamari and shrimp cocktails. After tonight, and the unexpected unveiling of their new romance, he wanted to take Twyla somewhere special. Meaningful.

He would take her to the one place in the world he felt most at home.

They sat on the bench seats of the catamaran and

watched the sunset while they ate. Funny, but before the accident, he'd never paid much attention to color. He'd listen to girls talk about the sunset and all the fancy descriptions of ribbons of red and gold. Once, when he and a few friends had missed the sunset, Noah had tried to lighten the disappointment by saying, "There will be another one tomorrow." It had been a while since he'd believed that.

Tomorrows weren't promised to anyone.

Will would be happy for them. Noah liked to think he would be, since he'd once thanked him for stepping aside. He'd give anything to have his brother back, and he didn't know that Twyla and Will would have wound up together anyway. Will claimed to be moving on to college and a new life.

Privately, just between brothers, Will couldn't wait to get away from their parents. Always being the good son hadn't exactly been *his* choice. Just like being labeled the stubborn one hadn't been Noah's. He'd walked around in a state of perpetual guilt for both what he had done and what he hadn't. Now, he could release the guilt. He'd tried to save his brother and failed. It was the biggest regret of his life, but Will had a part in the accident. He'd driven at high speeds, scaring Noah, laughing maniacally.

If our parents could see us now! Will had laughed.

Stop, Noah said. *You're going* too fast.

What's too fast?

It just wasn't fair.

Will had just been a kid, a teenager on the cusp of a new life in a town where he might not be labeled as perfect. For a moment, Will went against the rules in a complete break of character. And it had nearly killed them both.

"You're quiet. What are you thinking?" Twyla bumped his knee.

He pulled her into his arms, and her head settled on his shoulder. "About us."

"Yes, us. My favorite subject."

"Did you know I was going to ask you out first, before Will did?"

"No," she said quietly.

"To the junior prom."

"You went with Sabrina. I was *so* jealous."

"You would have been my first choice. Anyway, Will told me he really liked you. You remember that Will didn't date much and I…well, I did."

"Mr. Popularity."

"My popularity was based on the fact that I cared too much because I needed everyone to like me. I wasn't particularly intelligent and all I had was my personality. It was important for others to like me because Will… He was always my parents' favorite."

"That's not true." She clung to his neck. "Please don't say that."

But she more than anyone else understood because she'd witnessed it. Will was the kid eager to please his parents. The older and dutiful son, always doing what was expected. Schoolwork had come easily to him, while Noah always struggled. Will behaved, while from day one, Noah couldn't sit still.

"Just promise me one thing." Noah brought her hand to his lips and spoke through it. "Don't start treating me any differently. When I'm a stupid guy, and I will be, try to see me through the best friend lens. Know that whatever I fail to do, or forget to do, it isn't because I don't love you."

"Yes, okay. I can do that. You do the same for me. The best friend thing. Except... I will still talk to Zoey about you. She's also my best friend. I tell her stuff I can't tell you."

"What can't you tell *me*?"

She went still for a moment, and he got concerned. He didn't want to accept that she kept anything from him, which he realized was selfish. He already kept something huge from her.

"Like what I'm getting for your birthday or what I might get you. And I have to do the girl-talk thing. I have to tell her all the wonderful things you do to me in bed and how it makes me feel."

"Tell me that stuff, too."

"But I wouldn't want you to get too conceited."

"Fine. Just make sure you always talk me up. Make me sound even better than I am." He chuckled but the laugh died within seconds. "There's also...something I've kept from you all these years."

"I know. You liked me."

He swallowed the pebble in his throat and cleared it. "Yes, but not...not that."

"Noah, you can tell me anything. I don't want any big secrets between us."

"I know, but this... I never told anyone. It was better that way."

She stilled in his arms. "Maybe, if you can't tell me, you can tell someone else."

Such a sweet gift, giving him the permission *not* to tell her. There was such trust in that one sentence. Trust that he'd make the right choice.

"On the day of the accident? The thing is, I *wasn't* the one driving the boat."

She froze and met his eyes. "But…you said you were the driver, and the police investigated."

"Not very well. They believed what I told them and why wouldn't they when I took blame? 'Will let me drive the boat and I hit a sandbar going too fast.' It made sense to them."

"*Why*, Noah? Why would you take the blame?"

"Because I loved Will. Idolized him. He had one bad moment and paid for it with his life. I didn't also want him to lose his reputation. It was hard enough on my parents, and they were used to my being the one to blame. Used to Wild Noah, breaking the rules once again. I hoped their unconditional love would get my family through this, but my father never looked me in the eyes again."

"Oh, Noah." She buried her face in his neck, tears flowing now, wetting his skin.

"Some days I thought you were the one person in the world who knew it wasn't me. I thought you'd see right through my lie. You didn't and yet you still loved me."

"I will always love you. And your father loved you, too. Some men are not strong enough to show their love through the tough times. To stick it out, for better or worse. He was a weak man."

"Hey, didn't mean to make you cry." Noah reached to tip her chin. "But I didn't want the lie between us anymore."

"You should at least tell your mother. She doesn't blame you, but she does have Will on a pedestal."

"He might deserve to be. I lost a brother, but she lost a child. Maybe she has the right to do whatever she wants. It's easier to blame me and she needs to put the blame somewhere."

They sat quietly for several minutes, simply holding each other tight.

Noah closed his eyes and listened to the sounds of the water lapping against his boat, the woman he'd loved for half his life in his arms.

"Oh, my God, Noah! Look."

When he opened his eyes, fireflies danced just off the stern of the boat. Fireflies such as he hadn't seen in years, a shimmering display of lights.

"How many do you think there are?" Noah said.

"Hundreds!"

They stood and drew closer to them.

"Did you know that this is their mating call? Fireflies light up this way to find a mate," Twyla said.

"I thought it was to ward off predators."

"That used to be the case, but they've evolved over millions of years. They're near extinction now." She reached for his hand. "And a group of them are called a light posse…or a sparkle."

"Sparkle. That's perfect." He pressed a kiss to her temple and pulled her in front of him, wrapping his arms around her waist.

Noah wasn't one to believe in magic or fantasy other than in the books he and Twyla liked to read. But if he did, he'd think the sparkle was Will's doing, giving them his stamp of approval. After all, he had loved them both. Noah sensed in that precious moment that Will would want nothing more than their happiness.

They stayed and watched the sparkle for a very long time.

The closer they drew to Christmas Day the more anxious Twyla grew to give Noah her present. She'd been working on it for nearly a year now and had simply planned to ship it to him in Austin. But this would be so much better, so she could see his face light up at the book that had meant so much to the two of them over the years. It had added significance now, years later, because the grief had lifted and that had given them the possibility of a much brighter future than she could have ever dreamed.

Finally, five days before Christmas, she removed the book from behind the checkout counter where she kept it to add notes here and there as they occurred to her. Opening to the first page, she wrote the inscription:

For Noah, my whole heart. It feels like I've loved you for one hundred years.

It was the other copy of *A Dragon's Heart*, and though it would never be quite like the first—in which they'd honestly expressed their grief through a story—she had a feeling this, too, might serve a purpose. While "Silent Night" piped through the speakers and customers wandered around for last minute purchases, she carefully wrapped the book.

Tonight, she'd give him the gift early because she couldn't wait another minute. She was sure that like her, he'd missed the book which, in some ways, forever cemented their connection to each other. And what better book for two confused and hurting young people to read than a fantasy in which even dragons who breathed fire could be slayed?

So busy wrapping that she hadn't even noticed someone at the counter, Twyla looked up. "How can I help you?"

The man who looked vaguely familiar held out his hand. "I'm William Hart."

"Nice to meet you. I'm Twyla and my family runs this store. Can I help you find something?"

He shook his head. "I thought I'd drop this by instead."

He reached inside his jacket pocket and pulled out an envelope. "I wanted to personally deliver this check. I heard your speech at the Chamber breakfast and though I was leaning toward you anyway, those beautiful words clinched the deal for me. You should know that I'm a different kind of angel investor. I don't ask for anything in return. I want you to keep this bookstore around for many years to come."

Twyla stared at the closed envelope, then back to Mr. Hart. William.

Will.

It could be the coincidence of a very common first name, but delight pulsed through her anyway. First, after Noah's heartbreaking confession, the fireflies just *had* to have been sent from Will for both her and Noah. They couldn't see him, but he was still with them. Always.

Now this.

"Have we met before?"

"I don't think so, but I've been around." He patted his chest and smiled. "Merry Christmas."

"Thank you."

Twyla turned the card over in her hands, not wanting to open it in his presence. She would be grateful for any amount he'd given from the kindness of his heart.

"This means so much to my family. I want you to know—"

When she glanced up, the man was already gone. He had moved so quickly, and she'd been so engrossed, that she hadn't even heard the door chime as he left. And when she ran to the sidewalk, there were so many passersby that she didn't catch a glimpse of him in either direction. He'd melted into the crowd.

Walking back inside, she opened the envelope and took a look at the check. She blinked when more zeros than she could have ever hoped for followed the comma.

In the memo portion of the check, William Hart had written:

Books are forever.

Just like love.

When she got home, Twyla phoned Ganny to give her the good news.

"I knew if anyone could pull us out of this slump, it would be you."

"Well, it was actually Mr. Hart. *William* Hart. Did I mention that?"

"Yes, you did. And, honey, I don't believe in coincidences. That was a message."

Twyla's eyes were suddenly wet. "You think so?"

"I do. Am I to assume you'll be bringing Noah to my annual Christmas party?"

"Of course."

"Make sure Katherine comes, too. We'll have a big crowd this year. Dana, the yoga teacher, and all of the Almost Dead Poets Society members. Ava, of course, and Max. Valerie and Cole. Stacy and Adam may show up, too, if they can get a babysitter. Everyone who has gone out of their way to support us."

"You'd have to invite the entire town," Twyla said.

Twyla hung up and carefully placed Noah's book under the tree along with a few of her other presents.

Definitely on a budget this year, every single one of her gifts had been handmade. For Ganny, she'd put together an album filled with memories of the bookstore. Old newspaper articles going back to four generations when the store first opened. A photo with her parents and grandmother at the book signing of the first bestselling author they'd ever hosted. Photos of family and friends and books.

Bonkers came running out from wherever he'd been hiding today, stopped short when he saw her, then give her a dirty look and stalked away, his tail high in the air.

"That's fine. Go be in your bad mood. I know you like me, even if you act like you don't. What would you do without me? Huh? Yes, you'd starve, that's what."

She poured the dry food and set the bowl down. Bonkers sniffed it, then decided he'd rather starve.

The doorbell rang. "That will be my boyfriend."

Yes, her boyfriend. Noah Cahill.

Tonight, she'd give him the book and he'd know without words how much she loved him. She opened the door to a tired-looking Noah. His cheeks were ruddy and windburned, his gorgeous dark hair its usual tousled and wavy look. She took his arm and pulled him inside.

"What's wrong? Rough day?"

"You could say that. Tee got ahead of himself and took the dingy out without asking me. I would call that an offense worth firing him for, but Finn talked me off the ledge."

"Leave it to Finn. Does Tee know what he's doing?"

"Finn assures me he does. But Tee is going to have

to prove to me that safety is more important than impressing girls."

"I almost forgot to tell you. You're never going to believe this!" She went to her purse and pulled out the check. "The angel investor came through for us, and his name is William."

She told him the entire story and handed him the check to see. Even Noah's eyes widened.

He took her into his arms, then pressed his forehead to hers. "I'm so happy for you. He's right, you know? Books are forever."

Just like love. She'd loved Will as an innocent young girl, and she would forever. But Noah. The love for him was different and always had been. Deeper and wider.

And she'd like to think she and Noah were a forever kind of love.

"Come here. I have something for you." She tugged him toward the tree and pulled out her present. "It's a few days early, but I just can't wait another minute. I've been working on this for almost a year."

With a smile tugging his lips, Noah tore into it with the excitement of a little kid. But she couldn't miss the blank look on his face when he turned the book over in his hands.

There was almost a hesitance there. A flash of regret?

She felt the need to explain. "Remember? I lost our book and felt so bad about it. When it didn't turn up, I decided I would just recreate it. Of course, it's not the same but—"

She didn't get to finish the sentence because he grabbed her in a fierce kiss.

"Wait until you read the inscription," she gasped, a little out of breath.

"I love this, baby. But I'll read it later. *Much* later if you don't mind." Then he carefully tossed the book on her couch and hoisted her into his arms, carrying her to the bedroom.

"I don't mind at all."

Fresh and raw new guilt pierced Noah. He could only imagine the hours Twyla had spent recreating the book. The one she should have never had to replace. The one he'd taken and kept from her. It should be a simple thing to return now, to let her know the reasons he'd taken it. They'd be better received now. He hoped. But the lie, such as it was, or omission of truth, wouldn't go down as easy. He'd lost count of how many times Twyla had asked him whether he'd seen their book, and when and where he'd last seen it. She'd apologized to *him* for losing it. Apologized!

He'd almost broken down then and told her he had the book, and would she mind if he kept it? Hindsight being twenty-twenty now, he knew she would have understood. But she might have also *understood* that he'd loved her for years but didn't know how to tell her. That he loved her but had allowed an unnatural guilt to build a wall between any possibility of having more. And yes, she would have been disappointed to hear it, which was the risk he took now, too. He would still give it back to her, because now the original book would again be something they could hold between them. Their shared history.

A few hours later, Noah woke to the delicious scent of coconut tickling his nose. Wait. Was he on a beach in Hawaii? In a hammock on an island somewhere under a palm tree? When he opened one eye, Twyla's gorgeous dark locks were fanned over him, just below his chin. She'd burrowed into the side of him like a rabbit. Funny how he didn't mind, not in the slightest. It took great effort to disentangle himself from her sweet soft skin, but he heard scratching sounds right outside the bedroom. He climbed out of bed, pulled on his boxers and, as he drew closer to the door, identified the sound on the other side.

No surprise, he opened it and found Bonkers mid-swipe.

"I like you, dude, but you're not getting in here with us." Noah softly shut the door.

The cat probably needed to go outside and perhaps this was a regular nightly ritual. He and Twyla had been a little distracted for the last two hours. The kitchen digital clock flashed the time. Midnight. Come to think of it, Twyla had mentioned that her cat roamed the house all night and mostly hid during the day except for feeding time. He didn't seem like much of a pet to Noah. More like a vampire.

He walked to the back door, and Bonkers followed him, rubbing up against him and winding between his legs so Noah nearly tripped on him.

"What's wrong with you? You like me, and I don't really care much about you. But you don't like Twyla, and she's one of the kindest people I've ever known. She loves you, though I can't imagine why."

He held open the back door, and Bonkers slipped outside.

Now he could take another look at the book that had thrown him back into a guilt cycle.

He read the inscription, feeling his heart slam against

his chest like a wild animal trapped inside. Love shouldn't be this easy. He should have gotten over his damn self years ago and they could have been happy together instead of miserable with other people. A colossal waste of time and he didn't want to waste another second.

Noah crawled back into bed, pulling Twyla, who had rolled over on her side away from him, back into his arms. She made a soft sighing sound, then began to burrow herself against his body once again. Look at him, cuddling. He never thought it possible he would enjoy anyone invading his personal sleeping space, but leave it to Twyla to turn him into a cuddler.

"And I've loved you for a hundred and five years, and probably more," he whispered into her hair just before he fell asleep.

The next morning, disappointment clouded his senses because he didn't smell coconut anymore. He no longer had a gorgeous woman trying to physically attach herself to his body. So, he was alone. He'd spent the night, and he was alone in her bed. Great. Then he heard steps rushing back and forth outside the door of the bedroom and eventually the door swung wide open.

Twyla began to search through dresser drawers and under her bed.

"Lose something?" Noah rubbed his eyes.

"Bonkers! I can't find him anywhere. I used the can opener this morning and usually he comes running out of whatever place he's been hiding in at that sound. Maybe he's trapped somewhere? But I've looked everywhere."

Noah went up on his elbows and tried to shove away the layer of fog from his brain. He remembered letting

Bonkers out last night and must have forgotten to let him back in?

"Could he still be outside? Did you check?"

"*Outside?* He never goes outside. He's terrified."

"Terrified? That little monster? What on earth is he terrified of?"

"I don't know, but he never got used to outside so he's just an indoor cat. I'm so worried!"

Oh, crap. Realization cut through him like a knife. He'd let an *indoor* cat outside. It was a wonder he hadn't scratched at the door all night. Or maybe, just maybe, Noah hadn't *heard* him. Noah jumped out of bed and pulled clothes on. Great, now he'd lost her cat. First the book, now the cat. Before long she might learn to hate him. One he'd stolen and the other he'd apparently lost out of idiocy.

Time to confess and beg for mercy. "I thought Bonkers wanted outside. I heard him scratching at your bedroom door last night and when I opened the door, he went right outside like he knew what he was doing."

Twyla gasped. "He could be anywhere now. There's also a very mean cat a couple of houses down. If he gets to poor Bonkers, I don't know what will happen."

"Don't worry. I've got this. Do you have any idea how many calls I've answered for stranded kittens and trees?"

"Is that still a thing?"

On a slow day maybe.

If he was lucky, really lucky, Noah would find Bonkers, and he'd find him uninjured and possibly shivering behind a bush somewhere. Horrified to be set out into the wild. First, Noah went outside the back door in the direction he'd let Bonkers out. But for a scaredy-cat, it appeared that Bonkers had strayed from the roost. He wasn't in Twyla's small fenced-in yard, or behind any bushes or shrubs. And yes, he checked the tree.

He walked down the street asking any neighbor he saw outside whether they'd seen a gray cat, mean and with a lot of attitude. Noah went all around the block and was headed back when he noticed ruffling on the higher branch of a tree two houses from Twyla's. *Bonkers.* This should be easy. A no-brainer. The cat liked him, last he heard, which gave him an advantage. Shouldn't be too difficult to wrangle him out of that branch and back down the tree. Then, he and Twyla would carry him inside and laugh about this later, maybe even go back to bed for a little morning sex. His very favorite kind. Which he had notably missed this morning.

Noah started to climb the tree and scaled it quickly. The Fire Academy had taught him to endure both tight spaces and heights. He was fortunately afraid of neither. Yes, this would be a piece of cake. Or, it should have been, but just then the Texas skies opened up. They tended to do this at times without much warning so everyone could have a good old-fashioned drenching.

The cat, disgusted by the water, screeched and jumped from one branch to another, seeking better cover. And Noah got it. The branches were offering some shelter but, hell, Bonkers needed to be inside. Twyla wanted him and she would get him. The water fell hard enough that he wished he had windshield wipers for his eyes. Or at least a ball cap. With one hand, he reached for the cat, who should have been happy for the rescue. Instead, he retaliated with the only weapon he had.

"Ow. Oh, hell." Noah drew back his hand. Bonkers had claws.

Guess what? So did Noah.

"Come here, you idiot."

Then, in a death-defying stunt, the cat jumped to the ground and ran off. That's when Noah noticed a blur of black. Black, not *gray*. He might have had the wrong cat in the first place. Who could tell in this torrential rain? Noah headed back inside for a ball cap to resume his search.

When he opened the front door, there sat Twyla, Bonkers in her lap.

"Did you hear me calling you?" She stood. "What *happened*?"

"I think I got attacked by the wrong cat." He ran a hand through his damp hair. "But all's well that ends well. I see you two are getting cozy."

"He came home almost as soon as you left. And you know what? He's been pretty affectionate. I think maybe all he needed was a good scare to know he has a good thing going here."

"Looks like he missed the downpour." Meanwhile, Noah had been through a shower with his clothes on.

Twyla came close. "Why didn't you come in out of the rain, silly?"

"I had to get Bonkers. It's my fault he went outside in the first place."

"Oh, Noah." She framed his face. "Rescuer of cats and damsels in distress. My hero."

"Well, he's no dragon and you sure as hell are not a damsel in distress."

"I love you." Then she kissed him so deeply that he *wished* with everything in him that he'd slayed a dragon.

"Don't you know I'd do anything for you?" He took her hand and brought it to his lips to kiss the inside of her wrist.

She shook her head. "I didn't know, but I'm starting to believe you."

Later they'd find he had fresh scratches torn through his long-sleeved Henley. Twyla used antiseptic on each one and kissed the spot before she applied a bandage.

And as it worked out, he got his morning sex.

Twice.

Chapter Seventeen

With three days before Christmas, Noah realized his timing could have been better, but nonetheless this had to be done. He'd been a coward when he'd left Austin with the excuse that the roof collapse had forced him to reevaluate his life. That was true, but only to a point. The real truth was that he wasn't running from something. He was running toward the only person he'd ever truly loved.

Michelle had followed him here, which meant he hadn't been clear enough. He hadn't made a clean break. And yes, he'd been flattered by her actions, but now it was time to be brutally honest. Even if their relationship had failed, Michelle had been a good friend when he was far from home and missing the person who'd always been at the center of his heart. The person he told himself he couldn't have. Now, all that was in the past and he was moving forward.

He asked Michelle to meet him at the Salty Dog and now sat in a booth near the back of the bar for a little privacy. He couldn't discount the fact that he wanted to meet in a public place to avoid any big scenes, even if Michelle wasn't known for them. He also didn't want to lead Michelle on even in the smallest way. If he'd asked her to come over to his house to talk, she might have assumed things.

The moment she met his eyes, her whole face lit up and he realized he'd miscalculated. Meeting with her at all was misleading. He had never been any good at this. Will was the one with the silver tongue that always had all the right words.

He studied his hands and sent up a little prayer. *Mind helping me out a little here, buddy? I feel like I'm about to blow this and hurt someone I care about.*

"Noah," Michelle said a little breathlessly.

Maybe something in his gaze brought her up short because she blinked and then sat across the booth from him.

"Well, I'm thinking whatever this is, it isn't going to be a good thing for me."

Michelle wasn't a top-notch attorney in Austin for an inability to read social cues. She was an expert.

"Listen. You were a good friend to me when I was struggling. I didn't know anyone when I got to Austin, and you were good to me. I tried—I really tried—to make a go of this."

"But your heart was always with her. I just wish you'd been honest with me all along. *Both* of you."

"I wish that, too. Most of all, I wish we'd been honest with ourselves. I wasted a lot of time letting my guilt rule me. I'm not going to do that anymore."

"I don't think it's going to be as easy as you expect. Obstacles don't just move out of the way because you want them to."

"That's clear, but sometimes there are things worth fighting for. People worth fighting for."

Michelle lowered her gaze to the table and when she met his gaze, her eyes were damp.

"I wish you both luck. You deserve happiness. I'm just sorry I couldn't be the one to give it to you." She reached for his hand and squeezed it tight. "Don't let anyone ever put you in second place. Not even her."

The words surprised him, because he didn't realize Michelle had been so in tune with his own feelings of inadequacy. She was good. He'd give her that.

Over Michelle's shoulder, Noah saw Finn as he walked inside the bar. He quirked a brow in Noah's direction and his entire body became a question mark.

Is there a problem? Do you need me?

Thank God Noah had come back home. He'd forgotten how many true friends he had here. People he'd grown up with who saw him as more than someone who'd failed to rescue his brother. He had an entire "found family" in town, including Twyla.

Especially Twyla.

Noah gently shook his head in answer to Finn's unspoken question. Yeah, he was good.

And finally, for the first time in over a decade, he believed maybe he was worthy.

On the night of the Thompson family's Christmas party, Noah drove his mother. He'd been the first to tell her the good news of the angel investor that had rescued the bookstore. As usual, the Thompson family's beautiful ranch-style home had been decorated to the nines. Bright lights flashed from the oak tree and the shrubs, and they outlined each window. A Santa with his sleigh and reindeer was the lawn's focal point. Candy canes lined the pathway to the front door.

"Honestly," his mother said. "Look at this display. She's had so much loss in her life. Perhaps she shouldn't be celebrating."

Noah wasn't going to touch that remark anytime this year. It was that time of the year when he grew especially protective of every remark he made around his mother. Some days, it was like walking on landmines, afraid one word would set her off and she wouldn't leave the house for days.

Inside, they were greeted by Twyla, who hugged them both warmly. She led them toward the kitchen that was perfect for entertaining. Along the granite countertops, dozens of glistening crystal tumblers were set out around a tub of eggnog. Noah hadn't been to the Thompson family party in a few years, as the party often fell on one of his forty-eight-hour rotations. And as much as he'd loved being part of the emergency medical system, one of the things he'd never miss was answering calls during the holidays.

Roy Finch and Lois, along with their friends, were seated on couches watching the football game. Well, Mr. Finch was watching the game, along with Max and Adam.

Ella Mae stood and patted the seat beside hers. "Katherine, come sit beside me."

Noah walked his mother over to the gang and greeted everyone.

"At last, some more young people," said Patsy. "Valerie and Cole can't be here tonight. They have a thing out of town."

"A thing?" Ava laughed. "Valerie made teacher of the year and they have a ceremony."

"Yes." Patsy straightened, pride flashing in her dark eyes. "I wasn't going to say anything, but my Valerie won an award."

"Congratulations," Noah said.

Trays of hors d'oeuvres were passed around and Adam appointed himself as bartender, mixing drinks behind the bar.

"Everyone," said Ava. "We have an announcement to make."

She stood in the center of the room, beaming, Max beside her with an arm snaked around her waist.

"We're pregnant!" Ava announced happily, clapping her hands.

Stacy went to Ava. "Congratulations, sweetie."

"We wanted to wait until I was ready. And I thought I wouldn't be ready this quickly, but you know what? I am. Well, I'm going to be."

"Nice holiday surprise." Adam flashed a knowing grin. "There's just something about Christmas and babies, isn't there?"

"And to think we were in the room when Max wrote and recited a poem for Ava. And now we're here when they announced their precious child is coming," Patsy said. "I'm telling you, we need to rename our society. Something about love should be in the name."

After the conversation further evolved into babies and names, and all the equipment needed to make it happen, Noah thought it a perfect time to exit stage left. He whipped his head around, searching for Twyla. She was nowhere to be found, though a few minutes ago she had been tending to the food under heating lamps and she'd waved at him.

Honestly, with all this talk of babies, he remembered how much he loved the process behind making them. He realized for the first time that he wanted children. He hadn't before Twyla changed all that for him. If they had a boy, they'd name him William and Will would always be with them, but no longer something wedged between them. This time he'd be just one more thing that pressed them together into a deep and settling kind of love. A forever love.

He strolled through the rambling ranch house, peeking into open rooms, and, of course, the grand library. No Twyla. And then he heard the whispered sound of his name. The door to the guest room was open and Twyla beckoned to him. He followed her into the room where everyone had laid their sweaters and purses on the bed.

He winked. "What are you doing in here, Peaches? And did you lure me here for a reason?"

"Yes, of course." She moved closer and went up on her tiptoes, easing his jacket off. "I want you to take your coat off and stay awhile." She tossed it on the bed with the others.

"I don't plan on going anywhere."

"Good, see that you keep it that way." She fisted his shirt and pulled him to her, then kissed him with a deep and longing passion that matched his own.

The kiss quickly grew a little wild, him lowering his hands to her behind and tugging her against him. He lowered her onto the bed on top of all the soft jackets.

"Noah," she whispered, her breath warm on his neck. "What are you doing?"

"Don't worry. I'll remember my manners. I like looking at you sometimes. Just like this." He rose over her, bracing himself, looking at her sweet face. The girl he'd loved for half his life. "I love you."

"I love you."

He'd waited years to hear those words and, more to the point, to feel worthy of them. It was perfect, too perfect, and then the door to the bedroom opened softly, letting in the sounds of Christmas music, glasses filling and people chatting.

He winced. "Okay, this is a little embarrassing."

Then he noticed Twyla's expression, wide eyes and crimson tinged cheeks.

"Noah! Twyla! What on *earth* are you two doing?"

It was the shrill voice of his mother. One he would recognize anywhere. Noah knew before he turned around that he would not be getting a warm reception when he saw his mother holding her jacket.

Noah rose, offering his hand to Twyla to help her up. "Sorry, Mom, there's a time and a place. I know. This is not it."

He'd been worried about coming off like an unruly teenager all over again, who simply wanted to shock his parents into noticing he was alive. But instead, he saw a much deeper problem. There was more than disappointment in his mother's eyes. He witnessed pain and shock, and the kind of fresh heartbreak he'd hoped never to see again.

"How long has this been going on?" she asked, waving a hand between them.

Noah and Twyla glanced at each other, both coming up short with words. Noah wanted to say, "About fifteen years," but thought it best to take the fifth now.

I refuse to answer the questions on the grounds the answer might incriminate me. Yes, I've been in love with "Will's girl" for over a decade.

Because she's not "Will's girl." She's her own girl.

His mother shook her head, obviously not waiting for the answer.

Noah winced. So, apparently, she would not be as happy as Twyla's grandmother had been. Then again, it had to be embarrassing to have walked in on them. It wasn't exactly his finest moment. He decided that alone was the issue. She was disappointed in his timing, though maybe she shouldn't have been. It had been decided long ago in their family hierarchy that he was the son who would disappoint.

Dinner was tense, with Katherine barely speaking to anyone, acknowledging only Ella Mae and her husband. She wouldn't make eye contact with either him or Twyla. And not surprisingly, she wanted to leave early, thanking Twyla's grandmother and wishing her a Merry Christmas.

"Do you have to go so early?" Ella Mae asked.

"Oh, yes. You know me. I'll probably be in bed by eight o'clock."

"I'll call you," he said to Twyla as he followed his mother out the front door.

While he drove, Noah imagined the entire ride would be tense and quiet if he didn't try to explain. "I'm sorry that my timing was so bad. It was awkward for all three of us."

"It wasn't the best way to tell me. You're my main concern, Noah. I don't want to see you hurt."

"I'm prepared for that, and for anything that might happen. But I think I've loved Twyla for a long time. I tried to stop."

"Is that why you left for Austin?"

"Not the only reason."

He could tell her that he'd left because he was so tired of seeing the plaque. Tired of the reminders everywhere that he'd failed. Tired of seeing the pain in his mother's eyes. He was so tired of the lie that he'd told for so long, it seemed almost true some days. It had felt like the right thing to do in the beginning and instinct made him protect his brother. But the lie had settled on him like an armored suit he couldn't take off.

"All I want is for you to find a girl who will love you and put you first. Twyla has been your friend for so long and I've never seen the slightest bit of interest on her part. You're my only son and I want you to be happy. But Twyla? Won't she always compare you to Will? I know how much your father hurt you when he couldn't forgive you. When he left, it felt as though he was saying you and I weren't enough reason to stay." She closed her eyes. "That's why I thought the move to Austin might be good for you. Somewhere where no one will blame you for the accident. No one knows your past. A clean slate."

Whether or not she loved him and was loyal, she did blame him. And why not? He'd given her every reason. It was just the two of them left now. Half of a family once whole. The truth mattered. It mattered because he'd sacrificed a memory for his own happiness. The lie had festered until it was ugly and painful. Slowly killing him.

"There's something I think you should know about the accident."

Chapter Eighteen

The party went decidedly downhill after the awkwardness of Katherine catching Noah and Twyla kissing. And it definitely hadn't been the world's best timing, but it also wasn't the worst thing anyone could do. It wasn't like they'd been naked and rolling around on top of everyone's coats.

Even when Ava started to sing Christmas carols, starting with "Jingle Bells," the mood had lost its shine. Or maybe that was just all coming from her. She wished Katherine would have just looked at her across the table.

It wasn't that Twyla wanted to forget what amounted to her first puppy love. She wanted permission to move on. She firmly believed she'd been granted that grace. Not Noah. Poor Noah, caught between the past and the future he wanted. He was far more sensitive than anyone wanted to give him credit for. A good son, he did not want to hurt his mother, and Twyla believed he had never imagined he would by simply choosing to love her.

But this could change everything. Twyla wanted Katherine to accept her and Noah together, but she'd been foolish enough to think she didn't need her approval. She went back to the party, forcing herself to be happy. It wasn't any different than the way she'd lived the past ten years, so it came easily to her. Eventually, their guests left one by one, those with young children leaving first.

She and Ganny finished drying the dishes and putting away all the festive platters.

"Maybe you should spend the night," Ganny said. "I miss our sleepovers."

When she'd been a little girl, Twyla loved nothing more. There had been comfort in Ganny's soft cotton sheets and fluffy pillow. But somewhere along the line, she'd created all that warmth and familiarity in her own space. Now, she only wanted to go home to her own bed and slide under the covers. She wanted to read and fall into a world where she and Noah would be together with zero complications. If she could, she'd rewrite their story and he would have been her first love. Because whether true or not, it felt that way.

She got home and opened the door to a highly annoyed Bonkers who hissed and swiped at the air.

"I know, I know. I'm late." She removed her jacket and laid it on her living room couch.

Opening up a can of food for Bonkers, she set it down and watched as he circled it, as if he thought she might actually poison him.

"You need therapy," she said to her cat. "But I love you anyway."

Not long afterward, Noah texted her, I'm coming over in a few minutes.

Thank goodness. She needed to see him and be assured that he'd smoothed everything over with Katherine. They'd all be okay.

Twyla stepped outside into the brisk night and sat on the front stoop. Waiting like she had so many times before. For Noah. For Will. For both of them to show up together, wind- and sunburned from a day on the boat, ready to tell her all about the day's catch. She longed for easier days when love was simple and chaste. When love wasn't this giant boulder to carry everywhere.

Those days were gone. Love and loss were intermixed now and forever.

But anyone who'd ever lost someone could say the same. It didn't mean one couldn't love with all their heart and strength. Sometimes love was even stronger.

By the time Noah pulled up, Twyla had located both the Noah Dipper and the Will Dipper. She would look at the stars more often. Name new constellations. She'd see things in different ways all over again. She didn't have to go to New York to see something exciting. All she had to do was learn to notice everything around her, as though it was the first time.

Noah met her eyes as he walked up the porch steps to the stoop. His own eyes were slightly red. Not a good sign.

"Hey," he said, bumping her knee like old times.

"Hey, yourself."

He turned to Twyla and the utter pain in his eyes took her breath. All she'd ever wanted was to see those eyes shimmer with joy again and she had…for a little while. She knew in that moment he'd told his mother the truth of the accident. She held her breath and then asked the question.

"Did she believe you?"

"Yes."

Thank you, God.

"But I shouldn't have said anything. Not tonight, or maybe ever. She's already been through so much loss and now she's got even more to work through, knowing Will was to blame for everything. She made me sit down and hash out every moment of the accident. What Will said that day, what he did and how the accident happened. I didn't want to relive it again, but she asked for it." He rubbed his temples. "And then she sobbed and begged me to forgive her for blaming me. Because yes, she had. Even though she loves me and I'm all she has."

"It's okay." Twyla rested her hand on his thigh. "Now she knows."

"Even if the accident wasn't my fault, I always fell short when it came to my brother."

Her heart twisted because she heard the unsaid words. "Noah, you have *never* been second for me."

He seemed to ignore that.

"I'm going to find her some real help. Some counseling. Even if I have to drag her out of the house myself. I shouldn't have ignored her pain this long. I shouldn't have acted like it was normal to refuse to throw anything away. Grief is normal but she's…something different. She can't let go."

"Guilt can make it hard to let go, too. Not just grief."

"What does she have to feel guilty about? *None* of this was her fault."

"She must know on some level, Noah, that she failed you. She wasn't healthy enough to be the mother you needed. You suffered, too."

"I don't need to be mothered. I just need to fix this so she can be well. And happy. Somehow. If it's at all possible." Noah covered his face with his hands. "I don't know what else to do."

Every cell in her body hurt to see him in this position. She wanted to tell him it wasn't his fault, that he'd also lost someone he loved. Then he'd been left in charge when even his own father abandoned them. She wanted Noah to know he wasn't in charge of anyone's happiness but his own. But Noah, the rescuer, wanted to save his mother.

"I think we just need to..." Noah began, and then his own voice drifted and mixed with the sounds of the night.

"Break up." Twyla spoke through the sob in her throat. Why not make this easier for him.

"Right," he said, and took her hand in his, threading their fingers together. "We'll always be in each other's lives."

"Sure," Twyla said. "You take care of her. She comes first."

"I'm pretty sure she'll be ready to see you again soon."

"She...doesn't want to see me?"

Noah looked stricken. Maybe he'd meant to keep that tidbit to himself. "She's upset tonight. The news of us, the truth about the accident... It was too much for one day."

"Yes, sure, that makes sense." Still, the thought that Katherine had turned against her, even for a moment, was enough to cause fresh tears to form in her eyes.

She'd been like a second mother to Twyla for all these years. They might never be able to talk freely again. They might never just pull out a photo album and laugh and have cookies and eggnog and remember. It made no sense, but grief didn't have to make sense.

Noah stood and pulled Twyla up with him. "I'm going to spend more time with her. Get her some therapy. Maybe Finn will help more with the charters, so I don't have to spend all my time there."

He didn't have to add that he'd talk to Twyla every day, and he'd text. For a while, though, it wouldn't be the same. Not the wonderful way it had been for the past week when she'd literally had it all.

The world tends to take perfection and squash it to bits.

No. Turns out she didn't actually believe that. She did understand, however, that some people were incapable of seeing the beauty in brokenness. Once, she'd been one of them.

Twyla would no longer be that person. Not ever again.

Noah kissed her and held her tight for several long minutes, like he was trying to memorize the way they fit together. He might not realize he'd made this feel like a genuine goodbye.

Goodbye to the way he'd kissed her; goodbye to the way he'd made her feel loved and whole again.

Chapter Nineteen

It was the end of the day on Christmas Eve, and Noah and Finn were tying up the boats.

Once they'd finished, they all headed inside for the "all persons on deck" meeting.

All afternoon, Noah had been a grump and needed to apologize. He'd scared Diana and Tee was staying out of his way because the kid was far smarter than he looked.

Today, he wore a T-shirt that said: *It seemed like a good idea at the time.*

Not a good message for your captain if you wanted to be trusted with more responsibility. Then again, nothing was funny to Noah anymore.

"I want to thank you all," Noah said. "I'm sorry if I've been a grump, or a little distracted the past few days, but I couldn't ask for a better crew. Next year, Saturday pizza day is back."

Tee pumped his fist in the air. "Yessss!"

Diana smiled but studied the floor. She still hadn't met his eyes but at least she spoke to him occasionally.

"Yay." Finn gave a wry smile and leaned against the counter.

"And, well, Finn knows better than anyone that I leave shopping until the last minute—"

"I don't need any car freshener, thanks." Finn held up his palms. "And I'm full up on batteries, too."

"Ha ha, smart-ass. I've moved into the new millennium along with everyone else." He reached in his jacket and pulled out envelopes. "They're called gift cards. I hope y'all like books. And if you don't, it's time to change that."

They were all to Once Upon a Book. Approximately two hundred dollars' worth. Noah handed them out.

"Thanks, nacho man!" Tee had decided to call him by the ridiculous nickname and Noah had stopped correcting him. "Hope you don't mind, but I'm going to take my girlfriend to the store and let her go wild!"

Ah, another girlfriend who liked to read. Flashes of Twyla came back to him, curled on a pillow reading, but willing to drop the book for him. His chest tightened.

"Thank you, Mr...nacho... Captain, um," Diana stammered.

"Noah," he said.

"Noah." This time she met his eyes and in them he saw something...familiar.

A shy kind of sweetness that reminded him again of another girl, and of another time. Twyla had given him the same kind of bashful looks. Rarely meeting his gaze. He'd never imagined back then that she'd actually liked him as more than a friend which said something.

Maybe he'd put himself second before anyone else ever had.

"Okay, Diana. Let's get going if I'm going to give you that ride." Tee held the door open for Diana and when she went out, he turned to Noah and silently mouthed. *She has a wicked crush on you.*

Finn snorted, arms crossed. "Figures. They *all* have a crush on you."

"Shut up," Noah said and shoved him.

"Go have fun with your lady and I'll lock up."

"Nah, you go. I'm going to be here awhile longer."

"What the hell for?"

He may as well tell Finn now. "Twyla and I… We broke up."

"You're an idiot," Finn said, shaking his head.

"Tell me how you really feel."

"You asked for it." Finn scowled. "Who's good enough and who isn't? Nobody is good *enough.* We tend to think the women we love deserve better because we're not perfect. They deserve perfect but, brother, that's never going to happen. Twyla loves you. That makes you perfect the way nothing else ever will. You're perfect for *her.*"

"I don't feel like I am. I've made too many mistakes. Too much baggage."

"I can't believe I have to tell you, of all people, but none of us have the time we think we do. The point is, we don't know how much time we have left."

"Twyla understands me. This breakup is a mutual thing. She's always going to be there for me."

"She will, as a friend. There's no denying that. But I don't know how you can be so sure about the rest of it.

She's not going to wait around for you forever. If you want her, you're going to have to *choose* her."

Choose her.

It wasn't that simple. He already had but it didn't change the facts. She was too good for him. He would always be second best to someone who'd been better for her in every way. The last thing he'd ever wanted to do was take his brother's place. No one ever could. Maybe someday, someone else would come along and he'd find a way to be happy for her. The way he'd been happy for her and Will even when he loved her, too.

He and Twyla hadn't talked or texted much since the party, but they were still okay. Noah needed to believe that. He already missed her so much that his heart cracked every time he thought of her. Ridiculous. Once before, he'd stepped aside and lost Twyla to someone else. But he'd been someone Noah had loved almost more than he loved himself.

Will Cahill was good. Perfect. *He* deserved her.

But Noah still didn't believe that anyone else did.

Except maybe a reverend.

Finn was still yakking. "You've already had so much loss. I don't want to see you lose the best thing that's ever happened to you."

Noah swallowed hard. He really wanted to stop talking about this. He'd moved straight from the guilt of loving his brother's girl to the acceptance that he could never be good enough for her.

Eventually, Finn got tired of talking, which may have been around the time that Noah shot him a glare that indicated he'd had enough.

"Merry Christmas, idiot." Finn tossed up his hands.

"Don't let the door slam your ass on the way out!" Noah shouted.

But he followed Finn out and caught him before he'd gone too far. Noah didn't want to leave things like this. Not on Christmas Eve.

Not with Finn, one of his oldest friends. He'd been like a brother.

"Hey, but seriously. Sorry for being a damn grinch. Merry Christmas."

"Yeah," Finn said and pulled Noah into a man-hug.

They clapped each other's backs, and Noah lingered outside, watching Finn drive away.

A cool wind on the coast had turned the night chilly and Noah was glad he'd worn his jeans, long-sleeved shirt with a jacket and boots. He was about to go back inside when a beam of moonlight showed a string of Christmas lights they'd forgotten to remove from the night of the Snowflake Float Boat Parade.

"Guess I have to do everything around here," he muttered.

He was single, obviously, and had no one waiting for him at home. He didn't have to worry about his mother tonight, because Ella Mae and her husband were dropping by for a gift exchange. They were also bringing her dinner. He didn't know if his mother realized what a friend she had in Ella Mae, but Noah was grateful. Slowly, his mother was letting her friends know the truth. It hadn't been Noah driving the boat. It was as if saying it made it real to her, made it acceptable. She kept telling Noah the truth was important and she refused to live a lie. They'd get through this difficult time and on the other side of it. Someday.

Grabbing a flashlight from inside, Noah put it between his teeth and climbed the mast. He reached the top and worked the wires around. Funny, this had been much easier in the bright light of day when the wind wasn't rocking the boat. The mast swayed. Noah felt a wave of apprehension. He began to assess the situation. Worst case scenario stuff. No, but this was fine. He was good. Really, what could happen? He *could* fall and hit the deck. It would hurt his bum leg, but no serious harm. Noah had a good grip on the mast and just had to get this done faster. He wound the wire around, frustrated when it caught. Then he dropped the flashlight and it fell to the deck, making a cracking sound.

"Damn it!"

Now he'd have to shimmy back down and get the light. Halfway down, his weight must have upset the equilibrium and when a larger wave hit the boat it moved sideways. Noah lost his balance. He was airborne for seconds before he hit the water and went under.

His first thoughts under the dark murky water were of the fire. Similar to this moment, he hadn't been able to see a damn thing in the thick black smoke. But in the fire, he had equipment to help guide him, oxygen to sustain him. Still, the terror he'd felt had been far too real. It wasn't natural walking into a building fire when everyone else was running out. But it had been his job, and he'd done it to the best of his ability. Roofs falling could not always be predicted or avoided. But to this day, Noah could swear he'd been pushed out of the way. Now, he felt Will with him again, reminding him it was his job, and his gift, to live.

And damn, how he wanted to—and be forgiven for surviving.

Noah nearly swallowed a lung full of water but came up kicking with every ounce of strength he had left. On the way down the mast, he must have nicked his leg on the side of the hull. His bad leg. It was hard enough to swim to the boat wearing all his clothes and boots, but now he had an injured leg to deal with.

How ridiculous would it be to drown only a few feet from the dock? How ironic?

For one moment, he doubted he'd get back as he struggled against the weight of his boots. Noah hadn't been the strong swimmer that Will had been, which was why he hadn't been able to save him. With strength he didn't even realize he had, Noah managed to get himself back to the dock and somehow pull himself up into the boat. He fell to the deck, lying there sopping wet. Hands splayed behind him, he looked up at the stars.

This is ridiculous.

He was so tired of playing it safe with his heart, so tired of trying to minimize the risks since that day over ten years ago when he'd been shattered with grief. A memory came back to him, clear as a bright day in June.

I can't do it, Noah had said, an eight-year-old treading water and trying to beat his own record of sixty seconds.

Yes, you can, Will said, his legs dangling over the dock as he kept time. *All you have to do is try. Remember, you just have to beat your last record. Not mine.*

And it was true, Noah might have competed with everybody else, but he had never competed with his brother. He used to think it was because he could never measure up. But from the beginning, Will told Noah that as brothers, they would never compete with each other. And neither one would ever be better than the other. Funny how Noah had forgotten this. But the words had come straight from Will, and it was like a Christmas gift to remember them now, solid and real, like they were floating to him on the light fog.

He scrambled off the boat and grabbed a hammer and pliers. There was one thing he'd been dying to do for years, and he'd waited too long to do it. Soaking wet and mostly alone out here, he stalked to the plaque stuck to the entrance of the dock.

In honor of the heroic actions of Noah Cahill.

Slowly, he pried the damn thing off and threw it in the bed of his truck.

Twyla had closed the store early on Christmas Eve, but once she'd fed Bonkers—and he'd gone back to ghosting her—she had nothing else to do. Normally she'd spend the evening with Ganny, getting ready for the big celebration held at her home tomorrow. But everything had already been prepared. And surprisingly, because at the time she assumed Twyla would be busy with the Cahills tonight, Ganny accepted the invitation by Patsy Villanueva to an annual party held at the lighthouse. Twyla refused to allow her to change her plans.

She'd see Ganny and the rest of the family tomorrow for the Thompson family's white elephant gift exchange. Twyla's gift was always a book she'd read that she wanted someone else to enjoy, too. Her parents were flying in tonight and staying in a hotel by the airport, and they would drive to Charming early tomorrow morning. Ganny would have her annual pancake breakfast, one in which she invited all the people that didn't have family in town. Tomorrow would be great, and her spirits would be lifted to see everyone together again. One more year completed with their family bookstore. All signs appeared they would be around for another forty or so years, if Twyla wanted to continue the tradition. And she'd found that she did, because though New York City sounded wonderful, Charming was home.

Zoey was spending time with Drew's family this year, which meant things were getting serious. Noah, of course, would be with his mother as he should be. Finn? She had no idea, nor did it matter. He was a handsome guy and might have been fun to spend a little time with during the holiday season. But he'd never replace Noah in Twyla's heart. She was beginning to worry no one ever would.

When she couldn't sit still another minute, and didn't know what to do with herself, she headed back to the store.

She wanted to be in the one place where her heart had first healed, among the stories of amazing worlds created in an author's gifted imagination. It was more than any single book to her, but it had now become all of the books. All those spines lined up together, feeling a little like a family, bathed her with comfort. She unlocked the shop doors, turned on the lights and when a few passersby scurried by wondering if they might grab a last-minute gift, she relented and let a few of them inside. This led to another, and then another.

"I can't believe you're open on Christmas Eve," the young man who worked with Noah said. Tee? He wore a silly T-shirt again as seemed to be his custom.

"Well, I couldn't sleep, and my family celebrates

tomorrow, so I figured I'd just come here and hang out for a bit."

"Dude, lucky for me you're open. I leave my shopping till the last minute. And this year, I had no idea what to get my girlfriend. But then my boss gave me this gift card and the decision was made. This is perfect."

His boss would be Noah and she wasn't at all surprised he'd given bookstore gift cards to his staff. Twyla flashed back to the Christmas when Noah, always a helpless, last-minute shopper, gave her car fresheners and AAA batteries. She'd used some great mileage on that, teasing him over it for years. Eventually, he'd learned to be a more thoughtful giver, with a little help from her. Now he never failed to impress her. Last year, he'd sent his gift through the mail. A necklace with a pendant designed in the cover of *A Dragon's Heart*. If something could be made from one of her favorite books, he'd find a way to buy it.

Tee wanted recommendations. Twyla took care of the kid, then helped a couple of other shoppers find the perfect book for a loved one before she realized that her own purpose for coming here tonight was not to sell more books. She wanted some solitude to contemplate the end of another year. To plan how she would handle the rest of her life without Noah as a lover and only as a best friend.

After all the last-minute shoppers were gone, Twyla made sure the sign was flipped to Closed and shut off the front lights. She made her way to the back of the store and the fantasy section. Grabbing a pillow, she curled up in the nook, cracked opened a copy of *A Dragon's Heart*, and began to read.

She'd flipped to her favorite chapter, where the hero and heroine finally get together, when she heard the pounding on her shop door. More desperate last-minute shoppers. *Note to self: leave the store open later next year on Christmas Eve.* By then, shoppers knew it was too late to have anything shipped. Perfect chance to get their business. What else did she have to do? Bonkers didn't even want anything to do with her and she doubted a year would change that.

"I'm closed!" she shouted, but the banging continued, this time followed by yelling.

Someone was calling out her name and it sure sounded an awful lot like Noah. He was supposed to be at his mother's tonight. He told her that in an earlier text which had been short and sweet. It simply sounded like someone who felt guilty he'd suddenly cut off most of their communication.

Curious, she walked to the front of the shop and flipped on the light. What she saw there shocked her. Noah stood, hair wet, holding a wrapped package. One glance and her heart swelled with love. She let him inside.

"Hi," she said, trying not to look at him again.

"I dropped by your house, and you weren't there. I would have been here sooner, but I fell off my boat and had to go home and change."

"Wait. You fell? How did that happen? You're okay?"

"I'm fine, leg hurts a little but it's nothing serious. Still, I had to get your gift because I've waited too long to give it back to you." He handed her the wrapped present.

"Give it *back* to me? Is this a white elephant present? Noah, are you regifting?" she teases him.

Twyla wasn't going to lie. She'd made the lighthearted comment to distance herself from the emotions quaking through her. She didn't want to hope, but hope was this irrepressible wave rising inside of her.

She blamed it on books.

"You'll see when you open it. Go ahead." Noah cleared his throat, looking positively boyish.

She tore open the paper to find he'd given her the same book she gave him.

"That's funny. Great minds think alike."

"It's not just another book, it's The Book."

When she took a closer look, Twyla saw it was the copy she'd lost a year ago when she'd moved to her smaller rental.

"How did you…how did you find this? When? I've been looking all over."

She flipped through the pages, finding all the places where they'd written notes to each other over that first difficult year when the book was their escape.

"This is the embarrassing part, and I have to apologize in advance. Please forgive me, but I took the book when I left Charming. I'm still sorry I never told you—still sorry I kept it from you for so long. For a long time, I didn't know why I'd done it. Then I realized, it was because as long as I had the book, I still had a part of you, a part of us, that I could never lose."

"Noah, no matter what happens, you will never lose me. I love it. It is the perfect gift."

She held the book tightly to her chest. It was nice that if they had to break up, at least she had the book back with her now. And now *she'd* always have this part of Noah with her.

Noah pointed to the book. "Read the inscription."

Twyla turned the cover and flipped through to the beginning where Noah had written on the empty page:

I will slay every dragon for you.

Her finger traced the words and her eyes filled. "Do you mean it?"

He stepped closer and his big hand rested on the nape of her neck, pulling her to him.

"Finn said something that finally made sense to me. He said if I wanted you, I'd have to *choose* you. The thing is, I can't remember a time when I didn't choose you. I just never thought you should choose me back. I always felt like someone else could make you happier. Someone better. Someone…without all my baggage."

Twyla made a whimpering sound but didn't trust herself to speak against the sob in her throat.

He took her hand and brought it to his lips. "And then I remembered something else when I was kicking back to the boat wearing all my clothes—so what if I'm not the best man in the world? I'm only in competition with myself and doing the best I can no matter what. And if you say that you love me, then I'm the luckiest man I've ever met."

"I love you." Tears slid down her cheeks. "I always have."

"For a hundred years?" He winked. "Because I swear, I've loved you for at least a hundred and five."

Epilogue

Six months later

The grand opening of Nacho Boat Adventures was delayed until May—partly because of the weather, but mostly so that Noah could have more time to hire a full crew. Finn's brother, Declan, had joined their new and fledgling company. And when Noah's buddy, Tate, grew tired of running into burning buildings, he did, too. Tee and Diana were still with him, learning as they went. The company grew so quickly that Noah had forced himself to slow things down. A business could crash and burn if they took on too much and too soon. He'd joined the Chamber of Commerce and was getting plenty of business advice from people far more experienced than he was.

And besides, he'd wanted to spend time with Twyla and achieve the delicate balance of both work and family. He'd made one major decision just after last Christmas. Though the name of the company would remain the same, Noah took the unusual step of renaming a boat. He'd gone through the entire process. Though he wasn't the superstitious sort, many nautical types were. When they saw the new name, they'd be surprised she wasn't named after a woman—a normal custom. Not named after a goddess of protection, not after his mother and not after Twyla. He'd chucked naming conventions to the curb this time.

And on this bright, early spring day, they were officially christening her with the new name.

A small group of business leaders, residents and friends had gathered along the dock to watch and celebrate this new beginning.

Ava Del Toro, belly huge with child, stood in the crowd with Max. Nearby were Adam and Cole, fellow business leaders and people Noah relied on more and more. But Noah had his eye on only one person today. He only cared to see her face, wearing the sweet smile he now woke to every morning. Twyla stood sandwiched between her grandmother and his mother.

The past few months had been challenging ones for his mom. Between the knowledge and eventual acceptance that Will had been the one driving and understanding that she would have to accept Noah and Twyla as a couple, it hadn't been easy. But after the past two months, she'd finally turned a corner. The online grief therapy group she'd joined with Twyla's grandmother helped.

"Thanks for being here, everyone," Noah said. "As y'all know, this has been a labor of love from the moment we took over Nacho Boat. I have a lot of memories here, and plenty of them are even good, too."

Laughter from the crowd.

With a nod in Finn's direction, he communicated it was time to lower the sheet that covered the new name.

The Will Dipper.

Private little joke.

Not everyone here would understand, but Twyla did. And so did his mother, because while applause followed the unveiling, she dabbed at her eyes.

Love never dies, Twyla's grandmother had said to him shortly after Christmas. *It just changes form.*

Noah appreciated the sentiment and on days when his thoughts inevitably turned to his brother, he felt less alone. Someone else made him feel less alone. Twyla reminded him every day that true love was worth taking a risk. They were still friends, because they'd never lose that, but now they were lovers, too. Rather than change their relationship, they'd simply enhanced it. He was the luckiest man to be in love with his best friend. He understood that not many people were that fortunate.

Noah broke the champagne bottle over the ship's hull and on Ava's insistence, gathered his crew together, smiled and faced the photographers.

Finally, he and Twyla could head home. For now, they were living in her small rental. It suited the two of them and Bonkers, of course. He'd broached a friendly truce with the cat, who was going to help Noah today. He'd practiced this over the course of the past few weeks, every time Twyla was working late at the bookstore. Today, everything would be perfect. He had the second bottle of champagne chilling. He'd written the speech, with some help from Stacy. Words were important to Twyla, so rather than speak from the heart, he'd wrangled words into submission. Beat them into shape. But

Stacy refused to write it for him, unfortunately, so this wouldn't exactly be worthy of publication.

He could have done a loud and splashy proposal in front of everyone at the ship's christening. But Twyla would prefer something private and intimate. He'd wanted something, too, that would be clear, distinct and separate from the boat's renaming. One was a nod, a memory and an honor to the past.

This would be the start of their future together.

"Where's Bonkers?" Noah bent, as if that would encourage the cat to appear. "He always meets us at the door."

"Maybe he's hiding."

Bonkers would pick today to be the one day out of approximately one hundred days that he didn't greet them with his usual hiss. Very inconvenient. The ring box was tied to his collar along with his speech, rolled up like he was delivering the paper. Noah wanted to make this memorable and for reasons he couldn't fathom, Twyla loved this cat. God only knew why.

"You don't think he got outside again?" Twyla's eyes were a mix of horror and confusion, but they didn't match the fear churning in *his* gut.

His ring? Outside? With a pissed off cat?

What on earth was he thinking?

"No!" Noah shook his head. "I mean, how could he get outside? Now that I know he's an indoor cat, I never let him out. That only happened once."

Twyla rubbed Noah's shoulder. "Don't worry. He's in here. Somewhere."

And Noah had to find him. Now.

"Bonkers! Where are you, buddy?" Noah bent under

the couch, searched in cupboards—which Twyla left open for him—and in closets. "Come out, wherever you are."

"You really like him now, don't you? I knew he'd grow on you, just like he grew on me. He's not mean, just misunderstood."

"Yeah."

Noah smiled through gritted teeth. If Bonkers didn't show up soon with the ring, not only would Noah hate him, but the cat's days would be numbered. He'd leave the back door open…just in case he wanted to stalk into the great outdoors. Maybe this time he'd go farther than the shrub.

Noah bent under the bed when a streak of gray went flying past him. He followed Bonkers into the kitchen, where Twyla stood near the can opener.

"This always works."

Why didn't I think of that?

Food, a powerful motivator for the beastie. The box, barely hanging on, fell right at Twyla's feet. Not exactly the plan, but mission accomplished.

Twyla blinked, then stared wide-eyed at the ring box, then at Noah. Back to the box. She picked it up, and Noah dropped to one knee. He had a speech prepared, which might be lying in tatters somewhere in this house, so he'd have to go from the heart. It wouldn't be perfect, but neither was he.

And she loved him anyway.

"Twyla, I've loved you for at least half my life. And I—"

"Yes!" She tackled him to the ground and now lay on top of him.

Noah was vaguely aware of Bonkers swiping near his head after getting a full meal in him.

"You didn't let me finish," he chuckled.

"Oh, no. Did I get it wrong?" A look of fear crossed her gaze. She hadn't even bothered to open the box, after all. "Is it a necklace? Or earrings?"

Now, he laughed. "No. It's a ring. You read me right."

"Thank God!" she said, covering her eyes with one hand.

"I had this whole speech I wrote and rolled up in a scroll. Bonkers had the ring box and the paper attached to his collar. He always greets us at the door." He looked behind him and caught Bonkers midswipe. "What the hell is *wrong* with you, man?"

"You wrote something? For *me*?" Twyla's hand went to her chest.

"I know how much words matter to you."

"Oh, Noah. You don't have to be a *real-life* hero." She smiled and lowered her lips to his. "That's why we have books."

* * * * *

You'll love these other uplifting titles from Heatherly Bell:

A Charming Doorstep Baby
A Charming Christmas Arrangement
The Charming Checklist
Winning Mr. Charming
Grand Prize Cowboy
More than One Night
Reluctant Hometown Hero
The Right Moment

SPECIAL EXCERPT FROM

Sarah Williams jumps at the opportunity to work at Sierra's Web, the agency involved with the adoption of her beloved half sister. But the undercover office manager never expected to fall in love with her work…let alone her enigmatic boss, Winchester Holmes. What will happen when he finds out that Sarah isn't who she claims to be?

Read on for a sneak preview of
A Family-First Christmas
by Tara Taylor Quinn.

Chapter One

She was going to do this.

Wasn't she?

Stopped at the light, Sarah Williams folded her hands, tapping her thumbs together.

Her turn was just ahead. A block away on the right. She could see the clean asphalt drive of the upscale fifteen floor office building that housed the suite of Sierra's Web offices. The tall, perfectly manicured palm trees out front.

Was she really going to do this?

It wasn't illegal. She wouldn't tell any lies. It wasn't against the law to keep non-work-related personal details private.

She qualified for the position. Wasn't planning to steal anything. Or even act upon anything she might inadvertently find out—as long as sweet Kylie was okay.

The baby sister she hadn't seen in eight years, the

baby she'd raised, for all intents and purposes, alone for the first two years of Kylie's life, the baby she'd named, could be in need. Critically in need, for all she knew.

Kylie's adoption case was being revisited for some reason.

If Sarah could believe her mother.

Could she afford not to?

Lily Williams did have a history of telling falsehoods. But generally, they were only to cover up her falling back into addiction. Or to hide a lover.

Either way, what if her mother was right? What if Kylie's case really was being looked at again? Did that mean her baby sister's family life had imploded? Had she been abused? Neglected? Had her adoptive parents been killed in a crash, leaving the ten-year-old sweetheart without a family to call her own?

They were all things Lily had suggested the week before when she'd called Sarah in panicked tears, telling her what she'd heard. *I can't tell you how I know, Sarah. Trust me, you don't want to know how I heard, but Kylie's adoption case is being looked at...*

A closed adoption, to which they had absolutely zero access.

Sierra's Web, the firm of experts who'd assisted the county with the psychological evaluations of potential adopters eight years before, listed an office manager position at the same time of her mother's call. It had been timing she couldn't ignore. Yeah, as a nurse she'd been looking at their open positions for something in the medical field, but…

Being the first of November, it was a little early for a Christmas gift, but when the light turned green,

Sarah pushed the gas, signaled her turn and slid easily onto the lot.

Yes, she was really doing this.

"So how did you hear about Sierra's Web?" Winchester Holmes, financial expert, partner in the firm—and the man in charge of hiring at the moment—already knew he was going to offer the woman the job. Her résumé had been, hands down, the best they'd received. All seven partners had taken the time to vet the applications from their various locations across the United States. All had listed her as their top applicant.

And she was available to start immediately.

"I've been checking the job openings boards at the university since my first semester," she said, naming the major institution less than half an hour away. "Sierra's Web has been on there several times, mostly looking for experienced scholars, experts in their fields. Since most of the jobs were not entry-level positions, the firm caught my attention—not because I hoped to get a job here, as I'm definitely entry level—but because the positions always seemed to fill quickly. So, when I saw an opening for something I was actually qualified to do, I applied." She held his gaze as she answered him forthrightly.

"Universities are a great place to find experts," he told her. "Professors, researchers…" He shrugged, stopped himself from telling her the real story behind Sierra's Web. Didn't mention the college professor who'd helped seven grieving students solve the murder of their friend.

What the heck? He didn't get drawn into personal

revelations. To the contrary, his relationships, both romantic and otherwise, faltered due to his lack of sharing.

Except with the other six partners.

And Lindsay—the fifty-five-year-old woman who'd been running their office since the firm's inception.

The seven of them already knew his shortcoming, thus didn't suffer from his lapse…

He noted her Bachelor's degree. "What did you study?" he asked, to get himself back on track. The officer manager's position only required high school education or equivalent.

"Science, mostly," she said. "And business." Then, with a flick of her long dark hair back over her shoulder, added, "But I worked my way through high school and college in a variety of offices, starting with basic filing and moving up from there. I was employed at a real estate firm first. Then insurance. I spent a couple of summers as a girl Friday at a law firm," naming one of the biggest firms in the Phoenix valley. "And my most recent position was at a medical clinic."

Impressive. And all things he'd already gleaned from her résumé.

"Your variety of experience is a definite plus to us here since Sierra's Web partners all have different fields of expertise."

She nodded, sitting upright, back completely straight in the white blouse she'd paired with the navy pants and heeled sandals. Her hands, folded in her lap, were still but for the thumbs tapping against each other.

He noted those thumbs.

Getting the job mattered to her.

Which mattered to the firm.

"You met Lindsay on your way in," he said, holding her gaze directly as she nodded. "She'll still be the firm's contact with our clients and experts. She handles all phone calls."

Another nod, without hesitation or even a blink.

"And…it's quite possible that she'll be somewhat lacking in enthusiasm as you delve into the filing system and other things that have gotten away from us."

She shrugged one shoulder. A slim shoulder. Yet one that gave him the impression of being able to carry much weight. "My feelings don't hurt easily," she said.

"And I need to make it clear, you won't be her boss. The position is office manager, which means we need you to manage the office, literally. The organization, the paperwork, scheduling, phone system, mail…the way *things* are handled, not the people."

Another nod.

"She might disagree with the way you want to do things," he continued, outlining the lay of the land as clearly as he could, as he'd assured his partners he would. Lindsay's delicate positioning was why they'd put off hiring anyone to take over the running of the office for so long.

"We need you to be able to listen, to follow her edicts when they ring true, treat her respectfully, while still doing what you think is best and most efficient in terms of getting us organized."

Kelly, expert psychiatrist partner at Sierra's Web, had given him the verbiage on the phone a few nights before. He'd memorized it verbatim. But had never used it in any of the other interviews. He'd already determined the candidates to be no hires before he'd reached that point.

He waited for comment. Didn't get any.

"You have nothing to say to any of this?" he asked. He'd been prepared for conversation about what could be deemed a somewhat confusing situation leading to a potentially uncomfortable work environment.

The partners had already decided that if they couldn't find anyone who could work affably with Lindsay, they'd come up with some other solution. Like, maybe, the six of them pitching in and getting things in order and then…they didn't know what. Nor did they know who'd help all the hundreds of people they served between them each year if they weren't out doing what they did best.

Still, before they were a firm, the partners were family. And Lindsay was part of it. That's just how it was.

"I don't know what you want me to say," Sarah Williams replied.

"I want you to say what you think," he gave her back. "Not what you think I want you to say."

"I think that I want this job," she told him, her expression earnest. Serious. "If you think Lindsay will be a problem for me, then I can assure you she won't be."

"Have you ever been in a situation when you were both parent and child to the same person?" The words came out all wrong. The partners had discussed feeling that way with Lindsay. The conversation shouldn't have been shared with anyone but the seven of them.

"Every day of my life."

Eyes wide, he sat back. Absolutely hadn't expected that response. Uttered with a truth that couldn't be denied. He wanted to know more. Badly wanted to know more. Figured it wasn't within professional boundaries to ask.

He gave her time to elaborate, instead, to explain

herself—time that stretched into a long silence. And while a part of him was disappointed not to gain her confidence, at least pertaining to her comment, that same silence told him, clearly, that Sarah Williams was the right hire for Sierra's Web.

She kept her own counsel. Even when she was clearly eager to get something from someone. In this case, a job from him.

"If you ever want advice on how to handle a situation with Lindsay, you can feel free to speak with me or any of the partners. We're all aware of the delicate position we're putting you in, the lack of clear boundaries in terms of powers. We want you to understand that Lindsay has earned her position here. She's like family to us. But that doesn't mean you can't come to us. As it is with family members, we understand that everyone has their issues, and we'll run any interference you need us to run. At the same time, because it feels like I've misled you here in my attempt to get everything out in the open, I also want to make it clear. Lindsay's a sweetheart—she doesn't have a mean bone in her body. She's kind even when she's bothered."

He was babbling like an idiot. Saying far too much. But added, "She's just protective. And might not always be open to sharing…current case files and things…if she thinks you don't need to see them…" *Stop talking. Just stop talking.*

"Does this mean I have the job?"

He almost stared. Blinked just in time, and ruffled the sheets of paper in front of him. Piling them all together and stacking them neatly.

They weren't meant to go together.

That was it? His whole ridiculous soliloquy about

over-the-top potential job challenges, and she still wanted to work for them? "It does." He'd run a basic new hire background check, but he didn't have to wait for it.

He might be uncharacteristically off his mark, but he wasn't stupid.

And it would be a very, very stupid move to let this godsend get away.

Sarah liked Winchester Holmes. The man was a little stuffy with his tie and jacket in a thriving metropolis where customs were more laid-back. And the black hair was cropped beyond short.

But she wasn't there to ogle him. She was going to work for him.

She had the job!

As interviewers went, Winchester exceeded expectations. She hadn't even dared hope the meeting would go so well. She filled out paperwork, including a confidentiality clause that she would not break. Offered to head out for coffee and a bagel while he awaited background information. When he called to let her know everything had checked out, she presented herself for her first partial day of work.

Just like that. There she was. Within reach of Kylie for the first time in eight long years.

The knowledge was a breath of air so full and swift that she was light-headed. And it was an excruciating stab in her heart as well. She'd missed so much.

Would be missing it all still, if it turned out that Kylie was in a happy, healthy home and doing just fine.

And she hoped for that. With every fiber of her being

she prayed her little baby sister was healthy, happy, well loved.

Her own heartache was nothing if Kylie was well.

No one knew that Sarah had been planning to petition her mother for custody of the little girl the second Sarah had turned eighteen. No one knew, not even Lily, that she'd applied for a job at Sierra's Web, either. And her mother wasn't going to know. Lily's fragile emotions could only handle so much at a time, and Sarah wasn't risking another fall off her mother's rickety wagon.

She also wasn't going to miss the opportunity to get one step closer to finding out what had happened to Kylie, where she'd been taken, by whom. But rifling through files looking for her sister's name couldn't be the first thing she did in her new position.

She wasn't going to lose her sense of self-respect, or compromise her integrity, by not doing the job she'd been hired to do. She was going to work for Sierra's Web to the best of her ability.

And she was going to start with Lindsay Conch.

To that end, as soon as Winchester introduced the two of them, Sarah asked the older woman, "Do you have the time to show me around and let me know what you think I should focus on first?" The lines of concern on the woman's face turned into a smile—one that maybe didn't reach her eyes, but it was there. She showed Sarah the suite of offices, the filing room and the small kitchen with a farmhouse-looking kitchen table and eight chairs, suggesting that organizing the cupboards and figuring out a way to get in groceries regularly might be the best first use of Sarah's time.

She got right on it. Finished that task and assessed

the phone system. She researched more up-to-date models, found one at a decent price that would add cloud options to their landline, voice to text, touch-screen, cell phone forwarding and Wi-Fi. She wrote a report for Winchester, gained immediate approval for purchase and placed the order.

Then she wrote another report, explaining in detail all of the ways the new system was going to make Lindsay's day easier, more enjoyable and more efficient, and sent that as well. She stayed in the vacant offices after that, making up lists of potential improvements to the furniture—replacing ten-year-old secondhand desks and chairs with more ergonomic options—until she heard the older woman wish Winchester and Hudson, the only other partner in the office that day, good night.

Sarah had met Hudson briefly, as Lindsay showed her the offices. The married IT expert lived locally and was in the middle of a case he was working with the FBI. He'd had his door shut most of the day. Still had his door shut.

And so, figuring she'd done a fair day's work, and with the office quiet, Sarah allowed herself to make her way to what Lindsay called the filing room. A little bigger than a cleaning closet, the space could hardly be called a room. And the lack of square footage could explain the various filing cabinets she'd seen in partner offices and in the large reception area out front as well.

Heart pounding, she pulled open a drawer marked *W*. She didn't have any idea of Lindsay's filing system. But she figured, with Kylie's case being eight years old, and the firm just a little over ten, chances were good such an old file would have made it to the filing room.

Was it going to be that simple? One day on the job

and she'd have...something? What, exactly, she wasn't yet sure. Names of possible adopters who'd been interviewed at the very least. If she was extremely lucky, a note as to what interviewee had been targeted for final recommendation. Or even a couple of them who had been.

She could take it from there. Get on the internet. Do searches.

Something.

Which was better than the nothing she'd had for the past eight years.

Her fingers trembled as she riffled past old, faded and fraying folder edges on her way to the *Wi*'s. *W-i-l...* Wilbur, Wilhardson, Wilmington, Wilson, Wilt...wait.

Where was *W-i-l-l*? For Williams?

Nowhere. It was nowhere. Not in that or any of the other file drawers she went through in that room. She looked under *K* for Kylie, too, and still found nothing...

"I appreciate your willingness to give this job your all, but these files have waited around for years to get any attention. They certainly don't need you to work late on their behalf..."

She heard the words, oddly already recognized the cadence in the voice, and still jumped as Winchester's white shirt and tie took up her view of the doorway.

"I'm sorry," he said. "I didn't mean to startle you..."

Had he seen what she was doing? Seen what, the word *Kylie* in her brain? Even if he'd been standing there watching her the entire time she'd been in the room, it would only appear as though she was doing the job he'd hired her to do. Familiarizing herself with the filing system on her way to a complete overhaul.

And in her search, she had kind of done that. She

had discovered that nothing, as it currently stood and was labeled, made logical sense. Things were alphabetized, some by first name, some by last, some by company. None by type of case or expert who'd handled it.

Which is what she told him. In a voice that she hoped sounded like a newly employed office manager should sound.

"Lindsay, of course, would know far more than I do," he told her as she returned a couple of files she'd pulled from an overstuffed drawer just so she could get a look at others. "But it's been a work in progress from the beginning, with new systems outgrowing old, but older systems not being updated. We started out with two tall filing cabinets in this room. Those two." He pointed to a couple of old beige four-drawer units. "Each of the partners had a drawer and there was one left for Lindsay. From there, we expanded as we needed, making use of whatever space was there. Until it was determined that the partners should each have their own files in their own offices, for easy access. From there, each partner has his or her own system. To complicate matters further, some of us managed to get our old files out of here. Some didn't get around to it..."

She smiled, a day's worth of tension sliding off her shoulders for a second. She just couldn't help it. The self-deprecating smile, and more, the affection for his partners that came through loud and clear in the dismal filing tale, just felt...nice.

"You need me," she said aloud, surprised to hear herself. And yet...she was gratified to know that while she was using Sierra's Web for her own peace of mind, she also had something valuable to give back. Not because of her newly earned nursing degree, but from the years of office experience she'd gained while working on that degree.

And give back she would. Whether she found Kylie's file within the first few days of her employment or not. The nursing job she'd been dreaming about for years was going to have to wait.

She wasn't leaving Sierra's Web until she had their office firmly in order.

Until Winchester Holmes had received what he'd paid for.

It was just the right thing to do.

Chapter Two

Win stayed in town, working long hours at Sierra's Web corporate headquarters, during that first week after Sarah's hiring. Hudson was there for the first couple of days, too, handling a few cases that didn't require an in-person visit. But when Hud was called to Colorado for a job that involved an internal case of corporate hacking, Winchester was stuck. While Lindsay was often the only person in the office, with all the partners being called to other cities and states across the country, they'd determined that for the first week of Lindsay having to share her space, at least one of the partners should be present.

Win had been unanimously elected as the one to stay during the initial phase of the new hire planning. He'd just relocated to Phoenix, had closed on a home and was in the process of furnishing it and unpacking boxes, some of which had been in storage for years.

Everyone had also determined that he'd be the one to host their annual Sierra's Web Thanksgiving dinner—a feast that might or might not take place on the day itself depending on everyone's schedules. The dinner would happen. They'd been joking about him putting it on. He could do it. He was a decent cook. He had service for twelve—Hud could bring his wife and daughter, who were local. Mariah and her husband and newly adopted daughter could join them as well if Harper and Michael wanted to fly in from Arkansas and he'd still have a place for Lindsay.

Newly married Hud and Amanda could host, too, for that matter. In the past, the partners had always just had the meal catered. They sat around their conference table at work and ate off paper plates. They'd done this since their first year in business together, back when their office had been one big room rented in an old strip mall in a Phoenix suburb. Funny, they'd moved up in terms of office space, but had never bothered to replace the secondhand desks they'd all started with. None of them were generally in the office long enough to notice. Or particularly care. It wasn't like they ever hosted clients or had to woo anyone for business. They'd had more requests than they could handle almost from the first.

But he had to admit, his new L-shaped workstation, complete with wireless computer keyboard, mounted screen and table for spreading out financials was… nice. As was the chair that fit him as comfortably as his recliner at home. The others had moving in to do, but they'd all seen video of their offices with the new furniture in place and were eager to get to Phoenix and unpack the things that Lindsay had insisted on personally packing—carefully labeling each drawer and space—so that all the old furniture could be removed at once.

That first week Win saw Sarah every day. Met with her in one fashion or another as she moved quickly to get the offices into shape. The real challenge would come once the working space and facilities were up to par. He got that. But he couldn't help but be impressed by the woman's work ethic. Her abilities and attention to detail were wonderful, recommending that the partners pay for comfort, and work ease, but not for more than they needed. And she was wonderful with Lindsay, finding a way to stay out of the older woman's very busy way, to not impinge on or hamper Lindsay's responsibilities. She even enlisted Lindsay's help when it came to learning the partners' habits and preferences.

He also couldn't help noticing that he seemed to be smiling more as he drove to work thinking about their new office manager.

And that wasn't okay. The last thing he needed in his life at the moment was another woman to raise his protective instincts, which was what always happened when he started to fall for someone. Or cared for one in any way, for that matter. It was like he had some hidden superhero gene that, while denying him the hunk of a body or impressive physical strength, brought out a drive to protect in him that didn't bode well for relationships.

Or maybe it was his own history, his failure to protect the women he cared about, that was really driving him.

The idea was more credible than the whole superhero thing. And bottom line was that he had no desire, whatsoever, to be in any way attracted to the new godsend bringing comfort, order and efficiency—as well as stocked cupboards—to the Sierra's Web home office. Which was why, on Thursday of the first full week of Sarah's employment, Winchester eagerly accepted an out-of-state job request for a financial expert that could have been handled by any of the freelance experts on his team.

Running away didn't help his newfound predicament, though. Sarah called him on his first night in Washington State, Friday night, reaching him just as he got back to his hotel room laden down with a satchel full of old paper statements and a flash drive filled with newer but still old paper statements, with a room service order already on the way up.

The new phone system had been installed, days earlier than expected due to a cancellation, and she wanted to let him know to alert his partners that their new features, and access codes, were live.

He had no reason to keep her on the call. A thank-you and good-night would have been most appropriate. Instead, he asked how her day had gone. She'd given him a brief rundown of ideas she had for tackling the filing system, starting with his office as he was the partner soonest to return. From there he'd told her about a couple of open cases he was working and files that shouldn't be touched. Which had somehow led to the possible tax fraud case in Washington for which he'd been hired by the defendant to do an expert audit. The tax filings were the least of his problems. They were already in perfect order on his laptop. But the statements…

"Send me the electronic ones and I'll organize them

for you by month, year and type of expense," his new office manager said. Making a perfectly reasonable offer. His gratitude wasn't so much relative to the offer. It was over-the-top.

"I'm sure you have better things to do with your weekend than pore over pages of numbers and dates," he told her in lieu of the profound thanks he'd wanted to utter at her helpfulness. He could use the help. But it wasn't the offer itself that had him going.

It was that it had come from Sarah. That she, in particular, had offered to help him.

He had to get himself under control or one of them would have to leave Sierra's Web. And since he was a partner…

He couldn't be responsible for losing someone who was turning out to be a powerful asset to the firm.

"I wouldn't have said it if I didn't want to do it," she told him pragmatically—much the way she'd let him know that his Lindsay warnings hadn't bothered her during their interview the Tuesday of the previous week.

He wanted to ask why she wasn't going on a date, or whether she had family and friends who would mind that she was working overtime, and outside the scope of her original duties, after only ten days on the job—mostly because he wanted to know if she had a significant other in her life. But he accepted her help, made arrangements to download the files to her and hung up without any further conversation.

He might not be able to help his overwhelming reaction to their new office manager, but he could damn well make certain that nothing came of it.

That she never ever knew he found her manner disturbingly attractive. That he was drawn to her presence as he hadn't been since Sierra…

He would not fail another woman.

Period.

And if that meant he kept to his own counsel, then so be it.

His own pleasure wasn't worth the cost of possible failure.

Sarah did have other things to do with her weekend than pore over pages of numbers and dates. She had a life.

There just wasn't anything she'd rather do that second weekend in November but give her all to Sierra's Web—a payback for what she was still determined the firm would give her.

Some backdoor way in to find Kylie and know she was okay.

A week and a half of busting her butt and scouring files every chance she got had given her nothing yet, but she'd barely skimmed the surface of the information being stored so haphazardly all over the firm. Kylie's case was eight years old, had been through many filing renditions. There was no telling where it might be. Lindsay had filed by expert for a while, until the firm had acquired so many freelance experts. Then she'd switched to filing by type of case—court or other governmental agency, or private party—and then most recently, by date, changing as the firm had grown and ease of access had grown less…easy.

The older woman was giving Sarah access to all things firm related, other than the experts' desk drawers, but she was watching Sarah like a hawk as well, making it impossible for Sarah to dive into any kind of thorough search for her little sister's file. She'd hoped, with Winchester gone, and Hudson still away, she'd have time in the office to herself, but that hadn't happened.

But she knew that, since the time she was planning to spend looking for Kylie's file would be during working hours, she owed Winchester and the others payback time. And so, instead of heading out when friends from nursing class invited her to a club for some downtime, she sat at home in her little house in Tempe—the university suburb of the Phoenix valley that also bordered Scottsdale—making sense out of years' worth of purchases, payments and deposits. Eventually making a list so that she could get a clearer picture of the person whose accounts she was viewing. While the work was not the medicine she loved, she actually found it quite interesting. Studying a person's habits and lifestyle instead of their bodily functions—but basically looking for the same thing. Something that could be wrong. Or confirmation that all was right.

And on Saturday evening, she found something. A series of random withdrawals that seemed to go nowhere. Why would a man who never paid cash for anything, based on income deposits and credit, debit and check expenditures, suddenly be taking cash and using it nowhere?

The guy paid his bills on the same date every month. Ate at only three restaurants. Bought his groceries from the same retailer on the same day every week. Even at the same time. He golfed. Went to the movies every weekend and took a two-week vacation to various beaches during the summer. He wore nice, though not designer clothes. Paid to have his house cleaned and his yard manicured.

When she couldn't stand the niggling question any longer, she dialed Winchester. Listened to his phone ring. She didn't know why the guy Winchester was working for was being audited. She assumed it was by the IRS for taxes but didn't know that for sure. Her boss could have grave need of the information she'd uncovered.

And…she really wanted to please him. To live up to his expectations.

As she did with all her bosses. It probably just seemed more so with him because she felt guilty for having an ulterior motive.

Four rings and nothing…

That's why she'd been thinking of him so often. Wondering about his life. Smiling at things he'd said. Remembering the firm and yet tender grip of his hand when he'd shaken hers to seal the deal on her hiring.

Because of her guilt.

Five rings…

"Sarah?"

Was it wrong…that swirl of warmth that flooded her at his greeting? Of course, he'd have her programmed into his phone. She worked for him.

"I'm sorry to bother you…"

"No, it's no bother. I'm just in my suite, working. What's up? Is everything okay?"

Everything? What did he care about her everything?

No one cared about her everything.

Mostly because she didn't give them opportunity to look too closely at it.

She liked it better that way.

"I found something odd I thought might be important," she blurted out uncharacteristically. "In the material you sent for me to go over..."

Awkward! For no reason except that she was making it so.

Because of guilt?

Maybe she should just tell him about Kylie.

What? When had she ever told anyone about any of her problems? Or personal business?

And if she told him, she'd lose her chance to find out whether or not her little sister was in need. Because there was no way this man was going to risk his firm, or his partners' credibility, by knowingly turning over confidential information...

Another wave of guilt stabbed her at the thought.

So, should she quit, and abandon a ten-year-old girl? Her flesh and blood? Her sister who'd become her own baby girl, her responsibility, an hour after she was born?

Thoughts flew so quickly she was confused for a second when Winchester said, "What did you find?"

What? She hadn't found anything yet...

Her gaze settled on the computer in front of her. Right. The job...

She told her boss about the withdrawals. All large amounts. The same amount. Spaced two weeks apart.

"He was being blackmailed..." Winchester's voice trailed off, as though his thoughts had taken him on a road she couldn't follow.

"I just thought you should know. I've made a spreadsheet, can send it to you..."

"He wasn't hiding money...his family, they all said he wouldn't have done that..."

"He's the most predictable person I've ever encountered," she said, because she didn't have much more to offer.

"Was," Winchester said and then seemed to be off in his own world again.

Wait. The client was deceased? The man who she'd just spent twenty-four hours getting to know?

"He liked steak," she said inanely. "And bought a tux last March." As though those two facts meant the man couldn't die.

"For his daughter's wedding," Winchester acknowledged, and then said, "Daniel passed away six months ago and a business partner has accused him of hiding money in an offshore account. He managed to get far enough in his allegations to have an investigation opened, which included a subpoena for his tax records. Daniel's widow hired us to do an independent audit..."

Her heart rate picked up. "So...what I just found? This might help exonerate him?"

"It definitely puts an entirely different spin on the investigation," he told her. "Who deposits money and then withdraws it if they're attempting to hide it?"

"Sounds to me like he wanted to leave a trail of the blackmail..." Her mind raced along with her heart, and she told herself it was because she liked the work she was doing. "Maybe he was killed," she said, completely unlike herself as she bulldozed ahead with the fantastical thought. "Maybe there needs to be another kind of investigation going on..."

"He died of cancer."

Oh. Deflated, she sat back in the padded chair at her dining room table.

"But this...yes, please send me the spreadsheet, anything you've compiled… I'm going to put it together with the rest of what I've got and see if I can get this done in time to catch the evening flight home tomorrow."

Home. He'd be back in the office on Monday. No reason for that to make the coming week seem brighter.

"And, Sarah?"

"Yeah?"

"Thank you." His tone had softened. No way she'd just imagined that.

She couldn't help that her body filled with warmth as she told him goodbye.

Chapter Three

Sarah had herself better under control when she went to work on Monday. She'd spent Sunday with a couple of nursing class friends, walking the steep path up Camelback Mountain and listening to them talk about their new jobs. One had landed her dream job at Phoenix Children's Hospital, and the other was working in home health care.

They both assumed she was still at the clinic where she'd worked over the summer. They knew she'd had the job offer. And if Lily hadn't told her that Kylie's case was being revisited, that was probably where Sarah would be.

It wasn't her dream job. She wanted to do disaster work. Or something.

At the moment her only dream was finding her sister before it was too late to help her if she was, indeed, in need of help. There were systems in place to keep children safe. She knew that. Reminded herself of child services and school counselors, pediatricians and any number of other resources that watched out for endangered children, every night as she lay alone in the dark awaiting sleep.

Lord knew, she'd had enough of the child protection professionals in her life as a teenager to know how invasive they could be when they thought something wrong was happening.

Of course, in her case, it had been happening. She'd just been trying to fix it on her own, would have fixed it, but they hadn't given her the chance.

And…she'd blown the opportunity. She'd known the second she'd lifted the four-can pack of vegetable stew that she'd changed herself. Not in a good way.

But the idea of having four days of guaranteed meals for her and Kylie had just been too tempting…

Yeah, she could have had access to any number of resources that would have given them food. But that would have taken them from Lily, too. Splitting them up.

Which ultimately was exactly what her one bout of shoplifting had done.

Water under the bridge. In tan pants and a lighter tan cropped blouse with long sleeves and matching sandals—Arizona winter attire—she went to work on Monday with a renewed sense of urgency to find what she could about Kylie and be on her way.

No point in liking Winchester Holmes—he'd be out of her life in a blink.

As soon as he found out she'd had an ulterior motive in coming to work for him, she'd be out of his, too.

Keeping her thoughts firmly in check, she strengthened her resolve with the knowledge that the Sierra's Web filing system was up on her full-time radar that week. She wouldn't let herself think about guilt as she started in on a far more thorough investigation of the hundreds of paper files in desperate need of organization.

Yes, she started with Kelly Chase's office because the psychiatrist expert had been the one hired by the county to give testimony on child custody cases when the firm had first opened. But she also began there because the woman wouldn't be in the office until the following week, when all the partners would come to town for their annual fall board meeting and Thanksgiving dinner.

Lindsay had told her about the traditional gathering the week before, though whether she'd been intimating Sarah should be prepared to have something to do with the dinner, or to not be included, she hadn't been sure. And hadn't asked.

Didn't matter, either way. She had her own plans.

The drawers in Kelly's office were in order. Hospital charting order. Which made sense since the woman was an expert medical professional. What didn't make sense was that there was no mention of Kylie anywhere. Nothing under Williams. And nothing for Lily, either.

It was like, as far as the expert witness on Kylie's case was concerned, Sarah's little family hadn't even existed. Crushed with disappointment, she looked again, pulling files out, opening them and reading enough to figure out that they had nothing to do with her sister. Quickly passing over more recently dated items, she opened only those files dated at the time of Kylie's removal from Lily's home. Which had also happened to be Sarah's home, too, of course. Though no one had given her any consideration at the time of Kylie's placement. No one had interviewed her. Or seemed to factor her emotional duress into their game plan.

Maybe rightly so. As a sixteen-year-old shoplifter, she probably hadn't been the best influence on the toddler. Or didn't have much of a chance of giving the baby a great life. She'd have died trying, though.

One file then another...she perused...she put back.

Funny how the years brought understanding of some things, and yet the new perspective didn't ease the ache of loss at all.

"What are you doing?"

Sarah jerked, startled out of her self-pity as Lindsay's voice sounded from the doorway.

"Trying to get an idea of what type of files are labeled in which ways so that I can get them into one clear and easily discernible order." The words came. She had no idea from where.

Mastering her expression, as she'd learned to do at way too young an age, Sarah turned to face the older woman. "Is there something else you'd like me to be doing?" she asked.

"No...it's just... I spoke to you and you didn't answer."

She hadn't heard.

"Sorry, when I get focused I tend to tune everything else out..."

More likely she'd been lost in her painful past rather than being present as she was being paid to be. "What did you need?"

"Just wanted to let you know that Win is springing for lunch from LaJolla and I was wondering if you wanted the taco salad you've had the other two times they delivered..."

Lindsay's remembering her order almost brought tears to her eyes. Good Lord, she needed to go climb a couple more mountains and find her strength. Grow some of the leathery skin Arizona's hot sun had been trying to give her.

"Yes, that would be great, thank you," she said, but didn't miss the wary expression on Lindsay's face as her gaze lingered on the folder still in Sarah's hands.

Lindsay might suspect that she had stumbled upon something not quite appropriate.

And she was right.

Question was...would the infraction be enough to lose Sarah her job?

How could she have been so blatantly careless?

And yet...wasn't she being paid to go through files? To better organize them? How did you organize unless you knew what you were organizing? Right?

She'd thought maybe at lunch someone would say something, but everyone had eaten alone in their offices—she'd eaten alone in the kitchen. But she'd had her arsenal of defense ready.

She couldn't leave until she found Kylie's file.

Sierra's Web was the only place she had half a hope of finding anything at all about the closed adoption. No court in the state was going to grant her any access. Nor would a police department. Closed meant closed. For a reason.

Didn't matter that a big sister's heart was irreparably damaged.

Didn't matter that Kylie's biological family just needed to know she was okay.

For the rest of the afternoon, Sarah waited for a call to Winchester's office. Or Hudson's. The IT expert was back in town as well. Either one could fire her.

When the day ended, without a summons, she said good-night to everyone and, for the first time since her hiring, was out of the office earlier than anyone else. Breathing a small sigh of relief.

She could still lose her job. The call to a partner's office could come first thing in the morning. But until it did, she wasn't going to borrow trouble.

She was going to change into leggings and a T-shirt and climb A-mountain, the small peak a couple of miles from her home with the university's big yellow *A* emblazoned near the top. She could take the paved path up to the top, but she didn't. With an hour left until dark, she took the rugged, cactus-strewn rock and dirt short way up. Reminding herself with every step that she was made of strong stuff, too.

And trying to pretend that her only concern was Kylie. She didn't need the Sierra's Web job except to find her sister.

And she most definitely didn't care whether or not she'd disappointed Winchester Holmes. Or whether or not she ever saw him again, either.

No, definitely not.

She'd be just fine if she never saw him again.

Would hardly even notice.

Except that, maybe she would.

Win was…eager…when he left a message for their new office manager to let her know he wanted to see her in his office as soon as she got in Tuesday morning. He'd spoken with all six of his partners on a virtual call the evening before. First, to relay to them a conversation he'd had with Lindsay after Sarah Williams had left for the night—a concern that perhaps the new hire had been snooping in their files.

All six of them had lovingly dismissed the allegation—understanding Lindsay's mother bear protectiveness. She hadn't come to them a stranger, but rather, had been a single mother to a young man who'd lost his life much the way their Sierra had. If only someone had been able to follow all of the little facts that, alone, meant nothing… then maybe…

Shaking his head, he stood at his desk, having just shared with Lindsay the partners' hellos and thanks for having their backs, while at the same time gently letting her know that none of them were concerned that someone overhauling their files was actually looking at said files. She'd replied, as usual, with an acknowledgment that maybe sometimes she got a little paranoid.

She did. Maybe they all did, considering what they'd been through, individually and together. Maybe that was what made them so good at their jobs. And able to help so many people live longer, happier lives.

The second reason for his call to his partners was to get their buy-in for his use of their new office manager on one of his jobs. They all knew the assignment. And as he'd known they would, had all immediately agreed that if there was even a chance that Sarah could help it would be worth the hourly wage spent on her efforts.

The knock on his door was no surprise. He'd had a text from Sarah letting him know she was in the parking lot and would be right in. The seriously unsmiling expression on her steady features *was* unexpected. The blue eyes that he'd already grown used to looking at him with calm were anything but. Rather, they pinned him with an urgency he didn't understand.

And then thought he'd been mistaken as she calmly shrugged shoulders in another cropped blouse—white this time, over black pants that didn't hide her slim feminine frame—and said, "What can I do for you?" as though she didn't have rooms worth of files waiting for her to unscramble.

One by one.

"I have a request," he told her. Motioning her to one of the two new leather chairs in front of his desk.

"A...a request?" she repeated, lowering herself to the edge of the seat.

He sat down with a little more commitment, settling back in the most comfortable office chair he'd ever had and slid up to his desk. Picking up a pen he held it between his hands, end to end, fingers turning it back and forth.

Nervous for no good reason.

And a few bad ones.

Spending time with their new office manager mattered to him.

And shouldn't.

He was her boss, for God's sake. Sexual harassment issues alone meant that he could in no way see her as anything other than a capable employee. And beyond that was the respect she was due. Unwanted attention was not even remotely respectful.

Unless...she initiated something more...human between them?

Was he misinterpreting that look in her eye? As though what he needed might matter to her? Like his opinion of her mattered?

Yeah, right. He was the financial geek whose last girlfriend had lied to him so he wouldn't express concern over the safety of some of her choices and he hadn't even suspected.

Thinking he'd suddenly developed the skills to read women, or this woman, was ludicrous.

"I know you have a lot ahead of you with the filing system overhaul, and while that's important, I wondered if you'd be willing to assist with a current case I'm working. Based on the work you did for me over the weekend, you could be a great help..."

"You want my help on a case?" She sat forward, clearly startled. Even he couldn't misinterpret the raised brow, the complete overhaul of what had been a withdrawn expression.

"If you wouldn't mind." He had more to say. A lot more. Sat there meeting her gaze silently instead. Until he saw himself—the idiot he was acting like—and took charge. Of the meeting. And of himself. "I've been working on the job for a few weeks, thought I'd be in and done, but I've come upon hurdles every step of the way. The client requested me personally, but I've had a couple of other such requests come through in the past couple of days as well and need to get this one cleared."

She nodded. "I understand."

He liked that she did. Yet, how could she? She didn't even know what they were talking about yet.

"I'm tracing the assets of a man who's passed," he told her. A man believed to have been a pimp and drug dealer, but who had, apparently, gotten away from that life a few years before his death, due possibly to a terminal diagnosis. A man who'd appeared to have considerable assets—stating a substantial number in his will.

He'd trusted no one with the details of his assets. Not even the lawyer with whom he'd filed the will. Which threw up red flags for Winchester from the get-go.

But the client…the case had come from the county, back during Sierra's Web's meager beginnings when they'd stayed afloat with a small, local government contract. So Winchester felt…protective.

"The work you did for me over the weekend—most importantly, the way you compiled a character sketch of a man I'd never met—it really helped, and that's the kind of thing I need here."

She nodded again, settling back in her chair. Relaxing?

Because she was pleased with his offer?

He liked that she was comfortable with him.

"The work isn't going to be as straightforward as this weekend's was. I've been tracing accounts, but none add up to what they should, and none seem to have any obvious connections to others. That's where I'm hoping your talent will come in—helping me see the person behind the numbers in order to figure out what he might have done with various holdings. His will stipulates that all monies go to his heir or heirs and the state only found one. The heir is our client."

"What happens if you don't find all the money?"

"It goes as unclaimed and after a period of time—varies by state and foreign laws—it reverts to the state or government where it's housed."

"I'm in." She didn't show any concern at all. Just a willingness to help.

And he felt compelled to offer, "This is outside your job description, and none of us will think any less of you if you choose not to take it on."

"No." She shrugged. "I'm fine to do it. I want to."

He believed her.

And when she smiled at him, he smiled back.

Don't miss
A Family-First Christmas
by Tara Taylor Quinn,
available December 2023 wherever
Harlequin Special Edition books
and ebooks are sold.

www.Harlequin.com

COMING NEXT MONTH FROM

HARLEQUIN

SPECIAL EDITION

#3025 A TEMPORARY TEXAS ARRANGEMENT

Lockharts Lost & Found • by Cathy Gillen Thacker

Noah Lockhart, a widowed father of three girls, has vowed never to be reckless in love again...until he meets Tess Gardner, the veterinarian caring for his pregnant miniature donkey. But will love still be a possibility when one of his daughters objects to the romance?

#3026 THE AIRMAN'S HOMECOMING

The Tuttle Sisters of Coho Cove • by Sabrina York

As a former ParaJumper for the elite air force paramedic rescue wing, loner Noah Crocker has overcome enormous odds in his life. But convincing no-nonsense bakery owner Amy Tuttle Tolliver that he's ready to settle down with her and her sons may be his toughest challenge yet!

#3027 WRANGLING A FAMILY

Aspen Creek Bachelors • by Kathy Douglass

Before meeting Alexandra Jamison, rancher Nathan Montgomery never had time for romance. Now he needs a girlfriend in order to keep his matchmaking mother off his back, and single mom Alexandra fits the bill. If only their romance ruse didn't lead to knee-weakening kisses...

#3028 SAY IT LIKE YOU MEAN IT

by Rochelle Alers

When former actress Shannon Younger comes face-to-face with handsome celebrity landscape architect Joaquin Williamson, she vows not to come under his spell. She starts to trust Joaquin, but she knows that falling for another high-profile man could cost her her career—and her heart.

#3029 THEIR ACCIDENTAL HONEYMOON

Once Upon a Wedding • by Mona Shroff

Rani Mistry and Param Sheth have been besties since elementary school. When Param's wedding plans come to a crashing halt, they both go on his honeymoon—as friends. But when friendship takes a sharp turn into a marriage of convenience, will they fake it till they make it?

#3030 AN UPTOWN GIRL'S COWBOY

by Sasha Summers

Savannah Barrett is practically Texas royalty—a good girl with a guarded heart. But one wild night with rebel cowboy Angus McCarrick has her wondering if the boy her daddy always warned her about might be the Prince Charming she's always yearned for.